I0785147

WHERE HIGHLAND THISTLES BLOOM

Where Heaven and Earth Collide
Book 1

by

Paula Quinn

© Copyright 2026 by Paula Quinn
Text by Paula Quinn
Cover by Dar Albert

Dragonblade Publishing, Inc. is an imprint of Kathryn Le Veque Novels, Inc.
P.O. Box 23
Moreno Valley, CA 92556
ceo@dragonbladepublishing.com

Produced in the United States of America

First Edition February 2026
Trade Paperback Edition

Reproduction of any kind except where it pertains to short quotes in relation to advertising or promotion is strictly prohibited.

All Rights Reserved.

The characters and events portrayed in this book are fictitious. Any similarity to real persons, living or dead, is purely coincidental and not intended by the author.

AI Statement: No AI or ghostwriting was used in the creation of this story, or any story, published by Dragonblade Publishing. All text, structure, content, ideas, and concept are 100% human generated solely by the author whose name appears on the cover. It is prohibited to use this material, or any copyrighted material, for AI engine training.

ARE YOU SIGNED UP FOR DRAGONBLADE'S BLOG?

You'll get the latest news and information on exclusive giveaways, exclusive excerpts, coming releases, sales, free books, cover reveals and more.

Check out our complete list of authors, too!

No spam, no junk. That's a promise!

Sign Up Here

www.dragonbladepublishing.com

Dearest Reader;

Thank you for your support of a small press. At Dragonblade Publishing, we strive to bring you the highest quality Historical Romance from some of the best authors in the business. Without your support, there is no 'us', so we sincerely hope you adore these stories and find some new favorite authors along the way.

Happy Reading!

CEO, Dragonblade Publishing

Additional Dragonblade books by Author Paula Quinn

Where Heaven and Earth Collide Series
Where Highland Thistles Bloom (Book 1)

For All Time Series
A Promise For All Time (Book 1)
A Kiss For All Time (Book 2)
A Touch For All Time (Book 3)

Hearts of the Conquest Series
The Passionate Heart (Book 1)
The Unchained Heart (Book 2)
The Promised Heart (Book 3)

Echoes in Time Series
Echo of Roses (Book 1)
Echoes of Abandon (Book 2)
The Warrior's Echo (Book 3)
Echo of a Forbidden Kiss (Novella)

Rulers of the Sky Series
Scorched (Book 1)
Ember (Book 2)
White Hot (Book 3)

Hearts of the Highlands Series
Heart of Ashes (Book 1)
Heart of Shadows (Book 2)
Heart of Stone (Book 3)
Lion Heart (Book 4)
Tempest Heart (Book 5)
Forbidden Heart (Book 6)
Heart of Thanks (Novella)

CHAPTER ONE

Raigmore, Scottish Highlands
Late summer, 1657

"Now that the baron is dead—"

Ismay MacPherson looked up from her cup at her mother sitting across the dinner table.

Marjorie MacPherson was richly adorned in a damask silk gown of pale blue matching her complexion and giving her a bloodless appearance. Which was all too fitting. She stared at Ismay with hard, angry eyes, green with envy and sharper than glass. Those eyes hadn't softened toward Ismay since Lord John MacPherson saved her and brought her there to live as his daughter when she was eight. To spite Ismay, Marjorie, Lord John's wife, wouldn't call him what he was, her beloved father—though Ismay never considered him anything but her true father.

"—'tis time ye wed and start yer own family."

Ismay's heart halted, stopping her breath with it. "Pardon?"

"Ye heard me, girl. Marriage. Ye're four and twenty. The baron spoiled ye, giving in to yer every wish, even not to be wed. But things are different now."

Ismay stared at her in shock and dismay. She shook her head. "Father is not gone a month..." She swallowed back tears she would shed for Lord John MacPherson, Baron of Raigmore. "...It took even less time for ye to arrange fer me to be courted by Chief Alistar MacRae of Beauly, who is a mean-spirited—"

"Ismay—"

"Do ye hate me that much, Mother?" Ismay already knew the answer. Her father's wife had always harbored deep resentment and jealousy toward her—but to wed her when she knew...she knew Ismay would never agree to marry and she knew why.

"Pardon, m'lady." Andrew the butler stepped into the dining room, interrupting her thoughts. "Chief Alistar MacRae has arrived."

Ismay turned a hurt stare on her mother. How could she invite him here? Hadn't Ismay told her she never wanted to see him again after he'd slapped her?

"Excuse me," she muttered and rose from her chair. "I'm nae longer hungry."

"Sit down this instant!" Marjorie commanded with the authority of a general.

Ismay obeyed, a habit stemming from her days of serving the Clan Chief of the MacDonald of Glencoe. The days with her father's wife were bad, but nothing was as dark and terrible as her life before she had come to live with the MacPhersons. Those dark, early days had turned her heart against men in power, and men in general.

She sat in silence while Majorie left the table to greet their unpleasant guest.

Alistar MacRae, Clan Chief of the MacRaes of Beauly had tried to begin courting her a sennight after her father died. She refused him, of course, partly because it was completely thoughtless of him to attempt to woo her while she was mourning, and because of her hatred for clan chiefs. Whether she knew them or not, she hated them. She didn't want anything to do with any of them, especially Alistar MacRae, who after meeting her twice and being rejected by her as many times, grew angry with her and slapped her face. He didn't use any force. It was more like a quick sting on her cheek. Just enough to show her not to defy him in the future. She was afraid that if she was forced to live with him, she would kill—again.

She didn't look up when he entered the dining hall, or when Marjorie shone her coyest smile at him.

"Ismay," Marjorie's voice sliced through her like the edge of a parchment against her skin, "greet our esteemed guest."

If Ismay's father had been alive when their esteemed guest had put his hand to her, he would have been their deceased guest. But alas, she was on her own for the first time since coming to May Hall, her father's keep in Raigmore. He'd named it after the month he'd brought her here, inciting the wrath of his wife.

She finally looked up from the table. "Chief," she said in a small, soft voice, then looked away again. She couldn't help it. She hated the sight of him and the power his title unfairly afforded him. Men like him pushed others around, stepped over children, and wielded their power like a sickle against the more unfortunate.

"My dear."

The words rolling off his tongue sickened her. She would like to tell him, but she would not disgrace her father's memory by behaving like a miscreant. Lord John MacPherson had always been better than anyone else. She would strive to be the same.

"Is that how yer father taught ye to greet a guest?" Chief MacRae sneered as if reading her mind.

Her eyes flicked back to him like twin blades forged in fire. "Never speak of my father again."

"What did ye say?"

"Ye are no' worthy to speak of him," she clarified, still keeping her voice soft and low as he came near her chair. Would he slap her in front of her mother? She didn't care about his reaction. The venom poured from her. "I will—"

This time it was her mother who hurried around the table to slap her, and it was no tap. Ismay held her cheek while MacRae smiled as if the satisfaction was his. "Mother…" Her cheek stung but her heart burned. For a moment—just while her face hurt— she reconsidered her suspicions about Marjorie's part in her father's death. The house physician had blamed his death on the consumption of poison mushrooms. After confessing to the heinous deed, the cook was immediately executed under Marjorie's order.

"I have agreed to yer marriage to Chief MacRae," her mother dared to tell her. "As of today ye will be considered his promised bride—"

Ismay shook her head slowly. She felt as if she might break open, and if she did, they might find a girl who had been too damaged to accept anyone into her life, save for her beloved father.

"Lady," she uttered, doing all she could to keep her teeth from chattering, "I beg ye—"

Marjorie turned to the chief. "She will be willing soon enough. I promise."

"Willing or no', she will be mine," the chief promised, reminding Ismay of a snake slithering closer.

"I willna." She shook her head again. "I would rather join a convent than wed any man."

"Dear Ismay, ye are a fiery lass, like a fine red, an unbroken mare."

He lifted his hand and wound his index finger around a russet curl tumbling down her shoulder. "Ye are indeed intoxicating and lovely. Yer hair, like flames, makes me quite eager to have ye alone."

Ismay felt her face go red as she glanced at her mother. She felt ashamed and bare before her.

"But," he continued, dragging Ismay's attention back to him as he ripped a dagger from his belt, "the use of yer feminine wiles will no' be tolerated." He stepped behind her and pulled her hair into his fist. Ismay tried to move away, but he yanked back and began sawing at her hair with the dagger. Ismay didn't want to admit to herself what he was doing. She tried to stop him, reaching behind her and slapping at him. She fought him while the sound of a blade cutting through her hair scorched into her memory. When he finished, she suddenly became free. She spun around, feeling for her hair at the same time. Most of it was gone. Her heart thrashed within her. Her belly tightened until she was tempted to double over. He'd cut it off to just above her shoulders! Her natural cloak was gone. She wanted to weep. But she wouldn't. She looked down at her locks spilled across the floor.

He'd shamed her for everyone to see. She would never forgive him.

"I willna marry ye," she vowed on a slow hiss.

She expected another consequence of her words. There was none. He smiled slightly. "Aye, ye will."

Her worried gaze fell to her mother, and to Andrew the butler. No one interceded for her. What if this beast hauled her away to his home tonight and held her captive until he forced her to marry him? No one would help her. So, she had to help herself, as she had when she was a child.

Almost instinctively she looked around the hall at the windows, the doors, any way to escape. Her eyes caught a glimpse of her russet locks on the floor. She felt an unwanted tear slip down her cheek and swiped it away with the back of her hand. Never would she marry him. She would rather give up her life. What was there left for her anyway since her father was gone?

But while she lived, she would plan. In fact, her mind was already strategizing. She barely heard Marjorie and the chief planning her life. What did it matter what they said? She wasn't going to obey them.

She would leave tonight when everyone was asleep. She would go south along Loch Ness and board a ferry to Kiliwhimin. She heard there was a church there. She would become a sister of whatever order there was.

"Our priest has already been made aware of the nuptials," Marjorie announced heartlessly. "This morning I informed our dressmakers to create something spectacular for the bride."

Ismay said nothing. Concealing her contempt for her father's wife for planning everything so quickly and without her knowledge or agreement. Ismay knew that if she continued to refuse them, they would no doubt have her watched. Running away would be more difficult. She said nothing, nor did she eat. No one seemed to notice.

"I am happy to see that ye have accepted yer fate," the chief said to her. "'Twill make it easier to spend time with ye today."

No! Ismay briefly considered running for the window and leaping out. She could hit the ground running. The chief appeared to be at least twenty years older than her. How was his running? Would he catch her?

"What choice do I have but to accept it?" she asked quietly without looking up.

The chief grinned beneath his thin mustache and beard. "Precisely. Now, since ye are no' eating, let's take a stroll. I hear yer mother's gardens are like nae other. Or…perhaps 'twas yer hand that groomed such a variety of flora?"

Ismay shook her head slightly and lifted her gaze to his. "Nae, Chief. Everything I touch dies."

His smile faded a bit but there was no possible way that he knew who and what she was.

"Fear no', my dear Ismay, I willna allow anything to die in yer care."

Ismay breathed. What did he mean? Her belly flipped, making her feel ill. He was a cruel man so she didn't believe he meant anything that benefited her.

She would climb out her window tonight and be a memory by morning. She had to fight to stop herself from revealing her slightest smile.

"Chief," Marjorie said, resting her hand on the chief's arm. "When did ye want to take her?"

Ismay closed her eyes as a knife pierced her heart. They didn't have a good relationship but her words still hurt. Her mother couldn't wait to be rid of her.

"Can ye have everything ready in two days?" he asked.

Ismay reached up to touch her shoulder, bare for the first

time in four years.

"I am certain I can," Marjorie let him know.

"Very well then, I will take my leave after a walk with my quiet bride."

Ismay clenched her teeth. She wasn't his wife yet.

When he stood up and offered his arm, she reluctantly took it. She must not arouse their suspicions of her intentions.

During their stroll, the chief closed his much larger hand over hers, still set in the crook of his elbow, and didn't let her go. He chose their time in her mother's garden to tell her what he expected of her as his wife. She would be obedient, dutiful, submissive. She would always present herself as acceptable, and she must have a strong body in order to bear all his children. She was surprised he didn't mention her inheritance bequeathed by her father. Is that why Marjorie hated her? Her mother could have everything as long as she left Ismay alone and didn't try to marry her off.

Her feet burned to run. Every step taken at his side felt as if she were stepping over nails.

Finally, he announced that he would leave and bent to kiss her farewell.

She took a step back. "I hope ye dinna mind a shy wife." She cast him a coy smile that almost made her double over.

His snarl faded and a smile of naked male intent replaced it. "I dinna mind," he told her. "But I willna be patient if she continues to be shy."

When he left, Ismay fought the urge to kick him in the backside on the way out.

Without waiting for Marjorie to call for her, Ismay hurried up the stairs to her room. She packed a small bag with a pair of hose and things her father had given her, gifts for his beloved daughter; ribbons for decorating her hair or dresses, a small, polished mirror that must have been quite costly for him, a carved wooden comb, and various jeweled pins and brooches. She would not use them to sell, they were far too precious to her. For coin, she would take something less meaningful. She hid her bag in a trunk against the wall.

She couldn't be happier that the chief had left. By the time word would reach him that she'd gone, she would be on a ferry heading toward Kiliwhimin. She skipped her evening meal, claiming to be feeling ill. When her mother sent Murran, her chambermaid to check up on her, Ismay lay under her blankets in bed.

Knowing Marjorie would send someone, Ismay had knelt before the roaring hearth until her skin felt burned, then she had rubbed some water from her basin over her face and leaped into her bed moments before the door opened and Murran stepped inside.

"Oh, lady, ye are burning with fever. I best tell yer mother right away!"

"Nae!" Ismay sat up and grabbed Murran's wrist. "Dinna worry her. It has been a trying day. I just need some rest."

"Aye, of course, lady." Murran looked at Ismay's shorn hair and sniffed. "I asked yer mother if I could go to Beauly with ye. I canna fathom how difficult 'twill be living with an ogre like him."

Ismay smiled and slipped her hand around the chambermaid's hand. Murran had always been kind to her. Ismay would miss her. She couldn't bid the maid farewell or let her know she was leaving. Though she liked Murran, she didn't trust anyone. People who had treated her kindly while she lived with the MacDonald chief were some of the first to pick up stones when her death sentence was to be carried out.

"There now, Murran," Ismay said gently. "I will be alright. Dinna fret. Yer kin are here. I could never ask ye to part with them."

"But lady, ye are like my own kin."

Ismay pulled Murran's knuckles to her cheek. She said nothing but closed her eyes, aching to cry but not allowing herself the luxury.

Later, alone in her bed, she wept. She wept for her father,

who had saved her life and her soul. She wept for herself and her uncertain future. Wherever her path led, it would be difficult. She would be a runaway bride, a woman alone in a world ruled by men. She didn't know how to survive on her own, to hunt, or to fight. But dying out there alone was still better than living with another chief.

She reached her fingers to her hair. It was a good thing he cut off her hair. Now, pretending to be a boy while she traveled would be less difficult.

She left her bed and hurried to pack a bonnet that once belonged to her father. After waiting another hour, she climbed out the window and descended the thick vine trellis against the stone wall.

And ran for her life. She ran for days—weeks, until she reached the ferry in Dores. She only stopped to drink from a stream or cook what she trapped, like a chipmunk or a deer mouse. She was starving, but she kept going. Twice, some older men tried to take her and force her into servitude. They hadn't tried to touch her. Her disguise worked well. She escaped them and ran. Younger than the men, she managed to lose them quickly.

She had thought she could steal a horse somewhere and make quicker time, but there were none to be had. So, she traveled on foot, which was considerably slower, affording her no extra time to relax or rest comfortably. Chief MacRae, and even her mother would have their men out searching for her by now. She could not stop yet.

In the weeks it took her to reach the ferry, she felt as if she'd aged a decade. She had been chased by a bear—a most harrowing event, but less terrifying than when a man in Traslorr chased her. There was also a woman, as frightening as the bear when, after leaving her freshly baked peach pie on her window-ledge to cool, she lost it to Ismay's hunger.

Ismay had been robbed and then smacked around when the thief discovered she had nothing to take. With her hair tucked under her bonnet, the thief thought she was a lad and thankfully did not check for her riches under her clothes.

All the running was a blessing in disguise. It kept her warm on the cool nights.

Traveling by ferry wasn't any better. Since she had to stowaway or hand over Marjorie's marriage ring (that Marjorie had removed from her finger two days after her husband died), she couldn't leave her hiding spot to even stretch her legs.

As they were anchoring in the harbor, she was discovered but managed to escape her captor and leap overboard.

She didn't consider herself a braw lass. She did things to survive. Like killing the MacDonald chief long ago. Aye, she'd killed him. She had been sold to him and became his slave. He had always beat her, but one night he tried to have his way with her. She hadn't meant to kill him. She didn't even know what it was to kill a man. She wanted him off her, and grew desperate for a weapon to help.

Knowing where men kept their daggers, she reached for his in his belt. Without hesitation, she slashed it at him. She cut an artery in his neck and he bled to death in his bed. She screamed, alerting his men. She had been taken before the council and declared guilty, punishable by death. Immediately.

Dragged outside, they tossed her into the dirt and picked up stones to hurl at the murderess.

She was eight summers old at the time.

She'd heard from the priest at May Hall that murder would not be forgiven by God. If she lived out the rest of her days as a nun, mayhap then God would forgive her.

But the church in Kiliwhimin had no room to take her for more than a night. They advised her to travel to Aberchalder at the northern end of Loch Oich and visit the abbey there.

She set out the next morning and after getting lost for several hours, arrived in Aberchalder two days later, but the abbey there was closed. She couldn't stop. Chief MacRae could be in a village close by searching for her.

She reached Laggan, a small village in the Great Glen along the Caledonian Canal and remained there for another two days. By then, her feet were swollen and blistered. She was exhausted and starving.

Since leaving her home, she had learned how to read a compass, how to steal, lie, disappear, and survive without softness. Her life had changed. She was alone again the way she was when she was a child—and so far, she had kept herself alive. That was something to be proud of, wasn't it? She could do it. She could live on her own. But where? There were no vacant houses to inhabit, no abbeys to join. She had no idea where to go. She only knew that hunger plagued her. Catching squirrels or trapping a quail now and then was not enough. She longed for a full meal. Hunger drove her onward to a small hamlet on the southern shores of Loch Lochy. There were no taverns or inns where she could eat, but one of the fishermen from a nearby crofting settlement, gave her three of the fish he'd caught that day and he wouldn't take a pence for them.

"A lad must eat to grow strong," he said and gave her a friendly whack on the back.

She laughed and nodded, remembering that she was supposed to be a lad.

She didn't stay in the hamlet, or with the fisherman for longer than she needed to. She wasn't far enough away from Raigmore or Beauly. She had to keep moving until she found an abbey that would take her.

She didn't stop again, climbing up hills and walking through glens only to reach more hills and more glens. Her body had grown stronger during her escape with all the uphill terrain—and she quickly remembered how to swing a weapon without hesitating, when a ruffian leaped out from the trees and tried to grab her. She'd been using her stick as a cane for her tired legs, but when it hit the attacker in the head, it knocked him out cold.

She decided to keep the stick with her.

She kept going until she could see Ben Nevis jutting upward

in the distance, with gossamer mist swirling over its high crest. She would love to hide beneath the protective shadow of a mountain—just for a few days.

Making Ben Nevis her destination, she pushed herself farther along until a large castle loomed ahead, just beyond a field of heather, and in the midst of smaller, thatched-roof cottages and other structures. A chief's residence most likely. Of which clan she had no idea. She didn't know where she was yet, but she spotted an inn and as she moved closer, she smelled the salivating aromas of seasoned meats and honeyed bread wafting through the air.

Reaching into a pocket hanging from her breeches, she felt for the last trinket she could sell for food and a bed.

Despite its name, the Doomsday Inn & Tavern looked like any other inn and tavern in any other town or village. But, perhaps its name was a warning about staying in a place such as this, with its band of deadly looking ruffians sprinkled through-out.

With exhaustion slipping over her, Ismay decided that, rather than be molested by one of these men, she would turn around and leave. Safer to sleep behind someone's house than in a house full of men. Stepping back outside, the sound of roaring thunder broke the silence of the night. She looked up. Would she have to go back inside because of rain? But the sky was clear. The sound vibrated through her feet this time. Closer. She turned toward the loud sound and saw a herd of cattle running by about a hundred feet away.

She pulled her cloak closer around herself and walked away from the inn. There was likely someone's barn close by. She would sleep there. She was hungry, but the stale bread in her bag would have to do.

It was better than becoming wife to a chief.

✳

CHAPTER TWO

MIST SETTLED OVER the ground and covered Constantine Cameron, Chief of the clan Cameron where he and his men, most of whom were his kin, lay in wait for the pesky MacKintoshes and their cattle. Constantine had sent a warning to the MacKintosh chief that the Camerons would take any herd the MacKintosh brought through Cameron land. But his warning had gone unheeded.

Unforgivable.

He had received word last eve from his uncle Robert Cameron in Fort William, of the traveling MacKintoshes. Constantine would stop them here at the foot of Gulvain and make certain his point was made.

While he waited, clothed in gossamer thread and chilled to the bone in the late summer Highland dawn, he let the silence fill him. He welcomed it over memories of the accusing glares of his wife's parents and the prison of his past that haunted him.

Now, if he focused on the silence hard enough, all he heard was the breath of thirty-six Camerons hidden in the mist around him.

They were good at waiting. Patience had won his men many battles over the years. He and his men had held off hundreds of Cromwell's forces when the Camerons were called to act as an outpost to guard the Earl of Glencairn's army. They had waited almost forty-eight hours for the Cromwellians to appear. When they did, their enemies were quickly defeated. After that, they fought for two straight years of fearlessly butchering enemy Cromwellian forces. Their victories had earned Constantine the title of Deliverer of the Highland Army, and written praise from their exiled king, Charles.

With substantially fewer battles, the Camerons did what they had done before, they raided, striking unseen in the quiet dawn or the starless twilight of dusk—led by Constantine also known as *The Ghost* Cameron. He was feared and respected, but little was truly known about him, save that he'd fought eleven battles, he rarely smiled, and he always brought his men back home. No one but his closest friends knew the weight of his grief and regret over not being at his wife, Alison's bedside as she left the earth with their first daughter during the babe's birth. Or how so much death, much of it by his own hand during battle, tore the sleep from his eyes and produced cries from the depths of his heart when he did sleep and dream. He had seen much...too much for his heart to remain the same.

He rubbed his eyes, weary that his anguished thoughts found him again.

The ground rumbled, thankfully commanding all his attention. Immediately, his thoughts focused on what was happening. Only a herd could shake the ground. The MacKintoshes were coming. Constantine clicked his tongue against the roof of his mouth. The sound snapped his men to attention.

Peering down into the glen, the Camerons waited a little longer until the MacKintosh riders and their cattle came into view.

Constantine counted eighteen riders circling the herd. He blew a short puff of air through his lips, insulted that so few men had been assigned to keeping the herd safe from the Camerons. It proved the MacKintosh chief didn't take Constantine seriously. That would change after today.

Before he and his men raced down the side of the mountain

to retrieve their horses, he gave the signal for Lachlan, the youngest of his cousins and an expert archer, to ready his weapon. He wasn't to fire until he received a second signal from Constantine.

Now mounted, the Camerons almost reached the foot of Gulvain when their bold enemy spotted them. Constantine gave the signal and three consecutive arrows from Lachlan's bow struck the soil a few feet apart in front of the herd, startling the animals and driving them into a stampede.

Flying dirt, men shouting, and swords swinging made it difficult to see and hear. The danger of a horse slipping and being trampled along with its rider was very real and entirely possible if one didn't know what one was doing.

Constantine and his men were expert rustlers and despite the deafening clamor as the herd shook the ground around them, kicking up chunks of earth, they moved into their practiced positions. Some raced swiftly on their horses to positions of six feet apart in two rows with fifty feet between them. Geoffry and ten of the Camerons raced around the herd, shouting and pushing their mounts close to the cattle, drawing them into the narrow path made by their comrades, while Constantine and Lewis fought the MacKintosh riders.

Before the raid, Constantine had given orders to Lewis and any other one of his kin who found himself fighting. As was the case with raids, they were not to kill anyone in the MacKintosh clan. But they could break bones and knock out some teeth.

Dismounting, Constantine used his hands to pull MacKintoshes out of their saddles and beat them senseless. He was quick, precise, and merciful enough to stop before he killed them.

If the truth be known, he didn't like raiding and found fighting without the risk of death quite mundane. But it was a way to keep him and his kin rich. After today they would have three hundred head of cattle.

Taking a moment from fighting while his opponent fell, Constantine watched the thunderous herd slow under the direction of Geoffry and Fionn MacDonald, sons of Constantine's Uncle Richard on his mother's side, along with twenty other Camerons, including Lachlan, who had left his hiding place on the mountain and had come to join his cousins to lead the cattle away.

Constantine counted about fifty head of cattle.

Lewis, son of Uncle Robert, stayed behind with Constantine and the others to fight. They took down the MacKintosh riders, two by two but without killing any of them.

If this had been war, every one of them would have been cut down without mercy. But this wasn't a battle. This was a raid. There was a difference. He was an outlaw and a soldier, not a murderer.

He was tempted to yawn when the next MacKintosh came at him.

When Constantine discovered the chief MacKintosh's second eldest son, Kenneth, among the riders, he dragged him out of his saddle and hit him twice with his fists, almost knocking him out, but not completely. He wanted a message delivered.

"Yer father insults me by sendin' his son," he said, pulling the young man to his feet by the collar after his punches left him teetering. His eyes, with pupils as black and as cold as coal stared into his victim's eyes with dark contempt. "Does he think I willna kill ye if ye bring yer cattle through my land?"

"Ye will start a clan war," the MacKintosh's son reminded him quickly.

Constantine did not smirk or chuckle as his men did, but he continued to stare into his enemy's eyes with the pale promise of death glinting his gaze and unmistakable conviction softening his voice. "I dinna fear war. I'll kill ye and send yer headless body to yer chief just to prove it."

As he had hoped, his threat was enough to make his captive tremble. "But I willna kill ye today. When ye're well enough to return home, go and tell yer father that yer cattle now belong to the Camerons."

"When I'm…well enough?" MacKintosh asked nervously, still held up by his collar, eyes wide and haunted with worry.

Constantine said nothing but nodded and let him fall to the ground. When he stepped away to mount his horse, he passed Lewis and tossed him a slight nod. It was enough for Lewis to slip a knife from his belt and move toward their prisoner.

Without waiting around to see what damage his cousin would inflict—for Lewis was known and feared for his enjoyment in making men suffer—Constantine left the glen and rode to a small crest. Without dismounting, he let the wind blow his long hair across his face and eyes as he looked down into the glen at his kin herding the cattle, now under control, out of the mountain pass.

He heard another horse approaching, but he didn't turn to see who it was. He already knew it was the archer, Lachlan. After spending a lifetime—half of it on the battlefield—with his closest cousins, he knew the sound of their horses' gait, and the rhythm of each man's breathing.

"Geoffry counted fifty-three head," Lachlan let him know as he rode closer. "The men are herdin' them to the castle. Geoffry and Fionn will meet us at the tavern, with Lewis."

Constantine gave him a slight nod and shoved his hands into his leather gloves. It wasn't anything he didn't already know. Without another word he flicked his reins and rode away before his cousin heard him sigh or groan.

Once the cattle reached Tor Castle, they would be safe under Cameron care. If the MacKintoshes dared to come after them, they would be dealt with harshly.

But now was time to celebrate adding more cattle to the herd.

Constantine didn't much care for celebrations. He did it for his cousins. For him, life didn't offer much to celebrate. War, thieving, the deaths of those he loved—or could have spent his lifetime loving if he'd had the chance.

He thought of his daughter while he rode toward Geoffry's

tavern. Her name was Katherine. He would have called her Katie, which he did, even now five years after her death. He and Alison had chosen her name together when his wife first discovered she was with child. Katie lived for six hours after her mother's death. Alison's father and her uncles had buried her and her daughter.

Constantine thought of it now, every hour, every day. He hadn't been home to meet his daughter during her short stay on earth, or to put his family to rest. Guilt still plagued him, sorrow steeped deep into his bones so much that he no longer felt human. He found no humor in things that once made him smile, becoming instead morose and menacing.

When Gilbert, Constantine's older brother and former "Lochiel," as every Cameron chief was called, named him chief before he died last summer, Constantine refused the title at first. He didn't want to be responsible for so many. It was difficult enough on the battlefield, daily living in the Highlands of Scotland was an entirely different battle. But there was no one else willing to do it.

"I heard the MacKintosh chief's son was there," Lachlan appeared on his horse beside him. "Ye left him to Lewis?"

"Aye."

Lachlan didn't let Constantine's vague interest stop him. "Well, in truth, I…I…"

Constantine kept his gaze fixed in front of him and waited. He didn't care who knew it; he favored Lachlan. The lad had been found in the snow outside the castle seventeen years ago, orphaned at the tender age of two. At first, Constantine considered him a pest. The wee thing followed him everywhere he went with his other cousins, to do what ten-year-old boys did— mostly get into trouble. Constantine could not get into trouble with a babe hanging onto his ankle.

But one day, while the boys were searching for frogs along the riverbank, Lachlan pretended to be a frog and hopped off a rock and into the river. The water was not deep but was waist-high for Constantine. The babe went under and didn't reappear. But Constantine had already begun running. As he went, he realized he would miss the lad if he drowned. Once Constantine saved him, he barely let the babe out of his sight. He learned to love him as his little brother.

"'Tis just that," Lachlan began again, "do ye think 'tis…best to leave him alone with Lewis?"

"Aye. I trust Lewis no' to kill him."

"But, Lochiel…"

"Lad," he said, stopping him with the sheer, unmovable command of his voice. He loved Lachlan, but the lad should not forget authority.

"Fergive me," Lachlan repented with a bowed head. "Ye know I love Lewis. That was no' my heart speakin'."

Constantine smiled in the filtered sunlight and kept his horse at a canter.

"Have ye given any more thought to weddin' Millie Stewart?"

"Lachlan…" At the sound of his name coming from his chief's mouth, Lachlan lowered his gaze again and stopped speaking. His chief went on though. "I have nae intention of weddin' Miss Stewart or anyone else. Why would I?"

"To settle doun and—"

Constantine cast him a black look. His youngest cousin looked everywhere but at him.

"I dinna wish to settle doon. Dinna bring it up again."

"Aye, Constantine."

They rode on in silence, which was nothing new for Constantine, but obviously extremely difficult for Lachlan, judging from the way the lad opened his mouth to start speaking but then snapped his lips shut, likely remembering who he was traveling with.

Constantine didn't find it awkward. Talking just for the sake of conversation was awkward. Flapping his lips or listening to someone else do it did not silence the voices.

My love, you are to be a father. His heart had filled with joy. A father. He was to have a bairn of his own. A son or a daughter. He didn't care which. It would be tiny. How would he hold it?

Would his rough palms hurt its delicate skin? He had to care for him or her, and he would—all their life. The thought of another life…no, two lives completely dependent on a man could easily weigh him down. But not Constantine. How could loving others more than himself weigh him down? His life had been a blessing. He started building their house at the foot of Ben Nevis after she told him and took joy in watching them both grow.

But as dreams fade upon waking, his life changed almost overnight. War had broken out between the English, led by Oliver Cromwell, and the Scots. Constantine was called to fight for the Stuarts. He'd left his wife to go fight.

At the time, part of him thrilled at the prospect of fighting. He stayed alive in the midst of death and barbarism such as no eye should see. He stayed alive to see his family again. To finish their house and live tending cattle. But his family perished without him. And for that, he would forever reject having another family.

He felt the ground rumble beneath him and knew his kin were bringing the cattle to the castle.

"There's the tavern," Lachlan said, sounding as if it was an oasis in the wilderness—which it was, but Constantine's cousin was thankful to reach this spot of civilization because there were others to talk to.

They dismounted, and after seeing to their horses, were about to step inside the Doomsday Tavern when the sky lit up with bolts of lightning followed by peals of thunder.

Vaguely, his other cousins crossed his thoughts. Would they be safe getting here? Lightning was known to strike a person in a wide-open glen.

But as quickly as the thought appeared, it was gone, leaving him looking over the four faces of drunken patrons at two of the tables.

Constantine ignored them and pulled out a chair at an empty table. Lachlan sat next, offering the strangers an amiable smile. They ordered their drinks from Bea, one of the friendly servers and waited for the others.

When the door opened a few moments later, Constantine expected to see Lewis or the brothers, Geoffry and Fionn, but a lass hurried in from rain. It was a lass, was it not? Her features, as well as her hands were too delicate to belong to a lad. Though she—or he—dressed in breeches and a coat at least three sizes too big, moved like a woman, with soft, hesitant steps. The hair on the stranger's head appeared to be burnt auburn in color, though it was stuffed beneath a bonnet of dull green.

She looked around nervously, peering up the stairs where the rooms were. He understood why a lass would disguise herself as a lad. He didn't like it. Any man in Lochaber who put his unwanted hands on a lass would have his hands removed.

Or she could be running and hiding from someone, a husband or her father. Constantine didn't want to know or to get involved in things that didn't concern him and went back to his bread.

His rowdy cousins arrived, pushing open the door and almost knocking the emaciated soul to his or her feet.

"I think I saw a few teeth flying before I was finished with him," Lewis mused and the brothers laughed. "I also gave him a scar"—he motioned with his index finger down the length of his left cheek—"that will nae doubt get him more lasses. I did him a service."

They spotted Constantine first and then the new patron.

"What will it be, then?" Lewis asked her…him.

"I need a room fer the night."

"Pardon," Lewis demanded impatiently. "Speak up. I need a drink."

"A room. I require one fer the night."

"Look," Lewis said with distaste marring his brow. "'tisna safe fer someone such as yerself to sleep here."

She turned to cast a withering look at the front door being pelted with rain.

Constantine left his chair and blocked her path to the exit.

"Lewis, will ye turn her away in the rain? Get her a room." He turned his fiery gaze on the other men at the tables. "From this moment onward, she falls under my protection. If anyone goes near her room—"

My lord, fergive me," she croaked out, daring, albeit with a shaky voice, to interrupt him. "I am no' a she."

He bent his head to stare into her eyes for a moment. They were a clear, defiant gray, like mist over a loch, both haunting and unforgettable. He looked away for a moment, but then, as if he had no control over his own eyes, his gaze returned to hers. This time, he took in every inch of her face, with her delicate jaw, irresistibly plump lips, and a pert nose. This was most definitely a lass. But there was steel behind her soft features. He let his gaze rove over a stray, orange curl that had sprung loose from beneath her bonnet. He was mildly curious, unwantedly so, about the hair she tried to hide. Would it fall free around her shoulders like flames?

"I am corrected," he announced to the others who were watching.

When he set his gaze on her again, the slightest trace of humor flashed across his eyes. "Fergive me, lad."

Taking her turn, she let her wide, nervous gaze settle on him.

He felt the urge to look away, a warning to step away from her.

"Do ye remove yer protection from me then?" she asked in a voice so soft, he involuntarily moved closer to hear her.

As he looked down into her eyes, he felt an unfamiliar pull to stay close. Why should he? He began to shake his head.

"I...I need protection," she told him. "Just fer one night. If I dinna sleep soundly one more night, I will go mad."

Were those tears making her eyes glisten like starlight against a gray sky? She'd said for one more night. How many had she been traveling, and was she alone? All questions he didn't need answers to.

He broke eye contact with her and spread his gaze over the

men in the tavern. "He is still under my protection."

"Yer word, my lord?" She shifted on her feet at the weight of his stare. Then, "My father always said a man who gave his word and kept it could be trusted.

He only gave his word to his men and only when he meant what he said. "What do I care if ye trust me or not?" he asked coolly.

"If I trust ye, I can finally sleep."

Damn her, Constantine thought, searching her gaze for deceit. Why did shadows, like ghosts of things she had survived, fill her gaze? Why did she have to appear so pitiful in her filthy, oversized clothes?

She took a step to go around him and leave the tavern.

"Aye, I give it," he allowed.

She stopped and turned back to him. "Thank ye, my lord."

He wasn't sure if he'd finally gone mad—his cousins all stared at him as if they believed so.

"Give the lad a room that locks from the inside," he told Lewis. "Then return and tell me which room—" His words were interrupted by the loud rumble of the lass's belly. He looked at her and then sighed.

"Come." He crooked a finger at her. "Let's eat."

CHAPTER THREE

ISMAY WAS SHOWN to a table that only moments ago had been occupied by two rough-looking men. They hurried away from the table when the innkeeper told them to move.

The Highlander who gave his word to protect her didn't sit with her at the table, nor did he allow any other man to sit with her or even approach her while she was served mutton stew that tasted like it came from heaven, and semi-stale black bread, with ale to wash it down.

There were no words to express how happy she was to be eating a warm meal at a table.

She was also thankful that no one approached her or asked to eat with her, not because they all appeared to be miscreants bent on trouble of one kind or another. Nae, she was thankful they didn't approach her because then they might have asked her why she was weeping into her bowl. It was because, for this brief moment since her father died, she felt safe and cared for. She knew she was a fool. The Highlander didn't vow his protection and feed her for nothing in return. At the moment, she didn't care why he did it. She was overcome by the warmth flowing through her thanks to the kindness of one stranger. So she wept, unaware that all the ruffians lounging around the tavern were aware of her tears. A warning look from her benefactor kept them all from speaking a word to her.

She looked over at him, standing off alone, glancing at her every now and then. He wore a braided leather cord strapped across his body and supporting the sheathed sword at his back. A great plaid of red and dark green was draped over one shoulder and belted on his waist, where three more knives were tied. Underneath, he wore an ivory-colored thin, woolen tunic. His wrists were tied in strips of leather almost to his elbows, where more daggers were stored. His legs were bare and crossed at his booted ankles where he stood leaning against the wall.

Beneath his woolen hood his chestnut hair was long, spreading over his shoulders and falling across his deep, burnished brown eyes. He reminded Ismay of a wild stallion, a dangerous and unpredictable beast. But presently, he was all she had. As flimsy a thread it was, she held on.

She smiled at him through her tears.

He looked away, but not immediately.

Three times, one of the other men went to him to speak with him, or laugh with him. She watched his reactions, noting first that he held no drink in his hand, nor did he break out in laughter with them. He was quiet, seemingly preferring to be alone.

Seemingly—because she watched his gaze follow this one or that one as they returned to their seat. She caught the way his gaze softened on them, especially on a cherubic looking young man with a halo of golden curls framing his face, and a quiver full of bows slung across his back.

Her protector cared for the other Highlanders who'd arrived with him. But it was the barest glimpse of another side of him. She doubted anyone would see it if they didn't look hard enough. Authority and confidence rolled off him in waves, along with a detached to-hell-with-the-world air.

But he had stepped in for her—and seemingly of his own accord—when no one else, save her father, ever had.

In the course of eating and wiping her eyes, she learned the Highlander was Constantine Cameron of the famed Clan Cameron cattle raiders. And these men around him, no doubt, were the raiders.

Finally, when she pushed her bowl away and rubbed her belly in satisfaction, she opened her eyes and found Mr. Cameron standing over her.

She kept herself from trembling or gripping the armrests of her chair. She gave away no sign of the effect the sight of him had on her. He frightened her because he looked fast and fit. If she ran, she wouldn't get far.

"Would ye like anythin' else, lady?"

Lady. She hadn't felt like one in so long. She blinked back a fresh mist assailing her eyes. He knew then, yet he went along with her when she denied being a lass. Aye, his dark eyes shone on her, peering deep within her.

She blinked away, not risking the chance of him seeing her crimes. "I could not eat another thing."

"Then let me walk ye to yer room."

She wished she could trust him. She looked at his out-stretched hand. "I—"

"Come, then, lad." His deep voice settled over her like a comforting blanket. She thought his eyes warmed on her the way they warmed on his men, but she was sleepy and wasn't sure if she was dreaming.

She reached up and accepted his hand.

She tried to pay the innkeeper with her mother's ring, but her benefactor wouldn't allow the innkeeper to take it. She would have insisted, not wanting to be in any debt. But she was too exhausted, so she followed them up the stairs in silence.

The thought of sleeping in a bed made her sigh out loud three times before she even saw it.

"Look here," her protector said, calling her to look at the door, or more specifically, the lock on the door. "Here is the key. It locks from the inside. Once ye lock it, no one can get in. That is, if they get past me."

"What do you mean?" she asked. He didn't mean to—

Men's voices shouting threats and obscenities reached the

upper landing and the innkeeper's ears. "I'll wager a free supper that 'tis those two troublemaking brothers, Fionn most especially," he said to Mr. Cameron. "I'll whip their hides myself!"

Ismay watched the innkeeper storm out, leaving her alone with the handsome Highlander.

"What I meant was," he continued as if no interruption had occurred—at least not one he concerned himself with, "I'll be right ootside the door."

"What?" It took a moment to remember what they had been talking about. "What fer?"

"To protect ye, why else?" he demanded curiously while she yawned.

Ah, yes, he had promised to protect her. Had he meant all night? "I still dinna know why ye would do that."

"Why?" he repeated, eyes widening as if he could not believe she questioned him. "Why do ye ask that instead of thank the good Lord I was here tonight?"

"I already did that numerous times while you fed me, my lord."

"Hmm, I see," he said, sounding as if she had just blown all the wind out of his sails.

"I thanked Him, but I still dinna know why."

He captured her and made her go still with a gaze. A gaze from some deep place where he was not all hard and detached as he appeared. "I know ye're a—"

"Chief," the innkeeper returned.

Chief? Ismay turned to cast her gaze on Mr. Constantine Cameron.

"Ye settled that swiftly, Lewis," he said to the innkeeper, sounding a bit disappointed that the rumble was over before it started.

"I threw oot the whole lot of them," Lewis told him. "'Twas those four Anglos loiterin' about who started it, but I'll be lockin' up fer the night, so I sent them all home."

"I'll be stayin'."

Lewis stared at his chief after his declaration and then glanced at Ismay. The innkeeper didn't also know she was a woman, did he? She was certain the—oh, she had to swallow back a miserable groan that her protector was a chief—that the chief knew she was a woman. She suspected it was what he had been about to confess before he was interrupted.

Now it made more sense why he would offer to protect and feed her. Of course he wanted something for it. They would be alone.

Well, he would have to kill her first.

She waited while Lewis and his chief shared a few more words, then crossed her arms over her chest when they were alone again. "Chief?"

He nodded, perhaps noticing the sting in her voice, for his eyes narrowed on her.

"I didna know ye were a chief."

"Is that what angers ye? That I'm the Cameron chief?" He moved closer to her, making her heart thump loud in her ears. Just when she was about to back away, he handed her the key. She snatched it from his hand.

"I dinna trust men who hold power," she told him, walking to the door.

"That is why I got ye a room where the door locks from the inside."

She almost tripped over her feet.

"But ye trust me." His voice was lush and hypnotic falling against her ears.

"I will know whether I do or I do no' in the morning."

He seemed satisfied with her reply and turned to leave the room.

"Mr. Cameron, even if you prove to be trusted, I want nothing to ever do with ye after tonight."

He nodded without hesitation—which hooked Ismay in the belly just a wee bit.

She didn't worry about how she felt. She was bone weary and

almost forgot to lock the door. But she remembered, knowing he was out there.

She didn't have much time to think about him because three breaths after she climbed into bed, she was asleep.

She must have indeed felt safe because she slept until morning and more soundly than she had since her father died. When she finally did wake up it was due to hunger. She wondered if it would be safe to venture down to the tavern alone? Was Mr. Cameron still outside her door? She washed up in a small basin and dressed in the clothes she'd arrived in.

Then she remembered that she had locked the door from the inside. No one could get in to bring her food.

When she stepped outside her door, she was mildly disappointed to find that Mr. Cameron was not there.

A wave of panic rose over her. Would she be attacked while she filled her belly? Fear made her hesitate, but hunger drove her onward.

When she reached the foot of the stairs and looked inside the tavern, she saw the Highlander sitting alone at one of the tables. Had he stayed there all night as he said he would? What would he want in return? She waited there four stairs up, watching him in the early morning light streaming through the windows. His skin was golden, tanned from spending time outdoors. He was the Cameron chief. Was the castle she'd seen his home? What kind of chief was also a cattle rustler?

She thought about hating him, as she hated all clan chiefs, but this one had gotten her a bed in a private room that locked from the inside. He'd paid for her supper and didn't allow her to use her last trinket.

He was stunningly handsome in the filtered light, with smooth cheekbones and a sculpted yet gentle jawline. The slightest trace of melancholy shaped his lips. Natural waves and strands of his windblown hair framed his face and eclipsed his soulful gaze while he stared longingly toward the window and the great Ben Nevis beyond. He appeared distracted and mayhap…agonized by what he saw in his thoughts, what they made him feel.

He had likely done terrible things and suffered the guilt of it all. Was she his atonement? Did he still do terrible things? She shivered as a chill crept down her spine.

He turned toward her, and for an instant his faraway gaze fell on her. She felt breathless, lightheaded, incredibly sad.

Then he saw *her,* and his expression went a bit tender, evoking romance and mystery and compelling her to take another step down the stairs, then another, moving toward him.

He rose from his chair—like a mountain rising with the morning sun, though he was crafted in lean sinew rather than overly bulky muscle. How heavy was the weight he carried on his wide shoulders?

"Lady," he said, his voice sounding rough with the first word of the day. "Ye rested well?"

She nodded. He called her lady again. "I owe ye much fer keeping yer word and staying the night."

"Ye must be hungry." He reached a hand out to the chair beside him and dragged it out from under the table for her to sit.

She did and grabbed at the black bread on a plate close to him. She graced the male server with a smile when he brought her a cup of water. It was lukewarm but clean. She drank and then asked for more.

She felt the chief's eyes on her. One would have to be an incoherent fool not to feel the power of his gaze. But she was so thirsty for clean water, she could have drunk four cups. And the bread. It was the same she'd had last eve, so good she'd dreamed of it.

"'Twas two nights, lass."

"Hmm?" She looked at him and stopped chewing. "Pardon?"

"Ye slept fer two days and two nights."

What? What was he saying? He had not left her for over forty-eight hours?

"I wouldna have ye be confused aboot the days."

She swallowed, still staring at him. "I havena slept soundly but with one eye open and one foot on the ground fer some time now. I think I made up fer it these last two days." She smiled shyly before she realized what she was doing. When her blood warmed her veins at the way he was looking at her, she cleared her throat and darted her gaze to the door.

"No one will harm ye here," he said in a deep voice coiled in restraint.

"Have ye been home?" she asked after a moment of silence between them.

"All the comforts of home are right here," he said, turning his attention away from her to dig his spoon into his porridge when it arrived with hers.

He had stayed and hadn't gone home for two days.

"Thank ye, Chief," she allowed herself to say.

The faintest trace of a smile slipped across his features. She was glad he didn't smile more often. She would lose her senses too much.

"Now I am doubly curious why ye made such a promise to me." She ate a spoonful of porridge and then ended up scraping the bowl when it was all gone.

Feeling his gaze on her again, she looked up to find him watching. Shamefully, she set the bowl down on the table. "Fergive me, it has been a long—"

"There is nothin' to fergive," he said and went back to eating.

That was it? He was not going to scold her for eating so much and so quickly?

When he remained quiet, giving his attention to his bowl, she drank more water and smiled. Just a little.

"Ye were about to tell me what yer motive was fer guarding my door day and night for two days. What is it ye want from me? What do ye expect to gain, Chief?"

His expression darkened, frightening her for a moment. "I want ye to arrive safely at yer destination."

"What else?"

His brow dipped low over his eyes. His decadent lips arched downward. "Nothin' else."

"Am I atonement fer yer sins?" she pressed gently. She didn't want to push too much, but she wanted to know what he expected so she could refuse now.

Laughter bubbled upward and escaped him in a husky serenade that reverberated through Ismay's defenses and shook the walls. And while they were battering through, he grew serious again and asked, "From whom are ye runnin', lass?"

She breathed and set her cup on the table. "My mother and the man she intends fer me to marry."

"Why do ye run away?" he asked, appearing unfazed by her confession. But—

Did she note a thread of compassion in him? Or was she so desperate to hear it that she imagined it?

"The man I am to marry is a cruel man. Cruel men are capable of many things. I would rather be dead than tied to a heartless husband."

He said nothing while they sat together in the empty tavern—with the innkeeper, Lewis Cameron wandering about.

"Is he the reason ye hate chiefs?" the chief asked, wiping his mouth with his serviette and leaning back in his chair.

Ismay watched as if the passage of time slowed while the cloth rubbed across his full lips. Her heart thumped loudly in her ears. She swallowed, filling herself with the sound of her throat convulsing while she swallowed.

"No, I hated them long before him."

Again, he said nothing. Being caught staring didn't seem to bother him. It made Ismay feel awkward and she looked away.

"I dinna wish to speak of it anymore," she let him know.

"As ye wish," he answered kindly, quietly. Then, "Would ye like some chicken?"

Her eyes widened on him. Chicken? "Aye! I would love some chicken!"

Well, if he was trying to win her loyalties over to his side, food was the way to do it.

"Ye willna tell the others about me being a lass, will ye??" she breathed, feeling like a young girl sharing secrets with her closest friend. "Can I trust ye no' to tell them?"

He gave her an impatient look and nodded.

"I am called Ismay."

He took a moment to gather the sound of it in, then waited for the rest.

She didn't tell him. She couldn't. She knew Camerons and MacDonalds were distant kin. He would hate her and throw her to the wolves for killing the MacDonald chief when she was eight. The MacDonalds still hated the MacPhersons for harboring her.

"Drummond. Ismay Drummond."

He nodded, looking unconvinced.

"Fergive me," she repented again. "Knowing certain things could be dangerous fer ye."

His expression warmed on her, but barely. "Let me worry aboot myself."

"I would like to agree, Chief. But I dinna want anyone dying fer me."

"Miss Drummond," he said with a tender scowl, "ye insult me. I willna die. No' fer ye. No' fer anyone."

"I am glad to hear that."

He was silent. Letting seconds fade away. Then, "Why are ye glad to hear it? Because ye think I am a good person? Or is it somethin' else?"

She laughed, though it was a shrill sound that burned even her ears. "Aye, it is because ye are a good person. Ye have been kind to me. I dinna want to see ye die."

She held her breath until she decided he was done examining her words. She hoped he was. After all, she was not being truthful. She did not want him to die because then she would be alone again. She knew it was a selfish reason. That's why she could not tell him.

"Is that castle yer home?" She pointed in the opposite direction of Mount Nevis.

"Tor Castle. 'Tis where I live."

Where he lived, but it was not home. Home was the other way. Ismay turned to look toward the window and…Ben Nevis—the destination she had chosen when she had first seen its peak piercing the clouds. What was there for him that he ached to return to? His home, the place where his heart dwelled?

"I would not like to live in a castle or a keep ever again," she told him as their chicken was served.

"Where do ye plan to go from here then?"

Her eyes widened on him and for the space of a breath, she thought she would start weeping all over again. It was not like her. But she had never lost her father before. "I dinna have a plan, lord."

His lips parted like a flower rolling back its petals to greet the sun. "Are ye goin' wherever yer legs take ye then?"

"Aye, I suppose." And to the colossal Ben Nevis, she thought to herself.

"Well, they took ye here, and to Tor Castle."

"Fer what purpose?" She had to know.

"Ye will discover that when ye arrive, I suppose."

"I am no' going," she insisted.

He stopped and proceeded to eat his chicken. Ismay watched him covertly. Why would he believe that her legs took her purposely to him? Why didn't he insist that she go to his castle and serve him? That's what she expected. He was different. He didn't push her around or order her about. He didn't care if she stayed or left. In fact, he barely showed any interest in her at all. Was he married? Was she waiting at their home beyond the mountain?

The door to the tavern opened and two of the chief's friends from two nights ago came in from the morning cold.

"Chief!" The one with raven hair and bright-blue eyes greeted hurrying toward them. He offered Ismay a friendly smile and she returned it, though shyly. "Did ye sleep here again, then?" he asked.

The chief nodded and then turned to spread his gaze over them. "Why is Lachlan not with ye?"

"He stayed behind to have a word with the bonny Brigid Eloise Baker," said the other man with sandy hair and topaz eyes. Ismay remembered them and she knew which one was missing.

The chief paused chewing and appeared to be thinking about it, then he scowled. "Who?"

"The baker's daughter."

"Ennis, the baker from Mallaig?" asked the chief.

Both men nodded and the chief went back to his bowl. Soon, Lewis, the innkeeper joined them at the table, taking a seat near the one with sandy waves and large topaz eyes. He also inquired on the whereabouts of Lachlan.

"These men are my kin," the chief turned to her. "I didna introduce ye properly when ye last were with us. That's Fionn MacDonald," he motioned to the one with black hair tied back into a neat queue, "and that is his older brother, Geoffry. Ye already met Lewis."

Geoffry smiled at her and began to remove his bonnet. He froze when his chief glared at him.

All Ismay could think about was that these two Highland brothers would likely kill her if they knew who she was and what she had done.

"This is—"

"Joseph Drummond," she blurted, interrupting the chief. His kin didn't look happy about it. "Fergive me." She bowed her head before the chief without any difficulty in submissiveness. It had been taught to her in her earliest days. "I meant no disrespect."

"Again," he said without turning to her. "Nothin' to fergive. Quit that way of thinkin.'"

Quit...How? She leaned in close and whispered. "How am I supposed to do that?"

Finally, he lifted his head and seared brands into her soul when his gaze met hers. "Ye claimed to trust me. Start there."

---※---

CHAPTER FOUR

CONSTANTINE FINISHED BREAKING his fast and pretended to listen to the conversation around him. He wanted to look at *Miss* Drummond. Miss Ismay Drummond, but he would have to resist the urge to scowl.

She wanted to know why he helped her. He didn't have an answer. She had appeared so weary, so afraid and alone. He offered his help without thinking first. It was a habit he thought he'd broken years ago. When she wept while she ate, it tore at his resolve, though he did his best to ignore it. It tore at all the men's resolve. Without saying anything to her about it, they had guessed she was a lass early on. He was glad. He didn't want them to be fooled by anyone.

Yesterday morn they couldn't stop talking about her sobbing into her bread. Lachlan had asked if any of them noticed her shoes with the soles worn down to her flesh. They all agreed she was running from someone. Now, Constantine knew she'd been running from her kin and her betrothed. She'd been running for a long time, proving her fear and her resilience were real. He wanted to take her to Tor, where she would be safe for as long as she wanted to stay.

But she refused his offer.

What more could he do? She was not his responsibility.

"If ye're hidin' from the law," Fionn addressed her, "the chief will take ye in."

"I'm no' hiding from the law," *Mr.* Drummond told them in a voice soft enough to leave three of the four men oblivious to what she said.

"Ye will be safe at Tor," Geoffry assured her with a tender smile that tempted Constantine to kick him under the table.

"Safe from what?" She let out a short, high-pitched laugh that sounded more like the beginning of more weeping. "I told ye I am no' hiding from the law or anyone else."

She trusted Constantine not to tell his cousins about her plight. So he didn't. He turned and cast her an impatient look instead. Would she truly prefer to travel the Highlands alone than travel with him and men who would protect her?

He shouldn't have indulged his senses by studying her so closely, even for a moment. It was too reckless, too dangerous. She was beguiling, snatching the breath from his body—a malady he hadn't suffered in many years. It wasn't her large misty eyes, or the hundreds of freckles splayed across her nose and cheeks that made him forget for a moment his name, his past. It wasn't her straight, pert nose, or, Lord have mercy on him, her full, pouty mouth. He imagined what she looked like when her hair was set free from under that man's bonnet. No. It was the courage and resolve that made her eyes shine and her delicate jaw set that tempted him to offer her his protection until whatever end came to him. But that was all he would ever offer her.

"Chief? Are there lions in the vicinity?"

He wanted to tell her not to be afraid in his tenderest voice. But she didn't want to be treated like a woman. She was correct to travel as a man...if she insisted on going, and if anyone believed her. He wouldn't give away her secret, and neither would his men—if they didn't want to get trounced.

Without taking his eyes off her, he made another promise. "Even lions dare not enter Tor Castle, young lad."

"What do lions have to fear?" she asked, daring him with the slightest quirk of her mouth to take the bait and boast about himself, and appear a fool.

He took the bait, fool or not, delighting in the taste of it. "They fear my teeth."

"Lochiel doesna speak an untruth" Geoffry said raising his cup. "They do fear his teeth."

"His knives," Fionn clarified and laughed with the others.

"Lochiel?" she asked.

"Aye," Lewis answered, coming around to the table. "The Lochiel of Lochaber, deadliest man alive."

They laughed in agreement.

Constantine didn't join in the merriment. He didn't take any joy having to take down a mountain lion that thought to eat Lachlan five years ago.

Lions wouldn't come near any castle, but dangerous men would try. And they would fail. Always.

"Fer the last time," he said, rising from his chair and looking down at her, "ye will be safe with the men."

She let out a little mocking laugh and shook her head.

"With *my* men, ye will," he insisted.

"What about ye?" she asked him, gazing up at him. "Where will ye be?"

He finally looked away. "I have things to see to."

"Such as?"

She was bold, proving to Constantine she was of noble blood. Hadn't she said her mother had arranged her marriage to a chief? Chiefs didn't wed servants.

"Such as, doing work on my house—"

"Tor Castle is where ye live," she observed from their previous conversation. "Yer home is somewhere else."

"That is correct."

"Why can I not go there with ye?" she asked him, making him reconsider if she was bold or as innocent as a secluded maiden.

His gaze roved over his cousins to find them all slack jawed and waiting for his reply.

"I willna stay at Tor Castle if ye are no' there. I will continue on my way."

On her way? Where? Constantine wanted to ask her. "Is keeping yerself safe dependent on my presence?"

"Ye are the one who announced that ye would protect me," was her reply.

Should he point out that a public inn was far more dangerous than the home of a Cameron chief? He recalled her telling him that she hated clan chiefs. She'd hated them for a long time now. He was curious why.

But for now, he answered his own question. For her, the chief's castle was likely more dangerous than a public inn.

"I have been keeping myself alive fer a month now," she continued when he remained quiet and indecisive. "Yer assistance last eve was verra much appreciated, but yer vow was fulfilled. I willna hold any grudge against ye fer leaving now."

"A month?" he repeated in a low voice. He'd heard everything else she told him but *a month* boomed loudest in his ears. He heard Fionn echo her words. "Where have you come from?"

When she didn't answer right away, he glanced at his cousins and then at the door. "If ye must think about it, ye likely willna tell me the truth." He turned to leave.

Her voice stopped him. "Why should I trust a stranger and perhaps put my life in jeopardy again?"

Again. Constantine couldn't help but wonder how many times her life had been in danger.

"Did I not prove last night that I can be trusted?" he asked, pouting.

"Ye could be tricking me into trusting ye fer some secret purpose."

He scrunched up his face at her. "What secret purpose?"

She shrugged her shoulders and lifted her spoon to her mouth. He watched her for a moment, both in disbelief and in awe that he might forgive anything she thought of him.

"I'm goin' to find Lachlan," he muttered. "Drummond—"

"Thank ye fer yer help last eve, Chief, and fer feeding me. We will part—"

"Ye will ride with Fionn."

"Pardon?" She stared at him as if he had just grown fangs.

"Eat at yer leisure," he continued, softening his voice some, but keeping his tone commanding, "but dinna make me come and get ye."

Her lips parted on an angry gasp. Then, "I'm not going to yer castle without ye."

He didn't answer her but left the tavern alone.

WHO DID HE think he was?

Ismay knew who he was. The Cameron Clan Chief. His name was well-known even as far as Inverness. There were plenty of Camerons, even Constantine Camerons, but there was only one who was the Lochiel.

And now, he wanted to take her to his castle. Was he truly a criminal as was rumored? If so, what was to stop him from—what? Constantine Cameron was a criminal and he hadn't touched her. He barely looked at her.

"The Lochiel," said the one the chief had introduced as Geoffry, "has nae secret purpose in bein' kind to ye, though I have never seen him practice such hospitality before. Ye insulted him."

She? What? Ugh! She had been petty. She was sorry she insulted him after he had done much for her. She looked them all over. She should be a bit more afraid alone here with them, but she doubted they would risk their chief's ire if they touched her after he had given his word about them. Finally, she bounced to her feet and stormed out of the inn. Moments after she left, she heard the inn doors open and the chief's cousins come tumbling out.

She looked around for the chief or his golden-haired cousin

Lachlan, but not finding them, she followed her nose and found the stable.

The doors were open, letting in fresh air. Ismay stopped upon seeing the chief reaching up to fit a saddle over a horse. Beside him, Lachlan saddled another horse and chatted on enthusiastically.

Ismay didn't hear what the younger Cameron was saying, not because he spoke in a low voice, but because her gaze and her thoughts were fixated on the chief. In the golden lantern light, brightened by the sunlight streaming through the open door, he appeared almost other-worldly. He was tall and lithe, and quietly dangerous, like a blade sheathed in silk. She watched his long fingers work the buckles on his saddle. He pulled and yanked on the leather, mesmerizing her until the boisterous ruckus of his men approaching shattered her thoughts of her protector.

He turned toward the sound and saw her standing by the door. Ismay had no idea what to say or do as his men barreled past her and into the barn. She'd come to apologize for being so distrusting of him after he had stayed by her door for two days. But now, she suddenly felt more mortified than anything else. She had confessed to him that she was a woman. Why had she told him so much about Chief MacRae and her mother? She didn't even know him—

"Lad," his voice cut through her thoughts, "do ye need help gainin' yer saddle?"

She blinked out of her reverie, realizing he was speaking to her. "Hmm?"

"Come," he stretched his hand out to her. "Let us be off."

To his castle, she reminded herself. He'd promised she would be safe there, but he was a chief, a man of power and authority. Would he abuse it once they reached his home?

"I already told ye," she began as he moved toward her. Why did his potent, still gaze make her feel lightheaded? Best to be away from him quickly. She already trusted him a little too much. "I'm not going to yer castle without ye."

"Fine," he ground his chiseled jaw. "I'll remain at Tor fer a few days until ye're rested, then ye can leave—and so can I." He jutted his hand out and took hers, then turned and headed back to the horses with her in tow.

She stared at the back of him, his long hair falling between his shoulders. Why did it seem to be that the more she demanded, the more he gave in? Why help her? He never did tell her. Men didn't just offer their protection for nothing. But as of yet, he hadn't asked her for a thing in return.

When he brought her to Fionn and his horse, she turned around and went to the horse he'd been saddling. She didn't say a word about only riding with him, but looking at him as he came near, she felt her heart in her eyes, being poured out to only him. She was afraid. She was afraid of men, afraid of him, despite his protection. She didn't want the world to know what a coward she truly was, but she told Constantine Cameron, and she hoped he would respond kindly.

He stared at her for an eternal moment, looking hard and angry, breaking her heart and toughening it up at the same time. She was about to snarl at him and then storm out of the stable, when he fit his hands around her waist and hoisted her into his saddle.

"I have to retrieve my bag from the inn," she told him, about to slip down out of the saddle to go fetch it.

He stopped her by leaping up and landing behind her. "I'll drop ye off by the door and ye can retrieve it."

She felt his arm slipping around her and then held on when he steered his horse out of the stable. His chest felt like armor against her back—warm, malleable armor. His breath atop her head covered her in warmth and the scent of mint.

They almost reached the inn when a group of mounted men appeared from around the back of the inn.

The chief pulled on the reins, bringing his mount to a halt. Behind him, his cousins halted their mounts as well.

He took hold of Ismay's hand and lowered her from the saddle. "Go to the inn. Get inside and dinna come oot until I come fer ye. Go!"

She ran, keeping her eyes on the group of men. They didn't seem interested in her but kept their gazes fastened on the chief guarding her passage. Were they going to fight? Who were they? There were about eighteen of them. Surely the chief and his three cousins, not including Lewis the innkeeper, were no match for them. But when two of them moved to cut her off, the chief's horse was there, his sword gleaming against the morning sun.

She turned away, squeezing her eyes shut in time to miss the chief's blade from cutting down both men and spewing blood across his face.

Without a second look, she disappeared into the inn and ran for the innkeeper. "Lewis!" she shouted up the stairs. When he appeared, she told him about the group of men outside.

"Mackintoshes," he muttered, grabbed his sword, and ran from the inn.

She looked around at the empty tavern and then hurried to bolt the door. Feeling a bit safer, she went to the window. Was it wide enough for one of those men to squeeze through? More importantly, was the chief still alive?

She pushed the short curtain aside and looked out at the mayhem being inflicted on the MacKintoshes. Mostly by one man. Constantine Cameron moved like a mist in the cool wind, passing over the men and leaving those who opposed him bleeding in his wake.

Her eyes watched, both in horror and in awe, as he struck men down from his saddle. Why? Why had the MacKintoshes come here to pick a fight?

She realized quickly that she would never understand the ways of men. She turned to look away from the bloodshed and walked straight into the arms of a man. She didn't have time to look up to see who it was when she was struck and fell against him.

She woke up once, strewn across a man's thighs, bouncing

this way and that, making her head pound. They were on a horse. Her curls fell over her face, free of her bonnet. Where was he taking her? Was it Chief MacRae? Had he found her already?

She drifted back into unconsciousness. She didn't dream. She wished she had. She would have liked to have dreamed of living in a convent somewhere far away—or in home near Ben Nevis with a man who—. She came awake again hanging over a man's shoulder. Who…? Where…?

"Ch…Chief?"

He didn't answer. She wasn't surprised. She did not mistake this brute for the Cameron chief. Her captor was rough, almost throwing her to the hay-covered floor.

"Dinna bother trying to run away. Ye will find an arrow or two in yer back. Understand?"

His voice was gravelly and filled with fear and uncertainty. Definitely not the Cameron chief.

He crouched in front of her and locked his gaze with hers. His eyes were green but they grew darker as they roved over her with naked male intent. "I see why the Lochiel guarded ye so vigilantly. Though I wouldna have believed it if I hadna seen it with my own eyes. 'Tis rumored he hasna had a woman since he killed his wife years ago."

The chief had killed his wife? Did she believe it? She would ask him when she saw him next. She had no doubt he would come for her. For some mad reason, he'd given his protection to her. He wouldn't have stayed at the inn with her for two days if his promise meant nothing.

"I intend to discover what makes ye so special," the brute said in a thick voice.

"Truly?" Ismay mocked. "More important men than ye have sought to discover the same thing and it cost them their lives." There was only one, but she didn't doubt that she could have killed Chief MacRae when he sawed off her hair. "But I promise ye this; If I dinna kill ye, the Lochiel will fer certain. Am I important enough to lose ye life over?"

In the moments he took mulling it over, she flicked her gaze over his waist and anywhere he kept a weapon.

"Ye willna kill me, lass. Neither will yer lover. And dinna fear," he reached out and ran the backs of his knuckles over her cheek, "I will leave ye alive to grow fat with my child while he watches."

She wasn't sure if she could actually do it again. But if he came any closer…her heart raced fast and hard. She fought to keep a clear head. She prayed he wouldn't try anything. But she couldn't weep. Not yet. She wouldn't hesitate.

Spotting a six-inch dagger tucked under his belt, she grit her teeth and prepared herself to reach for it and slice his throat.

An almost deafening crash sounded as the door to wherever they were splintered and shattered to the floor. Her crouching captor spun on the balls of his feet to face a brooding Constantine Cameron.

Her abductor rose, but the Lochiel was faster, drawing his sword and swinging it across the MacKintosh kinsman's chest, killing him where he stood. He didn't wait for the man to fall but pushed him out of his path to Ismay.

Her protector bent to her, giving her a once over. He looked to be in pain at the sight of her. Momentarily.

His men rushed in next and stared at her, and her bare head.

"Are ye hurt?" he asked, his gaze hardening when it settled on the bruise forming on her cheekbone.

"Nae. I'm no' hurt," she assured him in a soft voice. Then she coughed to sound stronger, less affected by him.

He had come for her. Just as she knew he would. She wanted to smile at him, but… "Did ye kill yer wife?"

He stood up straight and lowered his hand to help her rise.

But he didn't answer her. He didn't deny it.

It seemed, she thought exhaustedly, her running wasn't over.

---※---

CHAPTER FIVE

C ONSTANTINE WAS SURE the lass could feel his agitated heart thumping against his ribs as they traveled back to the road leading to Tor Castle.

She had been easy to find thanks to the single hoof prints her abductor's horse had left.

The scent of her now, sitting in front of him on his horse, went straight to his head and soothed him before he kicked the unwanted thoughts away. He had no place for a woman in his life. No desire for one.

He hadn't answered her when she asked about him killing his wife. In a way, he had killed her by not being there with her, at her side to give her strength. He wasn't ready to speak of Alison or Katie, especially not to another woman.

When he'd gone into the inn to look for her and found her gone, he'd returned outside and threatened to kill the remaining three men if they didn't tell him who had taken her and where they went.

He'd discovered that it had been Reggie MacKintosh, the MacKintosh chief's eldest son who had taken her. Constantine hadn't cared if her captor were the chief himself. MacKintosh should not have laid a finger on his...his ward. He hadn't cared when he'd kicked down the door of the small barn in the hamlet of Muirshearkich and killed MacKintosh where he stood.

The sight of her alive caused an odd flutter in his chest. He hadn't kept his word to protect her. Still, he had raced to her. He had killed in a blind rage on account of her. It angered him that he would expend so much passion on her. He barely knew her. But she evoked a spark or light in him of some kind. Be it compassion, the gleam of strength and resiliency flashing in her gaze every now and then, or physical attraction.

When he'd found her, he bent to her. He shouldn't have. Were there always thousands of tiny brown spots strewn across the bridge of her nose? Was her skin always so pale? Were there always dark crescents under her eyes, as if she hadn't slept in…

He let out a little breath while they traveled and forced himself to breathe. He thought he'd forgotten how when he found her thrown in the threshing.

He wasn't moved by much anymore, not by beauty, nor by one's sorrows or sorry past. But he was moved by her.

"Thank ye fer coming fer me, Chief…I mean Lochiel," she said now in her dulcet voice. "I knew ye would."

He looked down at her uncovered head. She was a curious lass. She claimed to hate chiefs, but she clearly didn't hate him. She didn't trust him completely but enough to know he would come for her.

"How would ye know if I would come or not, lass? I dinna come to the aid of many."

"Aye. That is what made me stand out to that man back there."

"What are ye sayin'?" he asked, slowing his horse to a halt. "Look at me, lass."

She obeyed and turned in his lap to face him. He refused to be moved by her now. Something in him that had once been soft, told him to stand firm and never forget the pain of losing his wife and daughter.

"That man noticed how ye guarded me. He thought there was something between us. That's why he took me."

He kept his breathing steady—though it was much more

difficult than he'd imagined it would ever be. "Is that so," he said. It wasn't a question. He didn't expect her to answer it.

But she did. "Aye. He said, 'Though I wouldna have believed it if I hadna seen it with my own eyes. 'Tis rumored he hasna had a woman since he killed his wife.'" She finished and blinked up at him.

Constantine gave the reins a gentle flick and his horse began a slow trot.

"Fine, dinna answer." She brooded a bit and turned to face the road.

"I didna kill her," he offered after a moment. "She perished while giving life to our daughter."

"Oh," Miss Drummond lamented but didn't return her gaze to his. "Fergive me fer bringing it up. I—"

Maddeningly, he was tempted to rest his hand on her shoulder to comfort her. He almost groaned out loud at the thought. "I shouldna have mentioned it. I dinna want yer pity. But I would have ye know that I didna murder my wife."

His voice sounded rougher than he'd intended. She stiffened a bit in front of him.

Good, let her be angry, or think that he was. It was for the better. Once they arrived at the castle, he would keep his distance for a few days and then he would leave.

"Then…" she began, drawing him away from his plans… "ye have a daughter?"

"Nae," he told her, his hands tightening into fist around his reins. "She joined her mother shortly after bein' born."

She made a sound but it was muffled in her hand. She said nothing else until they reached Tor Castle.

It had been a while since Constantine had been back. He didn't particularly enjoy being there, and most times, the only reason he did return was because his cousins were here. But Alison was also here on every stairway, in the Great Hall and the kitchen. In the chapel and in his chambers. His brother, Gilbert was here in the study hall, the solar, the Great Hall. Ghosts roamed in every space, like sand seeping into every nook and cranny after a storm.

Their arrival—that was, the arrival of Geoffry, Fionn, Lachlan, and Lewis brought almost every female to the great doors to greet them home. They didn't spare Constantine a glance. Not that he saw, at least. They knew it was pointless. It was something Miss Drummond would come to learn. And then, she too, would remove her claws from him.

His heart was no longer available. He questioned if it even beat some days.

"Welcome home, Lochiel."

Constantine turned to his cousin Hugh MacDonald, steward of Tor Castle. Constantine's father Malcolm had taken him in sixteen years ago, just before Malcolm died in battle. When Gilbert became Lochiel he appointed Hugh to be their steward. Constantine saw no reason to change things when he became Lochiel. "'Tis good to see ye, Constantine." Hugh offered him a warm smile, then turned his sharp gaze on Miss Drummond.

"Hugh, this is Miss Drummond, my guest."

Hugh had always been kind enough to Alison—mayhap, sometimes a little overly protective. Constantine hadn't blamed the steward for wanting to protect her. Alison was alone often due to the constant warring between the leaders.

He felt the slightest twinge of something eating at his innards, like a fire licking dry wood when Hugh continued to stare at Miss Drummond. Everyone in Lochaber knew Hugh was a handsome devil. In fact, that was what most called him. Handsome devil.

Constantine didn't like the handsome devil shining his grin on Miss Drummond. But whatever he was feeling was terribly wrong, so he looked away at one of the chambermaids fawning over Lachlan.

"Joan," he called out brusquely, "bring Miss Drummond to a chamber on the second floor." The second floor gave Miss Drummond status. He gave her tattered breeches and coat a scowl. "And get her somethin' clean and proper to wear. Hugh," he called out, "she is under my protection. Make certain everyone knows."

"Aye," Geoffry boasted. "He killed the MacKintosh's eldest son fer thinkin' to take her."

A collective gasp filled the hall, but Constantine's gaze had fallen on Miss Drummond. She opened her mouth to say something to him, but before she could get it out, he held up his hand. "I'll see ye at supper."

He left her without another word, trusting in the care of his staff to see to her needs and his cousin to see to her safety.

He climbed the stairs, expecting her to call out to him, or mayhap chase him. He felt the infuriating urge to turn around to see what was keeping her from him. He didn't do it and was feeling rather good about it until he thought about the other men at the castle who didn't know Ismay or that she was under his protection. But he'd told Hugh to make certain the others were made aware. What if Hugh forgets to tell them? What if one of them tries to woo her right under his nose?! Wait now, the lass wasn't his. He wasn't sure why he kept thinking of her in such a manner. She wasn't his woman. Still, he had promised to protect her.

He pivoted on the heel of his boots on the dimly lit second landing. and started back for the stairs, ready to find Hugh and make certain he hadn't forgotten his command. He stopped when he heard Miss Drummond's voice.

"I have put the same question to him several times," she said to someone as she ascended the stairs. "He has yet to answer."

"Hmm, aye." Hugh replied. "The Lochiel does as he likes, including barely speaking to anyone."

Constantine scowled. Had he not told Joan to show Ismay to a chamber? And did he truly barely speak to anyone?

"I think he doesna wish to admit that he has a kind heart and took compassion on me."

"Aye, compassion on ye." Hugh was quiet for a moment. Then, "Tell me, Miss Drummond, have we met before, from where did ye come?"

Met before? Constantine inched closer to discovery, but he thought he should hear her reply.

"I'm certain we havena ever met," she told him in a voice so quiet, Constantine almost didn't hear her.

"Hmm," Hugh considered her further. Then continued. "About the Lochiel, I think ye have the wrong man. The Lochiel doesna have a kind heart and I wonder if the MacKintosh chief will agree with ye about compassion when they tell him his son is dead. What do ye think, Miss Drummond."

They reached the top of the stairs and one of them paled when he saw Constantine.

"Hugh," Constantine said, moving closer, "if the MacKintosh chief canna control his bairns, they become trouble fer Lochaber. Fer me. I willna put up with them much longer."

Without waiting for Hugh's response, he turned his attention to Miss Drummond. "Where is Joan?"

"She had an urgent matter to attend with Lachlan."

Urgent, as in she needed to tell him she loved him. She wasn't the only lass who did.

Taking Miss Drummond's hand, he turned one last time to Hugh. "Find Joan and tell her she is nae' longer needed at the castle."

Hugh nodded and risked a quick glance to Miss Drummond, who glared at Constantine just before he tugged her away from his steward. He didn't need someone putting him in an unsavory light.

"Damn it, what do I care aboot the light?"

"'Tis quite clear," Miss Drummond remarked. Making him bite his tongue. He wasn't used to anyone besides his closest cousins being with him all the time. He didn't realize that he had spoken out loud.

"How could ye let Joan go when all she did was fancy yer cousin?"

He stopped and turned to her, letting her go when he realized that he was still pulling her along. "I need the obedience of everyone who lives in this castle," he found himself explaining. "If I ever need her to help keep someone safe—" her, for instance— "and Joan is more concerned fer Lachlan, it could cause terrible trouble."

She met his gaze with the same intensity he offered to her. "Are ye letting her go because of me?"

He picked up his steps. His only reply was a low growl.

"Chief!" The cool authority in her voice stopped him. He pivoted slowly to face her, surprised that she had used such a tone with him. "Why do ye give them a reason to speak about ye as if ye were a tyrant."

"Mayhap that is what I am," he answered.

She shook her head. "I have known some tyrants, and ye are not one."

What was he supposed to say to that? Sometimes he was indeed a tyrant. Sometimes he was exactly what Hugh made him out to be: the kind of man who could kill another man's son.

"Ye dinna know me, Miss Drummond," he told her and then continued on to one of the chambers in the tapestry-lined, northerly wing of the castle.

"Nor do ye know me, Chief," she countered, hurrying to catch up. "And yet ye stayed outside my door at the inn fer two days to protect me."

"I didna stay ootside yer door," he argued, not wanting things to sound more complicated than they were.

"Ye risked yer life to find me when that MacKintosh absconded with me."

He looked around at the hall then drew in a deep breath before he gave her a brooding look. "I didna risk my life. I should feel insulted that ye think so."

"Ye agreed to stay here at the castle," she went on, ignoring his offended pout, "so that I would stay here where 'tis safe."

Constantine couldn't help but notice the little spark of excitement in her eyes. Did she enjoy challenging him? He had the ridiculous urge to laugh at her fanciful notions.

"Aye," he told her, his voice sounding too deep and too warm for his liking. "I want ye to be safe. Ye're a wee thing with a bold tongue and a bonnie"—he scowled and let his dark gaze rove over her—"face," he choked out.

She stared up at him and blew a curl off her forehead. "Does my bold tongue anger ye?"

Odd lass, Constantine thought she would question him about him blurting out that she was bonnie. "Why would it anger me? Does it do me any harm?"

"Only to yer pride," she answered.

"I may be prideful, lass," he told her, leaning in with a slight smile not many witnessed, "but I am more confident."

"That must be why I was so certain ye would come fer me."

Her breath smelled sweet, like the berries she'd picked and ate on the way here.

"Ye are a chief, who doesna demand attention but gets it all the same. I saw the quiet, not-quite-dispassionate man at the inn."

"Not quite dispassionate?" he urged.

"Aye, ye didna try to comfort me with false concern while I wept into my delicious stew. But ye kept watch over me like a guardian angel so that no one else dared take a seat at my table. Not quite dispassionate."

Constantine blew out a little laugh and stepped back. He remembered her weeping. He would rather forget. Her weeping was what had convinced him that she needed protecting. Something had made her run, and judging by her worn-down shoes, she had run a great distance. He now knew the reason for her traveling alone. Her betrothed. If he came to Tor, Constantine would not let him touch or take her.

He spread his gaze over her clothes and sighed through his teeth. "I will see that clothes are made fer ye."

"Made?" Her eyes opened wider. "Nae, dinna go through such trouble fer me."

He shook his head slightly, then turned for the row of doors.

"Follow me."

He showed her to the chamber three doors down from his room and left her sighing dreamily before the postered bed, its thick wooden headboard carved into an alcove between two windows.

He returned to the top of the stairs and shouted for Bethia, Tor's head chambermaid. She was an older woman who had come to Tor with Alison. She took her duties more seriously.

"Aye, Lochiel?" Bethia asked, leaving one of the other rooms, a bundle of keys jiggling at her waist. He should have asked her to see to Miss Drummond instead of Joan. "Would ye like me to bring ye a basin of water?"

He shook his head. A basin was not enough to get days of dust off him. He would bathe in the loch beyond the castle later. "Miss Drummond needs clothes and new shoes fer her feet. See what she likes and tell the seamstresses and the tanner to fashion whatever 'tis."

Bethia stared at him as if he'd just sprouted another head. Then, she nodded with a quick bow. "Aye, m'lord."

Constantine watched her hurry off and then went to his chambers to rest before supper. He shook his head at himself while unfastening his plaid as thoughts and visions of Miss Ismay Drummond danced about in his head. He refused to let himself think about her another instant, but when he chased her from his thoughts, Alison replaced her. He almost could not remember her face anymore. But he knew he had loved it once, just as he loved the sound of her soft, agreeable voice.

Miss Drummond was not agreeable. She was stubborn and contentious.

Not exactly true, he corrected himself when he thought about it for longer than a moment. She was braw, standing up to him when he would avoid or deny. Calling him prideful and then an instant later, admitting that his confidence gave her faith that he would come for her. He—

No. Cease. What was he doing? He shook his head again and

rubbed his hands down his face as he fell into bed. Could he not keep the troublesome lass out of his thoughts? But every time he did, other, even less welcome thoughts returned. It surprised him that Miss Drummond could keep Alison out of his head—even for a little while. No one could before her for five years now. And what about the accusing eyes of Alison's parents, the MacMillans? He hadn't thought of them in two days.

A slight smile crept over his lips. How had Miss Drummond managed to protect him from the glares and hateful stares of his wife's beloved parents?

And was it their absence that tempted him to smile more than he had since the tragedy?

He soon fell asleep with Miss Drummond's hesitant smile taking the place of one more easily given…one whose memory was fading. He reached out, trying to hold on to it. To her. *Alison.* She began to run away. He took off after her. They'd had so many plans that would never come to pass now.

He caught her in his dream and turned her in his arms, missing her face. He touched his fingertips over her soft, freckled skin. Freckled? Alison didn't have freckles. She didn't have storm-colored eyes and decadently plump, coral lips.

"Why are ye here, lass?" he asked her barely audible to his own ears. He meant here, in his dream, where Alison would otherwise be.

"I was trying to run away," she told him, clutching his forearms as if running was the last thing she wanted to do.

But she had infiltrated his thoughts. He could not let her invade his dreams, as well. "Ye cannae stay here," he said, releasing her.

She gave him a meaningful look before she disappeared and was replaced by the faceless image of his wife.

He woke up hours later, when the light outside his window faded to black. He stretched in his bed and almost smiled at how good it felt. He sat up. How long had he slept? What about Miss Drummond? He told her to leave. Was it a dream? Had she left?

She was prone to running, after all. He bolted out of the bed and to save time, threw on his night robe instead of tucking and tying his plaid.

He didn't run or admit to himself why he was walking with swift determination to her door. When he reached it, he knocked. After a moment of silence, he rapped on the wood again.

She would not leave the castle in the black of night, would she? He'd dreamed of telling her she could not stay. It was a dream. Of course she didn't leave. Still, he found himself racing down the stairs, making candles flicker on the wall as he passed them. It wasn't long before he ran into one of his cousins.

"Fionn, have ye seen Miss Drummond?"

"Aye, Chief, she is in the Great Hall. I just came from there."

Constantine hurried off, leaving Fionn to watch after him with a stunned expression on his face.

Swinging open the doors of the Great Hall, Constantine found her almost immediately with her short curls shimmering in all the colors of autumn in the morning. He felt such great relief that it made him feel lightheaded. What in blazes was the matter with him? Who was this lass who no longer wept into her stew but now laughed into her hands?

She laughed. With the handsome devil.

---*---

CHAPTER SIX

I SMAY LAUGHED WHERE she sat next to Hugh MacDonald at one of the long trestle tables in Tor Castle's Great Hall. She would much rather find Constantine Cameron and hit him over the head with something for leaving her alone for so long. She'd waited for him to show up all through their supper filled with some entertainment from musicians and jugglers. Hugh stayed with her the entire time. He was quite nice, but he behaved oddly, ofttimes alluding to a prior meeting between them. He also barely took his eyes off her, which made eating uncomfortable.

Lachlan and Geoffry came by several times, as if keeping an eye on her. Did they think she would bolt? Why would any of them care if she did? She wasn't a prisoner here. Was she?

"I take it from yer laughter," Hugh said with mild amusement, "ye are not watching the doors fer any sign of the Lochiel."

"'Tis a silly assumption."

"Aye," Hugh agreed all too easily. "Though I will say, he rarely sleeps this long. Two hours a night at the most." He turned to Geoffry sitting opposite them. "Ye are sure he hasna left his chambers?"

"I'm not dull-witted," Geoffry said woodenly. "Go check fer yerself."

Hugh began to answer, then looked toward the doors and

stopped.

Ismay followed the direction of his gaze. It was Constantine. The Lochiel, she corrected silently. Her eyes poured out on him, her heart beat erratically, her mouth went dry. Barefoot and disheveled, he was wonderfully, irresistibly handsome in his floor-length, blue velvet night robe, edged in black ermine. He stood in the doorway, staring at her table…at her, like a dark dragon ready to pillage.

Seeing her seemed to propel him forward. He took long, determined strides that fanned his robe out behind him.

He looked majestic and virile, and he made her blood go warm in her veins.

She had tried to learn more about him from his friends while he made her wait, but no one would say anything either good or bad about him. She'd seen him kill, and she had been told that he killed his wife. She could almost believe it since he was a chief. Unlike the chiefs before him though, he had not made any advances towards her. He kept his hands and his smiles to himself. And *this* chief was also a thief and a cattle raider.

She hated herself for being the least bit attracted to him. He offered protection. Not kindness. Not warmth. Just silence and steel.

"Miss Drummond." His greeting was heavy with unspoken relief. "I fell asleep."

She almost laughed again. This time it would have been kinder and more genuine than what she'd offered Hugh. She didn't know why his direct excuse sounded like the most innocent thing in the world. He fell asleep. According to Hugh, the Lochiel rarely slept. Yet she believed the chief. Partly because his eyes were sleepy. He looked as if he'd just rushed out of bed.

She felt a smile forming on her lips.

"I'm relieved to find ye settling in so well." His dark gaze slid to Hugh for just an instant. "Ye may go."

"Ye dinna look relieved," she interrupted when Hugh rose from his seat and promptly left.

Ismay wasn't bothered by Hugh leaving. She was happy about it. The steward's eyes lingered on her a wee bit too long—as if he were trying to see all her secrets. She had tolerated him because she wanted to wait for the chief. Fool that she was. "Ye look angry," she continued. "Did ye not wish fer me to settle in here—at least fer a few days?"

His eyes hardened further and he looked away. "No' angry. Nae."

He fell into a chair near her and motioned for a drink to be brought to him. With his brooding glare fixed on no one in particular, he remained quiet, speaking to no one, though no one remained but Lewis. When his drink came, he lifted the cup to his lips and guzzled its contents.

He set the empty cup down on the table and turned his gaze to Ismay. "I would know what ye mean by a few days? Where do ye intend to go when ye leave Tor?"

"Dinna concern yerself, Lochiel," she said, waving his questions away.

He stared at her, slack-jawed. He seemed to be deciding who spoke to him in such a disrespectful manner.

"Fortunate fer ye, lass," he said, "I *am* concerned."

Fortunate? Ismay decided then and there that, although everyone else considered Constantine Cameron a detached outlaw, uncaring whose son he killed—and they were all correct in their consideration—very few of his kin saw any other side of him.

She guessed she was fortunate indeed that he had shown her the man behind his mask of indifference. A man with a heart beating slowly and with its last shreds of warmth for a runaway bride with nowhere to go.

"Where will ye go, Miss Drummond," he repeated, proving her right about him. "I know ye have traveled a far distance alone and ye lived to tell me aboot it, but I dinna think yer luck will last withoot a plan. Do ye have one?"

"I am going to find a convent to join."

He stared at her for a moment, and then he burst into hearty laughter that drew the attention of the few servers still serving, and of Lewis. They stared with disbelieving eyes and ears, but no one spoke a word.

"What in the world do ye find so humorous about me wanting to live in a convent?"

He raised his cup for more wine, drawing a scowl on her lips.

"Ye will nae doubt hurl the holy sisters over on their arses."

"Pardon me?" she said with a stunned, insulted look.

"Come now, Miss Drummond, ye know ye are saucy."

She let out a short snort of disbelief. "I know nae such thing!"

"Now ye do." He took his freshly filled cup and raised it to his lips. He paused his hand in the air when she slammed her palm on the table.

"Cease drinking!" she commanded with such authority and anger he set the cup back down. "I willna sit here another instant speaking to a man who is too drunk to know what he might do later."

He dipped his gaze to his cup.

"Set it aside, please, or I will retire to bed."

"Are ye givin' the Lochiel orders, lass?" Lewis asked, surprised and offended.

The Lochiel did as she said and stared at Ismay while he spoke. "'Tis all right, Lewis. Go to bed."

Lewis remained for another moment or two and then stood up and smiled at the back of the Lochiel's head. "Aye, cousin."

The Lochiel was silent as Lewis left, his gaze still fixed on her. "I know what I might do later," he said when they were finally alone, "and it doesna involve ye."

He tried to make his words sound like an insult but there was a trace of regret lacing his declaration. Did he want his night to include her? Hadn't they spent the last three nights together—or, at least under the same roof?

She rubbed her eyes. She was weary. That had to be the reason she was entertaining such thoughts about a Highland Chief.

"That is a relief to hear," she didn't realize she sounded as regretful as he did until he lifted his gaze to look into her eyes.

"Ye dinna sound relieved," he remarked with a glint in his eyes, reminding her of her own words.

She cast him a wry look. "Should I feel sad or disappointed that ye dinna wish to spend the night with me?" Her eyes opened wider as what she said dawned on her. She choked out a feigned laugh. "What I mean is that ye dinna want to spend more time with me."

He raised his eyebrows but did not refute her claim. Instead, he looked around the emptying Hall, and then asked, "What are ye doin' here so late into the night?"

She blew out a slight sigh, careful not to seem disappointed by his careful evasion. So what if he did not want to spend time with her? She didn't care about spending time with him either.

Even as she thought the words, she knew she was lying. She enjoyed trying to break through his rigid indifference to spark that glint of curiosity and warmth in his eyes that she'd seen once or twice. A challenging task to remove that heavy mask, but she much preferred a man with self-control than a man without it.

"I was waiting fer my protector, who abandoned me. You can speak as much as ye like on the honor of the men here. Ye are seeing one side of them. Would ye have me ask one of them to escort me to my chamber? Joan is gone, thanks to ye, and the others are all busy with the seamstresses."

He was quiet for a moment, but his gaze never left hers. She had not broken through his indifference tonight. There was no warmth in his eyes. "Who did ye such harm that ye hate authority and power and dinna trust any man?"

She had opened up to him about her arranged marriage to a beast. At the time of the telling, she believed she simply needed to tell someone and he was available. He hadn't been shocked or overly concerned about any of it and that was strangely comforting. He had listened and then continued eating.

What more should she tell this stranger, and why did she

want to tell him everything?

"I was abandoned as a babe and taken in by an important chief. He abused me and when I was eight years old, he tried to force himself on me." She didn't tell him the chief's name or that she had killed him. She left out that Baron John MacPherson had saved her and taken her to her new home where she lived for the next sixteen years until he died.

For the first time, Ismay witnessed emotion darkening the Lochiel's expression. His jawline, stark and chiseled, trembled as his teeth grinded together. "Who is he? Tell me his name."

Why, Ismay wondered. What would he do if... "He is no longer a part of this world."

She didn't tell him how Chief MacDonald had left the world or how relieved it made her to know that he no longer shared air with her.

Constantine Cameron gave her a look that was like the one her father, John MacPherson, had given her when he came upon her about to be stoned to death by the MacDonald clan for killing their chief.

"Chief," she said softly, "I dinna want pity. The only time I ever wanted it, it was given to me by my father."

The Lochiel nodded, but he still looked sickened. "I will make certain no' to keep ye waitin' again."

No, she did not want a man who felt beholden to her because she was alone. "Truly, Chief—"

"Constantine," he urged gently.

"Constantine," she corrected herself with a slight smile. "I didna mean to make ye feel so responsible fer me. Ye are not. I chose to leave my home where it was once safe until my father died. It was my choice. I am responsible fer it. Ye are not my father nor my husband—" Why, oh, why did her cheeks have to go up in flame now?—"we hardly know each other. So please, let me release ye from any obligation pity has led ye to take up on my behalf."

She stood up. It was better to leave his company now and go

to bed. The more time she spent with him, the more she was tempted to throw caution to the four winds and trust him. Really trust him.

But he was not her father—the only man she ever completely loved and trusted even more. She'd vowed she would never love any man again.

"Please, stay where ye are," she ordered gently when Constantine moved to stand with her. "I can manage alone. I have come to prefer it."

He paused, taking the smile she offered him apart, seeing past it, through it. What did he see that made him stop? The truth? She preferred being alone?

She left the Hall and headed for the stairs. When she heard his footsteps behind her, she turned around to see him.

He looked to the west wall to examine the giant tapestry covering it.

"What are ye doing, Chief?"

He turned an innocent look on her that made the muscles in her lips ache.

"I'm heading to my chambers, as well," he explained.

She remembered that he had put her in the chambers closest to his. She gave him a slight nod and continued on. He didn't catch up to her to walk at her side, but stayed eight or ten steps back, and pretended to look somewhere else whenever she turned to look at him over her shoulder.

She suspected he still felt responsible for her and was escorting her to her chambers in his own subtle way—which was not subtle at all.

Oddly, it warmed her blood. She wanted to run the rest of the way when she saw her door. What lies was her heart telling her head? That there could ever be something between her and the Lochiel of the Camerons, kin to the MacDonalds? That he was worthy of what she swore never to offer to anyone? Her heart had learned too early the detriment of trusting anyone, especially a man.

She reached her door, and with the temptation to turn to see him too much to bear, she opened her door.

Before she stepped inside, she succumbed to temptation and turned to fill her vision with the sight of him, tall and lean in his silk-and-fur robe, watching her until she safely stepped into her chambers.

ISMAY STARED AT the ceiling, where people moved around in her imagination. Their lips moved but she heard their words in her soul.

Good fer nothing sot!

What devil brought ye and yer gloomy cloud here?

All she does is cry!

That was the oldest memory she had. She had to be younger than five. She had stopped weeping when she was five. She had only cried twice after that. When her father died, and when she wept into her stew at the Doomsday Tavern and Inn.

The MacDonald chief was fat and old—at least fifty. His cheeks and jowls often reddened when he looked at her. He would watch her being struck by his wife and the other ladies of the castle, and then hurry to comfort her, reminding her that he was the only one who cared for her.

She saw herself as a child running across the ceiling. She was always dirty and uncared for, her unruly auburn curls tangled from scalp to tip. But she was caught and brought to his chambers.

"Why do ye always try to run, gel?" the MacDonald chief had asked her.

"I dinna like it here," she told him. Let him kill her. It would be better than—

His thick fingers closed around her wrist. "I think 'tis time to punish ye in another way…"

Ismay closed her eyes and turned away from the last image of her slicing his dagger across his throat and running for her life, covered in his blood.

"Nae!" she cried out.

Almost immediately the door to her bedchamber opened and the Lochiel plunged inside.

He gazed at her leaving her bed. ""What is it? Why did ye cry oot?"

She lifted her hand to her temple. "I had a dream." Was it a memory? "Wh…what are ye doing here?"

"I was…ehm…passin' by yer door and heard ye cry out."

"And ye have the key to my chamber?

"Of course," he answered. "If ye need me I ought to be able to reach ye."

She was so tempted to smile at him, though he looked and sounded more serious than a deadly plague.

"But I told ye, I release ye from—"

He waved his hand around her face. "Spare me that drivel. I will be released when I want to be released. And there is nothin' to be released from. I want to protect ye and I willna be stopped by yer stubborn notion that I want somethin' in return. That is no' the kind of man I am. If I am drawn to helpin' ye, stop wonderin' why and just leave it to me to do so."

It was the most he'd spoken at a single time in three days. Could she do what he asked? She should at least try while she was here. If he wanted to keep watch over her, she would let him.

"Were ye guarding my door again, Chief?" she asked with a smile dancing around her lips.

"I wasna guardin' it," he explained, back to being wooden. "I told ye, I was passin' by."

"Walking the halls, were ye?"

"What? Nae, I was…that is, I couldna sleep." For a breath he appeared rattled, but then he scowled at her. "Miss Drumond, do I need to remind ye that this is my castle? Do I need to explain to ye why I am awake and was guardin' yer door?"

Her smile formed fully. She couldn't help it. She turned away to hide her amusement and to stop herself from reminding him that he had already said he had not been guarding her door.

"Ye are the chief," she said, growing serious, since being a power-seeking chief was no laughing matter. "Ye dinna have to explain yerself to anyone. Surely, I havena made ye ferget that."

She knew she was provoking him. One of the reasons she remained unmarried at the age of four and twenty was because she often provoked her suitors, letting her mistrust and dislike of men chase them away. Chief MacRae needed no provocation to become riled up, chopping off her tresses in the sight of her mother.

The Cameron chief was different. For the most part, he remained unruffled by whatever was taking place around him. She enjoyed watching him try to remain unaffected by her, and failing.

"Chief?" she asked, waiting for his reply that did not seem to be coming. "If ye are going to insist on guarding me then accept my gratitude."

He waited for more but she remained silent.

Finally he nodded and headed for the door. When he reached it, he turned to look at her. "Miss Drummond, tomorrow I may ask ye fer the name of the clan chief who hurt ye. Will ye give it to me?"

How could she? There were MacDonalds in the castle, in the Lochiel's bloodline. Geoffry and Fionn, and also Hugh to name a few. There was Hilary, Arabelle, Margaret, and Ann, just some of his female MacDonald cousins who Ismay had met at supper. They would hate her, mayhap kill her.

She shook her head. She could not tell him. She would never tell him.

CHAPTER SEVEN

I SMAY OPENED HER eyes several hours later to sunlight streaming through the window in the north wall, straight into her
face.

Squinting, she sat up and smiled. She'd slept soundly without
dark dreams plaguing her. She ignored the rumble in her belly as
she had learned well to do during the days she went without
food. Her thoughts were too fixed on the leader of the Camer-
on/MacDonald clan outside her door. Was he still there? Had he
truly been standing boldly in her bed chamber last night? She
could have dreamed it, after all, she had dreamed of him until she
opened her eyes a moment ago. He looked quite fine in his
bedrobe open at the waist. His chest was not bare but softly
concealed in thin beaten wool with breeches to match. His
underclothes.

She blushed a little remembering sitting with him in his bed-
clothes in the Great Hall.

She swung her legs over the side of the bed just as the door
opened and an older woman entered. She was Bethia the head
chambermaid of Tor. According to Hugh, she mainly served the
Lochiel. Her plaited hair fell between her shoulders in gray
streaks against black.

The head chambermaid carried an armful of skirts, and a
cream-colored corset expertly embroidered with tiny ladybugs

and shoes in fabric to match. "The Lochiel had these fashioned fer ye according to yer preferences."

Ismay eyed the clothes then remarked gently. "I do love ladybugs but as I told one of the chambermaids who asked last eve, my preference was breeches and a tunic."

"The Lochiel would not have ye run away and feels ye are more prone to do so in manly attire."

Ismay lifted a brow. "He told ye that?"

"Not in those words, but he made himself clear enough."

Ismay went to her and took the bundle from her hands, "He obviously doesna know me verra well. I will run in skirts as quickly as in breeches."

She felt the head chambermaid's eyes on her as she went to stand by a chair and set the gown on it. "Will ye help me dress?" she asked, looking up from the voluminous fabric.

"Ye will wear it then?"

"Of course. I used to wear fine gowns before I left home."

"So, 'tis true, then. Ye are a runaway." Bethia went to her and began to help her undress.

"It must have been quite terrible fer a pretty lass like yerself to leave the safety of yer home."

Ismay told her about her mother and her betrothal to the power-hungry chief of a powerful clan, but the chambermaid seemed only half interested in her tale.

"Most husbands seek prestige or power through marriage," the older woman told her. "I can tell by the way ye speak that ye are a lady, no mere vassal. This chief was gaining from a union with ye. There is nothing wrong with that. It doesna mean he would have mistreated ye."

Ismay swallowed and reached up to her hair.

Misreading her slight touch, Bethia examined her tresses with a kind smile. "'Tis short, but I can pin it."

"He cut it all off."

The head chambermaid stopped helping her into her corset and dipped her gaze to Ismay's. "Did I hear ye right, child? Yer betrothed cut off all yer hair?"

Ismay nodded. She felt a wave of sadness overwhelm her. Before she could stop them, tears welled up in her eyes. "He took out his knife and for a moment I thought he was going to cut out my tongue. He said my hair was like fire…it made him…" The shame of his words in front of her mother returned and heated her face. "He said my feminine wiles would not be tolerated and stepped behind me to slice it off."

Bethia took her hand and covered it with hers. She was silent for a moment or two, then seeming to gather her mettle, she smiled. "No matter, child. 'Twill grow back and in the meantime, I will arrange it so that no one will even notice that yer locks are missing."

Ismay swiped at a lone tear and smiled in return. She was surprised by how much better she felt just being able to tell someone what Chief MacRae had done to her.

"Is he out there?" she asked while Bethia helped her into a fresh chemise.

"Who, lady?"

"The Lochiel."

Bethia looked toward the window, then toward the door. "Is he oot where?"

Ismay leaned in closer to the older woman's ear. "Outside my door?"

"Ootside yer…?" Bethia pulled away to stare at her. "Why would he be ootside yer door, child? Is he so troubled about ye leaving that he—" She laughed and waved her own concerns away. "My, such a fanciful notion."

"What is so fanciful about it?" Ismay put to her, brooding just a little.

"Only that he doesna usually trouble himself with such things as lasses."

"Doesna usually," Ismay repeated. "Did he not have skirts fashioned fer me thinking I wouldna run away in them?"

Bethia caught her meaning and frowned at the door.

"There is no need to look disappointed," Ismay told her. "I dinna intend to stay here."

The head chambermaid's frown turned on her. "Where do ye intend to go, child?"

"Now that ye mention it," Ismay said, turning to look at Bethia behind her as the older woman moved to continue dressing her. "Where is the nearest convent?"

She took an involuntary step backwards when Bethia pulled on the laces to tighten Ismay's coral-colored corset. She pulled tight but the corset remained loose.

"Stay at least until I fatten ye up some."

Ismay agreed, happy that Bethia was the second person concerned about her well-being. Even if it was just what she put in her belly. It felt nice, and somewhat familiar to be cared for.

"As fer the Lochiel," Bethia said in a low voice, turning her around to face her. "He suffers, child. Mayhap too much fer ye to bear. Strengthen yerself, even more than before, against losing yer heart to such a man."

Ismay felt her heart thumping like a battle drum in her throat. "Such a man?" she asked on an offended breath. "Do ye know that he sat outside my door at the inn fer not one night, but two to keep me safe? He brought me here though had I another day to consider it, I would not have come. I asked him to stay while I remained and he agreed despite his plans to go to Ben Nevis. There might be more but at the moment I find my heart consumed with my words, so I will remain quiet. But if ye mean to insult him calling him anything other than what he has shown me, stop now."

The head chambermaid gave her a pitying sigh. "Very well then, he isna oot there. He left early this morn to bathe in the loch. He should be returning to the castle any moment now." She looked to the door and tilted her head. "Now, that I think of it, he did tell Lachlan to stay by yer door and have one of the gels check on ye every quarter of an hour."

Ismay smiled hearing the older woman's claim. She wondered if she hurried down the stairs and out of the castle could she reach the loch where he bathed?

Run to a man? Her?

She clenched her fists. She did not want to think about whether or not she was a fool and a traitor to her heart. She was not anyone special that the Lochiel would consider her anything but a poor sot. He pitied her. That's what it was, she told herself as the chambermaid finished tying all her laces and began pulling up her hair. She tried a number of different styles before deciding on one and gathering pins between her lips.

Ismay would not let thoughts spawned by the Lochiel hypnotize and tempt her with things she did not want, like a man in her life.

Temptation. Self-betrayal. Thoughtfulness. Pleasure. He was every temptation wrapped in sun-kissed skin and a heart laid out on the sleeve of his armor. Of course, she would do everything in her power to resist him, but she wasn't ready to leave Tor Castle yet. She had not wanted to come, but now that she was here, sleeping in a soft bed, eating more than one meal a day, not looking over her shoulder to see if Chief MacRae or Marjorie MacPherson were behind her, feeling safe, *being* safe in the company of Constantine Cameon, she resisted giving it all up.

There came a knock at the door. "Aye?' Bethia called out through clenched lips.

"Tis I," the Lochiel's deep voice seemed to seep through the wood. "May I enter?"

"Aye," Bethia allowed without checking with Ismay first.

Before Ismay had a chance to prepare, he opened the door and strode inside. He stopped when his soft, umber gaze settled on her. His dark hair was wet though no longer dripping down his shoulders. He looked especially pleasing to her eyes dressed in light-brown breeches and a rich, dark-brown tunic, belted low on his waist.

His feet were bare.

Bethia tugged on Ismay's unruly curls and pinned them to

Ismay's head with a pearl pin. Ismay didn't care if it were a diamond, it still hurt. But more painful was the way the Lochiel was staring at her. Was he…breathless? Ismay shook her head at her mad thoughts.

He blinked and looked away, ashamed at being caught admiring her. He was admiring her, was he not? He was difficult to read, always stoic and unruffled—unless he wanted her to see, like a bashful prince bringing his hidden heart into view.

Traitorously, Ismay was tempted to smile, but she sucked in a deep breath when the chambermaid pinned another group of curls…and Ismay's flesh.

"Bethia, leave us." His deep voice cut a rift through the air.

Bethia had no choice but to abandon the rest of her pins and obey. When she passed him, she cast him a disapproving glance. "I will leave the door open."

The Lochiel didn't reply to her but scowled so slightly, Ismay almost missed it.

Alone in her bedchamber, his gaze found hers again. "Ye look bonnie."

She blushed and reached up to touch her hair. She hated the MacRae chief more than ever for making her feel so ashamed in front of "such a man."

She didn't know in which way the chambermaid meant her words, "such a man," but Ismay thought of them in a good light.

"Thank ye fer the clothes—and my feet especially thank ye fer the shoes." She offered him a smile. He didn't return it. "What are ye doing here, Chief?"

He drew in a deep breath and seemed to compose himself. Had he not been composed before that? And had it been because of her?

"I left the castle to bathe."

"Aye, ye asked Lachlan to guard my door."

"Aye."

Her smile remained despite his best effort to contain his.

"I just returned," he continued, "and I wanted to make certain ye were well."

"Would Lachlan no' have told ye if I wasna well?" she asked gently, enjoying the effect her teasing was having on him.

"He told me," he confessed. "But I wanted to see fer myself."

"Why, Lochiel? Do ye fancy me?"

He finally smiled, but it was more like he was mocking her. And then he spoke, and proved that he was. "Nae, lass. I'm nae fool."

Her heart palpitated. What? "What are ye saying? That ye would be a fool for fancying me?"

"Correct," he claimed dispassionately. "I want nae part of my heart or any other part of me with another woman. Once was enough."

"Good." She sounded convincing, but she didn't feel it. Did he still love his deceased wife? If he did, why did it make Ismay feel like being sick? "Now that that is settled, let us go eat."

Instead of pausing to let him offer his arm, she walked past him and into the front sitting room that made up the rest of her chambers.

She slowed her steps only after he rushed in front of her and reached for the front door to open it for her.

"Did ye sleep well?" he asked as she reached him and stepped out.

She cut her glance to him. "Did ye chase away my unpleasant dreams too?"

"What kind of protector would I be," he answered, "if I didna chase away everything that troubled ye?"

Was that humor she saw in the deep-russet hue of his gaze? She looked away and laughed softly. She felt childishly giddy. She had no idea why, save that for the first time in too long, she was not burdened with thoughts of how to stay safe while traveling alone or what she would eat. It was all because of a man. A chief.

"Why did those men come to the inn and attack?" she asked him to chase the butterflies from her belly.

He sobered quickly enough. Regret passed through Ismay

momentarily. But it didn't remain. She had no desire to discover what made the Lochiel smile. What business was it of hers?

"They were MacKintoshes. We raided their cattle the day you and I met at the tavern."

"Why do ye do it?" she asked. "Why do ye steal other clans' cattle? Dinna they need to eat just as the Camerons do?"

"That is no' my concern, Miss Drummond," he drawled. "'Tis the concern of their chief. We have a duty to our kin. I will keep mine safe and well fed. Besides I dinna steal from the poor. We have a different reason fer raidin' the Mackintoshes."

"Oh," she lifted her brow at him. "What reason is that?"

"A feud."

Her belly sank. The same kind of feud his kin the MacDonalds had with the MacPhersons because of her father rescuing the killer of the Clan Chief MacDonald of Glencoe. It was the one feud her father had spoken of. "What kind of feud?"

"Once, long ago," he told her, "the lands of Lochaber were held by the MacKintoshes. After decades of neglect toward the land, and defeat in their battles against my kinsmen, we took hold of the Lochaber region and never let go, winning even the approval of the king. Still, it wasna enough for the MacKintoshes. They tried many times to take the land back and have kept the old feud alive. Which is fine with the Camerons. We live to battle and raid."

"And rob travelers on the road," Ismay added, needing more reason to resist him—hate him.

"Only the ones who ride in ornate carriages, foolish enough to take shortcuts through a forest. They deserve it. The rich send men off to battle because their pride has been wounded. Because of them, men—many of my own friends, have died on battlefields with no one to mourn for them."

Ismay looked up at him while they descended the stairs. Aye, this was who he was—all sorrow and loss covered in impenetrable armor. But it was not completely impenetrable, was it?

"What if ye get caught?" she asked softly, part of her hoping he never did.

"Lochaber is a refuge fer cattle raiders and thieves, like myself. As long as I dinna leave the region, I willna hang."

Hang? At the terrible thought of it, one of her feet tripped over the other and she began to tumble down the last four steps.

The chief's arms around her and pulling her close, stopped her.

For the space of a torturous breath, she remained still, not even blinking her eyes that were staring into his. He was vitally warm pressed against her. She had thought he might be cold, like his gazes sometimes were. She could feel the lean muscles in his arms, like steel from which nothing could snatch her away. They both teetered on the edge of a step and Ismay closed her eyes, expecting to fall with him. But he was well-balanced and righted them before they fell.

When the torturous moment passed, and she was safe once again, he let her go and continued to the last step as if nothing just happened. As if he hadn't turned her world on its axis and made her heart leap.

But his rejection was not too unbearable. In fact, she silently thanked him for stopping her from making an even bigger fool of herself by gushing and blushing over his closeness.

She stepped off the last step and practically into his arms, but he stepped back, out of her way.

She smiled, since her tongue felt as if it were stuck to the roof of her mouth, making it difficult to speak. What was this Highland chief doing to her? How was she allowing it? Did she have control over it?

They entered the Great Hall in silence. The Lochiel didn't return the smiles or playful jeering of some of his men when they saw them together.

Ismay was about to blush and look away when she noted more than half of the rest of his cousins, both male and female, wore stunned expressions at seeing their Lochiel enter the Hall for breakfast with his guest.

He brought her to one of the more crowded tables in the center of the Hall and motioned for Geoffry to give up his seat for her. Geoffry left before she could stop him. She wanted no special treatment.

When the Lochiel sat at the head of the table in a large chair to her direct right, the others all stared, not a word uttered by one of them. What was so odd about his behavior? Ismay wondered. What did Bethia mean when she called him *such a man?* She should have asked instead of getting defensive on his behalf. Why would she defend him anyway? He protected her and saved her from the man who had taken her from the inn and no doubt would have done unthinkable things to her if she didn't kill him first.

The Lochiel had put himself between her and danger on every occasion. She was grateful. She slid her gaze to him and almost sighed out loud. His hair dried over his shoulders, turning in large, damp waves around his face. He pushed them away, but they returned, insistent on flirting around his cheek and softening the chiseled cut of his jaw.

She swallowed, watching his lips close around his spoon.

He lifted his gaze from his bowl and looked right at her.

She coughed into her hand and died twice in her head at being caught admiring his mouth.

"Lass," he said, sounding neither cold nor warm. "Eat."

She was not hungry. For the first time in a month, she was not hungry. But she dipped her spoon into the bowl of porridge set before her.

"Miss Drummond?" Sitting across from her, Lachlan spoke, watching her while she ate. "Ye look verra bonnie this morn."

She heard a sound to her right. The Lochiel had set down his spoon. She cast him a quick glance to find him staring at Lachlan.

"Thank ye fer keeping watch at my door," she told him, ignoring his compliment. She was not unused to hearing such things about how she looked. Chief MacDonald had spoken of her beauty often, even as a child. Chief MacRae had told her she was like the sun rising in winter. Words meant little and usually were offered at a price.

Beside her, she sensed rather than saw the chief pick up his cup—for she refused to glance at him again. What had that glare directed at Lachlan been about? The chief had said nothing. Was he angry at his cousin or not? And if he was angry, did it mean he was jealous? Jealous of what?

She chanced another look at him, and this time, he was the one caught looking at her.

He didn't cough into his hand as she had. He did not appear mortified at all.

Rather, he stood to his feet and raked his diamond-hard gaze on the others.

"Perhaps my orders were no' clear. Miss Drummond is here under my protection. That means ye will speak to her with respect and ye willna try to win her favor. Is that understood?"

The men around him all nodded. Some regarded her as if she was something other than a lass, something other than human. She caught a few of the female inhabitants looking at her with envy narrowing their eyes.

She wanted to crawl under the table. But she was afraid that even under the heavy wood, she would feel the irresistible pull to take the shelter he offered and hide behind his strong shoulders.

She did not hide, either beneath the table or behind his back, but she did keep her gaze lowered to her bowl.

His broad, scarred fingers filled her vision when he held his hand out to her. "Come with me."

She was not hungry anyway. She went with him, but she did not accept the hand he offered. It was best not to touch a man. She watched him take an apple from a bowl by the doors and followed him out.

"Where are we going?" she asked, weaving with him through the halls.

"Ye are goin' to the sewin' chambers. The other women will join shortly."

She shook her head. "I want to go with ye."

His rich sable gaze warmed on her. "'Tis best if ye get to know—"

"What will ye be doing?" she insisted.

"I will be in the hills watchin' fer any signs of weather, game, or potential trouble comin' from across the glen. If all is well, I will sharpen my dirk and claymore"—she began to speak, but he spoke over her—"in silence."

"I will keep silent," she promised, eyes wide with hope. "I would much rather walk in the hills and sit in the peaceful quiet while ye sharpen yer weapons."

He looked like he was about to deny her request, so she clutched his arm. "Please. 'Tis better than me following ye, is it no'?" she added when he still looked about to refuse.

"Miss Drummond," he said with the slightest hint of amusement softening his expression, "are ye threatenin' me?"

"I simply want to go with ye, Lochiel."

"Why?" he asked, appearing sincerely perplexed. "Ye will need to be quiet or ye will chase away game, or give away my position, even in the mists."

"My appreciation of ye dwindles knowing ye regard me as a woman who canna keep her mouth shut."

"Perfect." He stopped at a set of doors and opened them to a large sewing chamber. Bright sunlight streamed in from the six high, pointed windows onto a dozen embroidery stands. "Then let us go our separate ways today."

She stared after him as he strode away. Truly, he was an unfriendly oaf. She stood at the open doors deciding whether to go inside and embroidery something beautiful for her fa—She had not picked up a needle since her father died.

She looked down the hall in the direction the Lochiel had taken, and then took off after him.

CHAPTER EIGHT

C ONSTANTINE LOOKED BEHIND him twice. The lass had said
she would follow him, and he believed her. She might be a
fool to have traveled alone for a whole month, but she was
courageous to do it, as well, and crafty to have made it this far.

It seemed she was not behind him while he made his way to
the exit.

Hugh stopped him before he left to remind him he had to
hold council with his tacksmen to discuss rents, the marriage
between Ennis Cameron and Ellen Stewart, and the crofters
wanted him to hear their grievances on the upcoming harvest
shares.

"I will meet with the tacksmen in two hours," Constantine
told him. "After that, I will meet with the crofters in the Great
Hall. Inform the cooks to have enough food prepared for
everyone."

"Everyone?" Hugh repeated.

"Everyone." He began to leave but Hugh called to him. Constantine turned back to him. His eye caught the swift movement
of a hem of a skirt edged in ladybugs disappearing around the far
corner.

"Lochiel," Hugh's voice pulled his attention back, "my duty
as yer steward is to manage and protect Tor's coffers. Feeding
everyone will drain some of the castle coffers."

Constantine flashed him a quick, practiced, disingenuous smile. "Yer concern has been noted, Hugh."

He left the castle and continued on toward the hills and the mist that would swallow him up and keep him unseen while he started many of his days looking out for his clan. Today was no different save that his day started later than usual.

He did not turn back to see if Miss Drummond was still following him. If she made it to the shrouded hills, he would go to her and scold her. He did not fancy anyone disobeying him, not because he wanted to feel powerful. He gave orders that were meant to keep his people safe. If everyone went around doing as they pleased, how could he protect them against their enemies?

And they had plenty of those.

There were the MacKintoshes, who were a part of the Confederation of the Clan Chattan, which included the Chattan Clan Chief, Angus MacKintosh, MacPhersons, MacGillivrays, and Davidsons. The Campbells, who sided with Parliament, came against the Camerons because of their Royalist sympathies. The Clan Fraser had tried to attack on several occasions.

He'd had much to prove since he had been fighting battles and hadn't been here for years while his brother was Lochiel. Enemy clans had not been as familiar and afraid of him as he would like. But they had learned.

It wasn't long after he entered the mist that he heard a sound, amplified in the silence. A soft grunt, a stifled cry. He should leave her alone for another moment or two—but she could get attacked by a wild animal.

With a scowl that did not reach his eyes, he turned and headed back the way he'd come. The sound of her shouting the words, "Get back!" caused him to break into a run. He found her wielding a large stick against a gray coyote, dripping saliva from its canines.

Constantine did not wait to see what the braw lass would do next against the beast. Without hesitating, he drew his dirk and in mid-run, leaped for the coyote.

The instant the animal spotted him, it turned and fled, leaving Constantine to look after it. He did not pursue the predator. If he didn't have to kill an animal, he wouldn't. Other than hunger, the coyote had no evil intent toward his clan.

Slightly out of breath, he turned to have a look at Miss Drummond. Damnation, she reminded him of a fierce warrior. He'd seen many. Never a lass though.

Some of her pins had fallen from her hair, leaving the fiery tresses to fall over her forehead and cheek. She blew them out of her face and stared at him, still clutching her stick.

He wanted to admonish her. He'd warned her not to follow him alone. What was he trying to keep her safe for if she was just going to do as she pleased?

But he remained silent.

Finally, she dipped her terrified gaze to her fingers and dropped the stick. "It seems all I seem to do is thank ye," she said in her soft, quiet voice.

Though she had been prepared to fight the coyote, she was terrified of losing. Something in his chest shook and made him want to go to her. Instead, he sheathed his dirk and walked past her. "I would rather ye stay alive and thank me than become a wild animal's breakfast."

This time, she did not try to conceal her presence but hurried after him. "The way ye described yer morning made me want to spend mine in the peaceful quiet too."

"So ye thought to disobey me and take a walk by yerself?"

"Nae!" she defended immediately. "No' by myself, but with ye!"

He stopped and set his gaze on hers. Mist curled around her, as high as her face. Looking into her eyes was like gazing into the charcoal sea before the storm.

"Dinna try to win my favor, Miss Drummond. My affections are long dead. In fact, I would venture to say, they have become ashes."

She stared at him and he thought he saw the oceans fill and

threaten to overflow down her cheeks. "I assure ye, 'tis not yer affections I seek. Just yer protection."

He nodded. "Then do as I say."

"Fine." She turned and took a step forward. "If ye dinna want me with ye so bad, I will return to the castle."

His fingers closing around her wrist stopped her. "I willna send ye off alone and I canna return yet as I still have things to do, so ye will have to stay with me."

She didn't argue. In this instance, he didn't expect her to. She was where she wanted to be—in the peaceful quiet—with him.

What would he do with her if she grew fond of him? Bethia had often told him that many of the lasses at Tor found him pleasing to the eyes. Some had even professed him to be more handsome than Lachlan, but they were afraid of his dark silence and intimidated by his cold demeanor. He was glad.

But this lass didn't seem to mind his terse replies, dangerous scowls, or brooding character.

Braw lass.

He continued walking upward without a sound. He was pleased that she remained quiet as well. Up here, he could hear a hare hiding in the bush, or the booming hoof steps of horses approaching his cattle.

After another half hour of listening and watching, Constantine began to think of his home. Not the castle, as the lass trudging alongside him had pointed out. His home, shadowed toward the east by Ben Nevis. Remarkably, he had not thought about the house—even while he was bathing behind the castle this morn. He also had not thought about Alison or all the hatred in her kin's eyes...

He turned to set his gaze on Miss Drummond. What had she done?

As if sensing his powerful stare, she angled her head toward his and let her face break into a smile that made him feel like some pitiful sot who would allow her to make him forget...

The warmth that curled his lips bubbled up out of someplace

he had forgotten. He let himself get a little lost in her and what she—it seemed only she—could do for him. She chased away his ghosts, even brandishing her stick against his demons.

"What was she like, Chief?" she suddenly asked. If the sound of her did not make him toss away reason, he would have better guarded himself against such a question.

Had he not told her he wanted quiet? Here she was not an hour in, talking.

"I dinna wish to speak of her."

"Ye loved her."

Despite the words piercing him, her voice soothed his wounds.

"Of course."

"Do ye miss her?"

"Lass," he said on a warning thread, "aye, I miss her. Why are ye askin' me these questions?"

She bent her knees and sat on the ground, then looked up at him. "I have never been in love as ye have. My father didna force me to marry without love. Neither he nor I thought I would ever wish to wed a man."

Constantine listened and folded his legs to sit next to her, his heart thumping madly as he remembered the reason she would not wish to marry. He also recalled her telling him the chief who had abused her was dead. By whose hand? The man who had adopted her?

"Ye said ye were taken in as a babe," he began. "How did ye come to know yer father, whom ye loved?"

"He saved my life when I was eight and took me in. I lived with him and his wife and he cared fer and loved me as his own daughter."

"I would like to thank him fer bein' a good man. But ye mentioned him dyin'."

"Aye, he fell ill this past summer. The clan physician couldna be certain what was the cause. He continued to grow more ill until he perished." She looked as if she wanted to say more. But she dipped her gaze to her hands folded in her lap.

What was she not telling him?

"Ye loved him," he said in a quiet voice, seeing the pain in her face, wrapped in foggy tendrils.

"He was the only man I have ever or will ever love."

She lifted her elegant fingers to wipe her eyes. It soon became apparent to him that she was doing her best to conceal her emotions. Normally, Constantine hated emotions. Weeping usually meant pain—and Constantine had enough of that in his life. But from the first night this lass had wept while she ate her supper, he felt pity and compassion—and understanding. It was as if she could not stop herself that night, but now she could.

"Lass," he said softly, not really understanding why, save that sometimes he wished there was someone who understood his pain, who would just listen. "Ye dinna need to hold back yer tears. Losin' the one ye love can be earth shatterin'."

She stopped sniffling and looked at him. "Has it been earth shattering fer ye too?"

Habit told him to shrug his shoulders and remain quiet. Some things he could not share. But he found himself being held steady by her gaze while he nodded and then spoke. "It shatters anew every day."

He shook his head, gazing at her. "Nae. No' every day." *Not anymore.*

A wave of guilt washed over him. His wife and child were lost to him forever and he hadn't even bid them farewell properly. How dare he take interest in any other woman?

He watched her rest her tear-stained fingers on his forearm. "Lochiel, ye dinna need to hold back yer tears either."

Of course, he would not weep. It would not bring his family back.

"I didna have a chance to mourn my father," she said, looking off in the distance. "Almost immediately his wife arranged fer me to be courted. A se'nnight after my father's final farewell, my betrothed swore that the more I mourned my father, the crueler he would become toward me. My mother spied on me, I am certain of it and reported my tears to him. Despite the chief keeping his word, I still wept fer my father." She blinked away from wherever she was and gazed at him. "But it was always in fear. I dinna feel afraid right now."

He was glad. Even when she bent her head and wept into her hands, he was glad she was not afraid of him. He did not weep with her, and was barely familiar with comforting anyone, especially a lass.

But he had known how to comfort Alison.

This was not Alison.

He looked at Miss Drummond's bent head. One of her pins was dangling over her ear. He lifted his fingers to it, then, without thinking, he slipped his hand around her shoulder, bypassing the pin, and pulled her a little closer.

He sat that way with her in the mist, on the ground in the hills, unseen by anyone else while she wept for her father.

Finally, she wiped her eyes then her nose, and sat up straight. The gratitude in her smile warmed his blood.

"Shall we go?" he asked, looking past her smile before he lost more than his logic.

Her gaze spread over the hilt of his sword, his dirk, and his boots, where more knives were hidden. She knew where everything was.

"But ye havena polished yer blades yet, Chief."

He chuckled softly. "Ye would rather sit here while I do such a tedious task then return and sew something pretty?"

"Aye," she said without hesitation. "I used to sit with my father while he polished his sword. I found it verra peaceful."

That was what she wanted, Constantine told himself. Peace. But there was something she was keeping from him. Something that haunted her.

He repositioned himself on a rock and produced a cloth from his belt. He started with his sword, wiping it clean of any dried MacKintosh blood.

She kept her word and remained quiet, watching him.

She tempted him to smile back at her—or get up and run for his sanity. He did neither but ran the rag down the soon-shining blade.

When he finished with his dirk, he found her bending to a patch of blooming thistles. She looked at him at the same moment. Her smile widened, along with her eyes.

"Look! Are they no' pretty?"

He slipped his gaze to the thistles. He never noticed them before. "Aye, they are," he said, returning his gaze to her.

"I have only seen thistle twice before, when I traveled with my father. 'Twas late summer. And they were dying. But these are blooming so late," she marveled. "I willna pick them, since this is not my land, but—"

He put down the knife from his boot and rose to go to her. When he reached her, he bent and plucked one thistle from the bunch and held it before her. "As long as ye stay here, this is yer land as well as mine."

She offered him a beguiling smile in exchange for the thistle, making him both thankful he gave it to her, and angry with himself for the same reason.

He stepped back, afraid that if he didn't move, he might go forward. She held the aromatic thistle to her nose and looked up at him. He almost reversed his tracks. He didn't want anything save to be a little closer to her. He told himself it meant nothing. He didn't have to fret over it or feel guilty.

"Lochiel—" she began.

"Constantine," he corrected. His voice sounded deeper in his ears than he intended.

Her fading smile shone to life again for a moment, but she did not speak his name. "What ye offer is tempting, indeed. Nae man but one has ever invited me to share his home and his land. I would venture to say that I could nae doubt be happy here, mayhap bloom like these thistles if my life had been different. But I canna risk being found and dragged—"

"Do ye think I would let anyone drag ye anywhere, lass?" he asked with a darkening expression.

Severing her gaze from his, she laughed, but there was no mirth in it. "Why do ye think I would let ye fight fer me?" She turned back to him and looked him straight in the eye when she spoke again. "We are nothing to each other, Chief. I didna agree to stay here. I have thought about it and decided to keep moving and get as far away as I can from my past. I will find a convent and spend the rest of my days there."

He wanted to say something. His jaw clenched with the need. But he fought it and won. He did not know what to say anyway.

"I will never ferget ye, Constantine."

His heart lurched within him, making him involuntarily reach his hand to his chest. He looked down at it and then raised his gaze to her. "Let us head back. I have things to see to."

Without another word, he turned on his heel and started back. It was good that she was not staying. The sooner she was gone, the better. He didn't like that something about her attracted him. He hated how out of control his reason and emotions felt around her. Let some convent have her. He scoffed in front of her. She would never master meekness or obedience.

He had the mad urge to turn to her and tell her to never change.

She wanted to forget her past. He never wanted to forget his.

And yet, once again, he had not thought of Alison all morning. He had not felt her in the mists or heard her laughter in the wind. Instead, he'd heard another voice.

I will never ferget ye, Constantine.

It felt like a hook piercing him in the gut. He wanted to forget her. He wanted to forget the possibility of being happy again. Too many of his fellow patriots had died in battle against Cromwell's forces. His wife died giving birth to their child, who left the earth soon after. Too much pain and loss had seeped into his heart. He had learned to live with it, never wanting anything more.

He still did not want more. His life was just fine.

He scowled and aimed it over his shoulder at her. The more he had, the more he'd be afraid to lose.

"Am I correct to believe yer pout is aimed at me?"

"Pout?" he asked incredulously. He did not *pout*.

"Whatever it is ye are doing with yer face," she clarified…sort of.

"Nae, ye are no' correct. I am no' *scowlin'* at ye." He returned his attention to the unseen dirt road in the fog.

"Do ye know where ye are going in this mist?" she asked. "'Tis getting thicker."

"Do ye intend to insult me every time ye open yer mouth?" he asked, brooding fully.

She hardly noticed and hurried to catch up to him. When she reached him, she clung to his arm.

He almost pulled away. No woman had touched him since…but he let Ismay Drummond cling to him. From the moment he met her, he let her cling to him.

It was not such a terrible or forbidden thing to do. In fact, it was a wise decision on her part, he thought. Rather she clung to him than try to foolishly go off on her own again.

He let her hold on, ignoring the blaring warnings going off in his head and led her down the hill.

Like a curtain parting, the mist rose above them, leaving them in the bright light of day. She did not release him immediately. He crooked his arm and laid her hand on his elbow.

But as if she were just coming awake, she moved away from him.

He kept going and only paused when she stopped behind him. "Are ye comin'?"

"With ye?" she asked.

Instead of a reply, he gave her a look that asked if she was dull-witted.

"Where are ye off to, Lochiel?"

She was back to calling him Lochiel then, he thought with an impatient sigh. "I am meetin' with the council."

She nodded and hurried to him.

Continuing onward, he smiled despite himself. He was eager to discover the effect this breath of fresh air had on the elders of the clan.

"Are ye smiling, Chief?" she nagged beside him.

"Nae," he answered, tossing heaven a patient look.

Then he smiled again.

CHAPTER NINE

"I DINNA CARE if the land was handed down to Angus Cameron," said the brutish looking Highlander standing before the Lochiel. "He lost the deeds in poker fair and square!"

The Lochiel looked at who was none other than Angus Cameron. "Is this true?"

Angus lowered his head and nodded. "But Lochiel, that land wasna mine to gamble away. My late father left it to me, and his father—"

"Angus," the Lochiel said, stopping him from any more speech. "If that land was important to ye, ye should no' have bet against it. Hand the deeds over to Jamie MacDonald and go home, thankful that ye didna bet that too."

Ismay watched and listened to the chief. He was just, concise, and each decision was handed out with authority. His was the last word. Jamie MacDonald got his land, the widow Abby Cameron would have her roof repaired by four of the village men. Old Ennis Cameron was given the Lochiel's blessing to marry Ellen Stewart, and Magnus Ranald received the chief's commendations on his written agreement with the MacMartins of Torlundy to be their chief butcher and have Cameron's best beef delivered to them monthly.

The Lochiel's attention was demanded on a dozen different matters, over the next pair of hours. For each one, Ismay watched him make wise, fair decisions. He was not swayed by begging, station, or a bonnie face.

He looked toward her more than once and Ismay was certain he would have been swayed by her. Not because of any way he gazed at her, for his expression barely changed in two hours. He was as unchanging as steel before it was dipped into fire. But so far, he had done everything she'd asked. He had even granted her wishes when they were not what he wanted. And…well, he did, in fact, look at her more warmly than he did with anyone else. Even his scowls lost some of their fearsome warning on her alone.

It was most likely why he did not look at her overlong. It would do him little good if others knew he favored her.

He favored her. How did she feel about that? She believed he was a better man than the monsters of her past. But what did she know? What if she made him angry? She thought about it. Had she not made him angry already when she followed him and almost got eaten by a coyote? Or how about when she disagreed with him or insulted him? His demeanor toward her had not changed.

"Lochiel," an elder called out from where he sat at the table after the tenants left the Hall. "We must discuss the lass Hilary, daughter of our esteemed Sir Richard MacDonald's wish to marry John MacBain."

"She should be banished from the clan for such treachery," another elder cried.

"A MacBain of all people, part of the Chattan!" shouted someone else. "She might as well have run off with a MacKintosh!"

One of the other ten tacksmen slammed his fist down on the table, riling up the other men.

Ismay sent them all a scathing look. These were the men who would toss her out and stone her if they knew she was the cause of the MacPherson/MacDonald feud.

"Miss Drummond?"

She turned her eyes in the Lochiel's direction.

"What do ye think? Hilary MacDonald is Geoffry and Fionn's sister. She wishes to be wed to a man from an enemy clan. Most here are against it and want to banish her. What do ye say?"

"Lochiel, who is this woman ye invite into our council?" an elder demanded.

When another of the men elbowed the first in the ribs to quiet him, Ismay wondered what had just been silently conveyed between them? She moved her gaze over the rest of them to find them all staring at her.

"I think"—she began without hesitation. She knew what kind of stuffy old fools these were, for there were plenty of them in her father's council. "—if she is banished, she will more than likely be taken in by yer enemy, and in fifteen to twenty years yer sons will face her sons in battle." She let her gaze rove over the men. "Is any one of ye willing to sacrifice his son today? Let her remain with ye without changing how ye feel about her. Let her husband live with ye—" At this, the elders went into an uproar, waving their hand and wagging their fingers at her. "Stop thinking only of yourselves and yer stubborn thirst fer battle and think of the future of yer clan. Let her husband live among ye and gain an ally whose sons will fight by your sons' sides one day."

Six of the ten continued to shout that her suggestion was madness. Four others stared at her and each other, taking her words into consideration.

There was only one opinion that mattered to her. She turned to the chief. He was staring out at his council and then, as if sensing her watching him, he flicked his gaze to her and smiled.

Ismay's heart had no right to feel as if it might pop right out of her mouth if she opened it. Her head did not want anything to do with a man, especially not a man as powerful as the one lounging in a chair to her right.

How had he managed to penetrate her strongest defenses? No. She convinced herself it was not too late. She did not think he was terrible. She still wanted to leave his castle.

"Lochiel, ye are no' considerin' this lass's words, are ye?"

Did his smile mean he agreed with her in front of these old, rigid men?

"She is correct," he told them, then waited for them to settle down before he spoke again. "I have listened to yer complaints on this matter for two months now. This is my final judgment. Hilary is our kin. She will no' be banished from the clan because of who she loves. Better an alliance with the Chattan than more enemies."

Ignoring the arguing around her, Ismay grinned at the Lochiel when his dark gaze found her again.

He appeared as affected by her smile as she was by his. He tempted her to abandon her fears and…no. Even if she could somehow get past the hatred in her heart, her body was another matter. She did not want a man in her bed. The very thought of it would repulse her the rest of her days.

She sighed and looked away.

"All right," he pushed his chair away from the table and stood up. "We are finished."

"Chief," one of the older men stood with the rest. "Hear us on this matter at the next council. We—"

"Nae. I have declared my judgment. Do ye contest me?"

"Nae, Lochiel. I just—"

"We are done." He pushed his chair aside, and reaching for Ismay's wrist, pulled her to his side and out of the Hall.

"Have ye truly been hearing their complaints on the marriage fer two months?"

"Aye," he breathed, sounding weary of it.

"Did I sway yer decision?" she asked, peeking up at him.

He let go of her wrist and headed through another short corridor with doors.

"What ye said made good sense to my ears," he admitted. "We usually think in terms of fighting. Considerin' my"—he stopped walking and turned to look at her and then at the ground—"our"—he closed his eyes and clenched his jaw before trying again—"their sons made me see things differently."

"I'm pleased to hear that ye would admit a woman's decision was the correct one."

He gave her one last stare then continued on toward a door at the end of the hall.

"What is next?"

"Can ye ride?" he asked, opening the door and surprising Ismay with a view of the back of the castle. And the stable.

"Aye," she told him, stepping outside.

"Why did ye walk here then," he asked her, leading the way down the narrow stone steps to the stable.

"If I had taken a horse, they would have overtaken me. My journey consisted mostly of hiding rather than riding. 'Tis more difficult to hide on a horse."

He thought about it and nodded. "Ye can ride today. If anyone has followed ye, I will keep them from ye."

"Where are we going?"

"To inspect the herds. Geoffry and Lachlan will accompany us."

Did he actually want her tagging along? She didn't want to overthink it. She wanted to be outside, riding freely and without worries weighing her down. So she followed him. She was beginning to think she might follow him anywhere.

He had an almond-colored mare called Radiance saddled for her and when the others joined them, they set out for the vast grazing glens, with the chief keeping up a steady trot beside Ismay and Radiance. When they reached the massive herd, there were more heads than Ismay could count.

"I must get closer and move within the herd," he told her at the gated edge of the glen. "'Tis much more dangerous than ye can imagine. Stay here."

She didn't want to stand and watch, but she didn't disobey him.

Even atop his horse, he looked small within the pulsating herd. Still, he commanded authority over the beasts, weaving in and out of their giant bodies, the Highland wind blowing his hair off his shoulders.

His eyes found hers more than once, eclipsed by strands of dark hair when the wind settled down.

Finally, he broke through the herd and rode his horse close to the gate where she waited. He motioned for her to leave her mount and climb the wooden fence. When she did, he lifted his arms to her and caught her easily when she stepped off and into his safe embrace.

He set her atop his thighs and closed his sinewy arms around her.

For a moment, terror gripped her at his touch. What did he mean to do? Her heart told her he meant no harm—but how could she be sure? Her head told her to jump down and run.

"Dinna make any loud noises or sudden wide movements," he said, as if sensing her thoughts—or mayhap it was the way she turned as stiff as a board in his lap that made him suspect she might try to flee.

He lowered his head and dipped his lips to her ear. "Though they are used to us bein' here by now, caution is safer."

She closed her eyes against the heat of his breath and the deep cadence of his quiet voice. How could she like it? How?

She nodded, unwilling to say anything and risk crying out something that might shame her, like *Dinna touch me! Ye are a monster. I'm afraid!*

He kept the horse's pace steady with the cattle as he rode close to a group of ten, grazing in the grass.

"That one," he told her, keeping his voice soft near her ear and motioning with his chin to a large coo with a white patch between its eyes and on its chest, "is Fraya. We took her from the MacKintoshes eight years ago. At the time, she hated bein' touched and would often cause a stampede by bellowin' and sometimes even screamin' if we went near her. Finally, I separated her from the others and put her in a smaller enclosure, where she could still see the others. Fer days I simply sat in the grass waitin' fer her to graze near me. She refused to eat fer a se'nnight."

From where she was perched on his lap, Ismay gazed at the coo. Her heart went out to the animal. Ismay understood how it felt to be so afraid that fighting back or even killing became the only option for escape. "Poor thing."

"Aye," the chief agreed behind her. "I feared she would starve herself to death. But on the day I had decided to leave her alone, she came near me and lowered her head to the grass. We became friends after that."

He started walking the horse closer to Fraya, but the coo met them the rest of the way and rested her giant head in his lap—on top of Ismay's thighs.

"Ye taught her to trust ye," Ismay noted while he scratched the coo's nose. "Not many would be so patient."

"That is why she belongs here. With me."

Ismay's heart froze. With him? There was no *with him*. Nor would there be. She would not have another man make plans for her life. She would make her own. In a convent.

When she turned away, he took her hand and lifted it to the top of the coo's head. "Let her know ye are her friend. She isna used to lasses."

Ismay thought about pulling her hand away from him, but she wanted to pet the beast. Besides, he released her the instant she touched Fraya's thick fur.

"Greetings, bonnie coo," she practically sang, her smile wide. "I hope ye will accept me and never try to crush me under yer mighty hooves."

Behind her, the Lochiel chuckled, making her belly flip before she turned to him. "What?"

"Is that how ye win her favor, lass? Move slowly, respectfully while fillin' her with compliments?"

Her wide smile intact, she nodded. "Does she deserve less?"

"Mayhap more," he countered with amusement lighting his poignant eyes.

After a little while getting to know some of the herd, he rode them back slowly to her horse.

"Ye have confidence, lass," he told her. He'd moved back, away from her ear. But she still heard him. "Ye know yer worth."

She shook her head. "I had no worth, Chie—Constantine. None, whatsoever before my father. He taught me that although I had no riches or noble title, I had worth to God and to others on this earth. One of them was him. I felt it every day in his presence." Like she felt it in the chief's. "My father knew what I had become, and he didna care. He understood what my early years had done to me and let me decide if I wanted to marry or not."

"What had ye become?" he asked.

"Hmm? What?"

"Ye said, he knew what ye had become and he didna care. What had ye become? Will ye tell me?"

She trusted him, did she not? He would be the only soul, besides her father, who knew of her crime.

"I became a murderer." A sound in her head like a door slamming shut—or a guillotine coming down made her heart lurch. Did she just make a terrible error? She told him nothing else. Not the name of her victim. She could never tell him that.

He didn't ask her what she meant or demand that she tell him everything. When they reached her horse, he helped her dismount.

She would have preferred to remain with him. Her head was still spinning from her confession when he set her feet on the ground. Her knees nearly buckled beneath her. He caught her and held her close against his chest while he stared into her wide eyes.

"Are ye feelin' ill?" he asked, concern marring his dark brow.

"Nae," she told him and righted herself. She took a tentative step away from him. When dizziness did not overcome her again, she made it to her horse.

But the chief stopped her when she fit her foot in the stirrup.

"Ride with me," he commanded gently, while seizing her wrist.

Ismay's heart thumped madly in her breast. That was what she wanted in the first place.

"If ye fall from yer horse, ye will be injured and stuck here longer. Ye dinna want that, do ye?"

Her heart slowed. "Nae," she answered dully and returned to his horse. "Yer consideration of my desires is appreciated, Chief."

He lifted her to his saddle, then leaped up behind her.

"What about Radiance?" she asked, trying to turn without falling or having to hold onto him.

"The men will get her."

"I am fine, by the way," she let him know when he flicked his reins and they began to move. "I was a bit shaken because I—" She stopped, unable to say it again.

"Because ye told me ye were a murderer?"

She stiffened and nodded. Now she *really* had to run away.

"I am certain whoever ye killed deserved it."

Of course he would say such a thing. He was a soldier, a chief with many enemies, and a thief.

"I had never killed anyone before," she cried, wanting to curl up in something soft, yet safe—like his arms. "I was just a child."

His arm coiling her waist tightened just a bit. She fought not to panic while the warmth of his touch spread into her. She would tell him…she stopped. He was clever. How long would it take him before he figured out who it was she had killed?

"I prefer not to speak of it any longer."

"Whatever ye wish, lass."

She was quiet while they rode to the castle. She didn't realize her back rested against him until it was time to dismount and she grew cold at their separation.

He walked her into the castle and then looked around. "I will have Bethia see to ye. Ye can rest and then freshen up fer supper."

It was all he was going to say, proven when he turned on his heel and was ready to walk off with her stammering behind him.

"Will ye send fer me later?" she asked, hating herself for appearing so pathetic, always chasing after him.

He turned and stared at her for a moment, as if he were trying to decide something about her that made his brow dip over his eyes. Then, he nodded and left. "I will teach ye how to fight."

"Hmm?" Did she hear him right? Why would he do something like that?

"If ye're ever alone again, ye willna need me to save ye."

Her brow dipped. He didn't seem to notice and turned away. She stared at his back growing smaller as he disappeared down one of the corridors. What if she liked when he saved her? Where was he off to? Had he grown weary of her? She couldn't complain and she wouldn't follow him. He had spent the entire morning, making her smile, allowing her to weep freely for her father, bringing her into his herd—cautious in keeping her safe.

She smiled now, despite herself.

"I take it that the precious grin ye wear is evidence of a pleasant morning."

Ismay turned to greet Hugh. Was he always just a moment away? "Aye," she admitted with a slight blush.

His dark-green eyes dipped to the thistle in her hand. "Did ye pick such a thorny flower when there are others which will not cause ye pain?"

She held it up to study the thistle again. She didn't tell him the Lochiel had picked it for her. She had a feeling the steward was not speaking of the Highland flora and anything other than that was none of his concern. "Everyone wants to push their noses against those other flowers," she told him, then looked up from the thistle. "I much prefer the bloom that will prick yer nose if ye get too close."

"Hugh," Lewis, the owner of the inn, called out, approaching them. "Dinna ye have anythin' better to do than follow the Lochiel's bonnie guest around?"

"He leaves her alone in this shadowy fortress too often," Hugh told him while wearing a friendly smile. "She should have an escort to her chambers."

"The chief promised to send Bethia to me," Ismay let him know.

"And in the meantime," the steward gazed at her, "ye wait alone."

He had a valid point. Ismay had no rebuttal, but Lewis did.

"Hugh," he said in a slightly whiny voice, "ye know I dinna have the patience the Lochiel has. Ye are close to haviin' me drag ye into the trainin' yard and beatin' some respect into ye."

He sounded as if it was the last thing he wanted to do, but if he had to, he would, and he might even enjoy it. The choice was in Hugh's hands.

At the threat, Ismay could not help but feel sorry for the steward. Lewis had a mad-in-the-head sort of look about him—as if it took all his control to stop himself from killing anyone he fought with.

Hugh was not so easily intimidated by him and moved a hair closer to her.

"That is enough." Ismay put her hands between them and pushed gently. "Let whatever this is end now."

"Fergive me, Lewis," Hugh backed off.

Lewis smiled and pulled him against his chest—and out of the path of the Lochiel standing a few feet behind him. Ismay's gaze found him at the same time she heard the innkeeper's low warning to the steward.

"If I hear ye speak poorly of the Lochiel again, I will remove yer tongue."

"Lewis," the Lochiel called out, making his presence known. "There is a lass present."

Lewis gave him a soft chuckle and looked at her. She retreated a step, guilty of disguising herself to appear as a lad when she first met them.

"Ye may go," the Lochiel commanded his cousin softly.

Lewis did not pause, but bowed to her and then left, the heels of his boots clicking on the stone floor.

Hugh stood facing him.

"Stop temptin' him to keep his word," the Lochiel warned. "He will. Now, tell me," he said as if everything before this very moment was forgotten, "have ye seen Bethia?"

Hugh shook his head. "No' since this morning'"

Ismay heard a girl's laughter and turned to see Joan restored to her position beside Lachlan.

Seeing them, Ismay looked up at the Lochiel and beamed at him. Only his order could have brought Joan back.

He shifted in his place and looked at the wrought iron wall sconces lighting the walls, then at the arched windows—anything but her. "Come," he said, placing his hand on her back. "I will take ye to yer chambers."

She was glad he had not abandoned her as Hugh had tried to convince her. He had looked for Bethia to tend to her, and not finding her, he'd returned to Ismay.

"Chief?"

"Aye, lass?"

Why did his voice have to send tremors through her veins, and quakes throughout her heart?

"I am sorry to be causing ye trouble."

"What?" He stopped when they came to the stairs and turned to her. "Who told ye that ye were trouble?" He shot a murderous gaze to Hugh over his shoulder.

Ismay rested her fingers on his arm to capture his attention and veer it off slicing his blade across Hugh's belly the way he had to the MacKintosh who had taken her from the inn.

"No one told me. It is obvious to my own eyes."

"Ye are nae trouble to me, Miss Drummond. Even if ye were, ye are leavin' soon. I havena fergotten. Have ye?"

The warmth in her gaze vanished and was replaced by a cold sheet of ice. "Nae. I havena fergotten, Lochiel. How could I when ye take every opportunity to remind me!"

They reached her door. She opened it, stepped inside, and slammed the door in his face.

Inside, with her back pressed to the cold wood, she squeezed her eyes shut. Why was she angry? Why was she hurt that he wanted to get rid of her—when it was the same thing she wanted?

She had to go. She had to leave him before—before she didn't ever want to leave his side again.

Oh, Lord, help her, she mourned. 'Twas too late.

CHAPTER TEN

CONSTANTINE SAUNTERED AWAY from Miss Drummond's door, wearing the hint of a smile that widened the farther he moved away from her chambers. Her fire sparked something in him to life. Other lasses shied away from him, afraid to touch the bear. All the men, including his closest cousins, would never think of betraying him and rarely disobeyed him.

But this wisp of lass, who journeyed on foot for a month to Tor, was not afraid of him. He almost breathed out loud with relief.

He enjoyed getting her angry by giving her exactly what she wanted: the freedom to leave. Of course, he didn't fancy the idea of her leaving, nor was he certain he would let her go so easily. If her betrothed or her mother were after her, a convent would not stop them.

He would. But that meant she would have to remain at Tor Castle. There were plenty of folks living here who weren't necessarily kin, but Miss Drummond was different. Was she not? He thought about her...often. He didn't think about anyone else in the castle.

She made him want to smile—and a few times, he had. The only other people he felt any inclination to smile with were Lewis, Geoffry, Fionn, and Lachlan—and even with the four men he'd grown up with, he didn't do it often.

Miss Drummond kept him occupied watching to see what she was up to next. Even in the silence of the misty morning, she had gone traipsing about in the thistle, marveling at purple flowers while he marveled at her. She hummed often. It was mostly done just under her breath, but he could hear it. How did she still sing after being so mistreated by a man and finally killing him as a child? After losing her beloved father, being hated by her mother, and treated cruelly by her betrothed, her resilience shone like a beacon.

She had an unwelcome effect on him and he had no idea how to stop it. He could send her away, but he didn't want to do that.

He was acting like a fool. He'd never put himself in the path of deliberate danger before. But Miss Drummond was making him feel and do things he had not done in years.

He felt the beginnings of another smile, then stopped when he saw Bethia hurrying toward him. He stopped and waited for her to reach him.

"Fergive me, Lochiel. I heard ye were looking fer me."

"Aye," he said, picking up his steps again. "Where did ye disappear to withoot tellin' a soul? Ye know 'tis dangerous to go oot alone."

Truly, he thought of the lass he just left at her door, did he want another foolishly fearless woman on his hands?

"We needed some supplies from the market and I took Fionn with me."

He paused, then nodded. At least she had some sense—unlike a certain lass who had run into a coyote.

"Lochiel, if ye dinna mind me saying," the head chambermaid said, "ye seem ill at ease. Is it the lass who darkens yer countenance?"

He looked at her, sincerely surprised. "Is my countenance dark? I feared I was smiling too much."

Now Bethia was the one who appeared utterly astonished. "Smiling too much, Lochiel?"

"Aye," he confessed. He'd often confessed to Bethia, who was the one who tended to him through the quiet times and the times when nightmares covered him in blood and he woke up crying out into the night, when he drank too much and told her too much while she undressed him and put him to bed. He didn't remember her ever cowering from him after his drunken confessions of the men he had killed fighting in the royalist army, and how he'd felt killing them. How he'd tried to kill one hundred a day. A hundred for every one of his kins' lives they had taken. She'd never admonished or judged him outright, but she thought he was a monster. She didn't have to say it.

"I have been feelin' more…light-hearted," he said after a moment of pondering it.

"Light-hearted?"

She moved slightly closer and gave the air around him a sniff. "I havena been drinkin', woman."

She contemplated him for another moment. "Hmm, come to think of it, ye havena been drinking at all since ye returned with her."

He thought about it, continuing onward. She was correct.

"Chief," his trusted chambermaid said, stopping him again, "is she making ye ferget Alison and Katie?"

"What?" His heart thrashed wildly. "Nae! I could never ferget them! But am I to pay fer my sins fer the remainder of my days?"

It was the first time he had ever complained about feeling responsible. He was not surprised by Bethia's slack-jawed stare. She loved Alison and doted over her. She even left her home with the MacMillans and came to live here with Alison when she married Constantine. It was because of her devotion to his wife that he'd grown close with her.

But he did not appreciate her trying to hold his guilt up to his face.

"That is between ye and the Good Lord, Lochiel," the head chambermaid told him.

"Then let me feel the weight of His decision. Not yers."

She bowed her head slightly. He kept walking.

He descended the stairs, then, sensing her behind him, he turned at the last step. "Find Joan. Remind her this is her last chance and tell her to tend to Miss Drummond."

"I will tend to the lass—"

"Nae," he said, cutting Bethia off. "Have Joan do it. Yer feelin's are too raw. Ye may say things ye should keep to yerself."

"I would not—"

"Send Joan," he cut her off again and went on his way.

He found Lachlan and Fionn in the courtyard, practicing with their heavy swords. When they spotted him, they exchanged a nervous look. No one wanted to practice with him. He had no idea why. He had not killed anyone during practice.

He waited and bit into an apple he'd plucked from a bowl in the kitchen when he passed it. He watched his cousins while he ate, calling to Lachlan when the younger Cameron should have blocked left, doubled around, and struck from behind.

Then, shouting at Fionn to strike with more purpose. If his opponent did not block, parry, or evade, let him suffer the consequence. He did not care if the one to suffer was Lachlan. They could not keep him from fighting forever because he did not know how to keep himself alive other than with an arrow. He had to learn.

He watched until Lachlan seemed to be doing better against Fionn, then Constantine called them to a halt, tossed his apple to Fionn and stepped into his place.

Facing Lachlan, he pulled his sword free from the scabbard at his side. "Get ready," he said ominously.

"I am not ready to face ye yet, brother," the younger of the two admitted nervously.

It hurt Constantine to be so cold toward him. But how much worse would the pain be if Lachlan were ever to be killed in battle?

So, giving his cousin no further reply, he advanced and swung hard. Lachlan had no choice but to block, crashing his blade into Constantine's and shooting sparks above their heads. The lad paled. Constantine swung again from the other direction. Their swords clashed again, and then again, and then, yet again.

Lachlan made a painful expression when he lifted his arms again. He was weary and likely in some pain. An opponent on the battlefield would not give him time to rest.

Constantine jabbed and nodded when Lachlan leaped back and blocked.

They practiced until Lachlan fell back on his arse and begged for mercy.

With a heavy sigh, Constantine reached down to help him to his feet. "Ye did well."

That seemed to be all the accolades Lachlan needed to restore him. He grinned at Constantine and thanked him.

"Where is yer lady?"

"She is no' *my* lady," Constantine assured him with a scowl. Mayhap he was not hard enough on the lad.

"Ye must admit," Fionn chimed in with a smile, "she is bonnie with all them red curls tumblin' 'round her face."

Immediately. Constantine imagined her hair like a wild lion's mane around her bonnie face. Aye, of course she was bonnie. He was not blind.

"Since she isna' yer woman," Lachlan pressed, "would ye mind if I—"

"Aye, I would mind," Constantine said through his teeth. "Are ye rested now? Should we continue our lesson, then, whelp?"

Lachlan cast him a loving grin. "That willna be necessary, Lochiel. I will consider her—"

"—my guest, whose favor ye willna try to win."

"Aye," Lachlan agreed and looked at his boots.

Constantine gave him one last look of disgust and then sheathed his sword and left the courtyard.

His lady. He almost laughed but then a shadow drifted across his eyes. What was he doing that made Bethia and his men— because while Lachlan was going on into territory that could have gotten him trounced, Fionn was smiling—believe he fancied Miss Drummond? He'd left her alone for the afternoon, had he not? It was not as if he kept her by his side an instant longer than he needed to.

Unbidden thoughts of his guest filled his head as he strode back inside the castle. Was she resting? Had Joan tended to her needs this time or had Hugh—

Before he realized where he was heading, he stopped on the stairs. Why was he about to check and make certain Hugh was not with his la—guest. What did he care? He had not cared when Hugh spent time with Alison. Why would he care about a strange lass who was on the run? Had she run? Was she still here? She spoke often of leaving for some convent God knew where. He was too busy fighting in the courtyard to notice if she had slipped out. He thought her departure would be welcome because he no longer had to worry about her. But he found himself taking the stairs two at a time.

When he stepped onto the second landing, he looked around for Hugh. His steward was nowhere to be found.

Continuing to the door of her chambers, images of her wrapped themselves around his head. Her with her eyes bloodshot and the tip of her nose red from crying, or her holding a prickly thistle to her nose as if it were the most delicate of all the flowers.

He swallowed and knocked. A few moments passed. Enough to make his heart stall and his legs ache to kick the door down. If she had left, he would—what? What would he do?

The door opened, keeping him from finding out. When he saw her freckled face and curious gray gaze, he couldn't think of anything but how relieved he was that she was still there.

"Lochiel?" she urged when he said nothing. "Is something troubling ye?"

Aye! He wanted to tell her. Aye, something was troubling him, all right. What was he doing at her door, wanting to smile like a halfwit that she had not run away?

"Are ye hungry?"

She offered him a smile as hesitant as his own and nodded. He turned and began to walk away and then looked over his shoulder at her. "Are ye comin'?"

She hurried to catch up and kept pace at his side. After a moment she turned slightly to look up at him.

"I was happy to find Joan tending to me. It was kind of ye to allow her a second chance."

"She has ye to thank fer that," he let her know. "I dinna usually hand out second chances."

He felt her eyes on him and chanced a glance her way.

Her smile softened, making his belly flip and flutter as if it had just come to life. He turned away, and in doing so, noticed the folks coming to and fro in the halls. All their gazes lingered on him and his guest. He moved a step or two away from her, lest they imagine the preposterous.

She would never be more to him than his guest. His wife and bairn were gone from him but five short years—short according to her parents and to Bethia. How long was an acceptable time for him to mourn his family? And once the grieving eased, how long would the guilt take to fade? Would it ever?

Was killing more important to ye than being present at yer wife's deathbed? Alison's mother cried out when he had finally come home.

We buried our daughter and granddaughter without ye! her father had practically growled at him. *Ye will have no part in where they rest.*

His closest cousins had thought Alison's parents were too harsh.

Ye were her husband and the babe's father, after all, Lewis complained.

It isna that ye didna want to come home! Fionn agreed. *The choice wasna yers.*

Constantine could have argued that no matter what, he should have been here with his dying wife. She—

"Chief?" Miss Drummond's soft voice pulled him from his thoughts of Alison. "After we eat, and ye teach me how to fight, would ye show me where ye bathed this morn?"

"Bathed?"

She nodded. "I used to bathe in the stream close to my father's house. There was a waterfall—"

"Alone?" he asked incredulously. Was it so safe in her father's house that she felt safe bathing in a stream? Or was she just a careless fool?

"My maids were with me." Immediately seeming to realize what she said, she grew quiet.

"Was yer father a nobleman?" he asked, too curious to remain silent. He suspected she was no servant since she'd been promised to a powerful chief. But for her to have had more than one maid to accompany her while she bathed, suggested her father was a man of title.

"He was…a wealthy landowner."

"Where?" He knew nothing about her. If she told him, he might figure out who she killed.

"Dalneigh," she told him after she thought about it for a moment. He guessed she was not telling him the truth. Then, she did not trust him fully. Good. Full trust was not earned by keeping your word once. "Near the River Ness."

She knew where Dalneigh was though, and that told him that she likely came from somewhere in Inverness. Wealthy landowners were usually prominent men. It would not take Constantine long to find out the wealthiest landowners in Inverness who had died this summer.

"Did ye walk here from Dalneigh then?"

She dipped her gaze. "Aye."

He shook his head in stunned admiration. He knew she had travelled long, but he was not sure how far. Suddenly a wave of protectiveness washed over him. She had told him her promised groom was cruel, but what had he done to her to make her fear she could not get far enough away from him? His mouth opened before he could stop it, but he was not certain he would have stopped himself if he had time to think about it.

"Lass, I will keep ye from ever goin' back."

She lifted her gaze to his and stared into his eyes.

He should look away. He tried, but his eyes refused to obey.

"Ye have already done so much fer me," she said meaningfully. "I could never repay ye."

Images invaded his thoughts. Images of leaning in closer to her and kissing her plump, slightly parted lips.

He blinked, severing their gazes and looked toward the stairs. "I wonder what is fer supper?"

He rubbed his belly and continued on, quickening his pace to move away from her.

As they descended the stairs and neared the Great Hall, the aromas of freshly baked bread, braised duck, and hare stew filled the air. Constantine and his guest inhaled deeply at the same time and then smiled at each other in silent agreement.

Neither of them saw Lachlan and Fionn entering the castle from a set of side doors leading to the stone stairway outside or their stunned expressions at seeing their Lochiel smiling at a lass.

"Chief?" Lachlan called out to him.

When Constantine turned to see him, the lad grinned at him and then at Miss Drummond, and then back at him. "Will ye be eatin' with us today then?"

With an almost silent sigh of annoyance, Constantine nodded, his smile fading.

"Our practice wasna long enough today," he murmured low as Lachlan passed him to enter the Great Hall first.

The young lad turned to toss a worried glance over his shoulder. Fionn laughed. Miss Drummond was still smiling when he looked at her again. Seeing her, Constantine stopped caring about what his cousins thought and smiled back at her.

CHAPTER ELEVEN

A LISTAIR MACRAE, CLAN Chief of the MacRae's of Beauly, stepped out of the Dueling Princes Inn in Glenelg, belched, then looked around at the horses tied to the nearby posts.

Lady Marjorie MacPherson had told him her daughter had not taken a horse. Was it possible the lass was on foot? Had she procured a horse somewhere else? He didn't even know which way she'd gone. North, south, east... He sighed with frustration. Did she run away with the help of a man? Alistair would find out. He thought cutting the wench's hair off would keep men away from her. But if she was offering herself for aid in escaping, he would kill whoever was helping her. Rage filled him, balling his hands into fists.

Her father, the baron, had been a very wealthy man. At his death, he bequeathed everything he owned to his daughter, unbeknownst to her.

Baron MacPherson's estranged wife offered her newly wealthy daughter to Alistair as a bride. If he accepted her, he would lay claim to her father's fortune. He only had to sign a promise that he would give Lady Marjorie half.

Of course, he had accepted, especially after he laid eyes on Ismay. She was beguiling and bewitching with her long, fiery tresses flowing all about her. Her temper flared like a hellcat he ached to subdue and tame. He'd wanted her but had agreed to wait, like a fool. When he found her, he would not wait another instant.

Aye, he would still take Ismay as his wife. He wanted what he was promised. As for giving the baron's wife half the fortune, she would wait for it until she died, which, if he has his way, will not be long after her daughter's death.

He went to his horse and checked the saddle, then pulled himself up on the stirrup. He was going to find her. If he searched until his last day on earth, he would find her and have her and her father's fortune.

First though, he had to ride into the forest and find his men's camp. Of course, the ruffians could not spend the night at the inn. Who would pay? Certainly not him. Besides, they were dirty, rowdy men who would draw attention and offend.

Alistair did not always want to be associated with them. He would soon be rich and his image would be important.

As he entered the forest, he had the sinking feeling that they were going the wrong way. How could no one have seen her with her sun-colored hair, short or long, it stood out. She could be traveling with her hair covered, but who would not remember a lass traveling alone or with a man? Women did not often travel far from their home.

What if she'd gone from Raigmore northeast toward Culloden or south, toward Kiliwhimin? Had she not mentioned joining a convent over becoming someone's wife? Was Kiliwhimin not Saint Cummein of Iona who had built a church there?

What made him travel west? He had decided on going west, toward Skye because it was mostly a desolate place, with the clan MacLeod in the north and clan MacDonald closer to the mainland. She could hide on Skye without being seen or found for years.

He found his eleven men clearing up their campsite when he arrived. Unlike Ismay, who had either gone in a different direction or did not leave a trace that she had camped anywhere, they left a good amount behind for anyone to find them.

Alistair did not care about cores, or pits, or bones scattering the grass. He cared about catching his defiant bride, and that was all. His men were there in case she had help in escaping.

"Any leads at the inn, Chief?" one of the men asked. He was Ramsey Fergusson, one of the meaner looking men of the group, with a long scar running down his face, two teeth missing, and dark stubble covering half his face.

Alistair shook his head. "Today we will head south."

No one questioned him. They knew better after he ran Brodie Graham through with his sword after the miscreant made a crude remark about mayhap having a go with Miss MacPherson for all the trouble she caused.

He would kill any man who touched her or even spoke of touching her. If they tried to stop him from finding her or questioned his ability to do so, he would kill them. They were nothing but hired mercenaries anyway. Who would miss them?

"Let's go." He didn't wait for any of them but flicked his reins and took off in a southern direction.

"Kiliwhimin," he said to the air. "Are ye hiding in an abbey, my dear? I am going to find ye and then I will cut off the rest of yer hair." He chuckled to himself.

His mirth was dashed to pieces when they reached the abbey in Kiliwhimin days later and were told that there had been a lass here looking for a permanent place to live.

She had been there! He gritted his teeth thinking of the time he had wasted traveling toward Skye.

"We suggested she go on toward Aberchalder."

"How long ago?" Alistair demanded.

"Almost a fortnight now," the abbess answered.

Alistair did not care who this woman standing before him served. He cursed, spat, and stormed away.

He wanted to keep traveling without stopping to eat. He had already lost too much time. But the men murmured under their breath and rather than make enemies of them, he gave in and let them fill their bellies.

Soon though, soon he would catch up to her.

And then he would make certain she could never run from him again.

ISMAY CLOSED HER eyes and breathed. She had to tell herself to inhale-exhale-inhale. At first when Lochaber's Lochiel stepped behind her and fit her neatly against all his hard angles so he could show her how to hold a dirk, she thought about breaking free of him and running.

But, mayhap sensing her fears, he leaned his head in and spoke softly in her ear. "Dinna fear me, lass. Dinna fear any man. Stab. Jab. Duck." With each instruction he gave, he moved her hand gripping the dirk to show her how it was done and made her forget her fear. "Slice at the neck, the thigh. Here, and here."

His voice filled every nook and cranny within her where fear lurked, chasing it away and replacing it with belief in herself. He held her and had her mime him for the first hour and then he faced her as an enemy and taught her where to strike with a weapon or without one.

She would admit, watching him so close to her, so intent on his lesson, she was tempted to smile and sigh dreamily. She didn't.

"If I come at ye from this angle, 'tis best if ye use yer knee to kick me in the groin."

"Nae!" she exclaimed, horrified.

"Ye canna have mercy, lass. Yer life could depend on it. Now, here, dinna—

She jerked up her knee and smashed it into his groin. She threw her hands to her mouth as he went down.

After that, he avoided her kicks, knowing they would come.

Later, Ismay sat on the wide stump of a tree in the yard behind the castle. Before her, about ten feet away, the Lochiel lifted a heavy axe and brought it down on a piece of wood making it two in one clean strike. Several times she found her gaze settled comfortably on him while he worked.

Sleek muscles in his arms danced and glistened under the autumn sun while he brought the axe down. She blushed twice as many times when he caught her staring at him with dreams in her eyes. Dreams of things she had thought were impossible. Dreams she had never dared allow herself to dream before, like, kissing a man's lips and enjoying it. Was it possible? Dreams of laughing with him, lying in bed with him. And other things she didn't allow herself to ponder too long else she might burst into flames.

It had been a wee bit over a sennight since Constantine Cameron brought her here to Tor Castle. At first, she was convinced that she had to leave. Now, she was not sure she could go. Nothing but her own head and heart were holding her prisoner.

She had made friends, mainly with Joan and Hilary MacDonald—soon to marry a member of the enemy Chattan Confederation. Bethia was kind to her, but for some reason, Constantine kept her from tending to Ismay. Of course, Lachlan and Fionn were always friendly and pleasant. Geoffry kept to himself most of the time and when Lewis was not at the Doomsday Inn and Tavern, he was always somewhere nearby, seemingly ready to trounce anyone into the nearest wall for speaking ill of the Lochiel.

Ever since he'd been warned by Lewis, Hugh was cautious about what he said and whom he said it to.

But the one who made Ismay want to stay at Tor, despite her fear of someone from her past finding her, was the Lochiel. She was more surprised than anyone else would be if they knew her past and how she was beginning to feel about her protector.

The way his gaze grew warm on her when she laughed, and the way he gave in to her every whim—even those whims he did not agree with, drew her to sink deeper, find a closer place within him, and never let go.

Could she go to a convent and live a life trying to forget this virile man? Would God not reject her for her covetousness? Could she stay here and ever be happy with a clan chief?

"Lady," he called out, dark eyes on her free of his hair, neatly tied at his nape.

He called her "lady" as if he knew who her father was. She prayed he didn't know. Among the MacDonald clan, they knew it had been a MacPherson's bairn who had murdered their chief. Constantine could not find out. She had told him she was a murderer. She should have included being a fool to her confession. What if he had guessed the truth? He was clever.

He went to her, setting the axe against the tree stump. "What is it that darkens yer countenance?"

She smiled, trying to forget her worrisome thoughts. "I always knew what my future would look like. Me, unwed and happy living at home with my father, and then it became me, living hidden behind convent walls. Now…"

He knelt before her. "Now—?"

Should she confess even more? She felt as if she was a geyser ready to blow. She had not told anyone what she felt or what she thought in months. Now Constantine Cameron knew.

She gazed into the chief's eyes. She wanted to tell this man. "I dinna know what my future looks like anymore. I dinna know what is best fer me, or if I even care if 'tis good fer me or not."

She didn't realize she wanted him to say something reassuring like, stay here with me behind my castle walls. When he said nothing, it trumpeted much. He didn't want the same thing she wanted. He was not over his wife.

"Mayhap," she began, "I do know and that is what is darkening my face."

He stood up. "Ye are still considerin' leavin."

"Should I not?"

He looked down at her and then looked up and away at the castle turret looming overhead. "I'm goin' home soon. I have things to get in order."

She stared at him. …His home. He did not want her to tag along.

She swallowed back a rush of emotion and disappointment. She would not stand in his way then.

Nodding, she let him know she understood, then laughed softly. "My belly just cried out fer food. I told Hilary I would eat with her." She leaped off the stump and hurried away before she was tempted to beg him to stay by her side. She had no right to expect more from him than what he had already given her.

She would never forget him. No matter if she spent the rest of her life in a convent, or if she was killed on the road by some madman. She would carry her memories of the Cameron Lochiel, her protector, with her. He was the first man in her life she ever let her heart beat for.

She felt tears spill over the rims of her eyes and swiped them away. When she could see clearly, she saw Bethia in her path.

The older woman did not say anything but put her arm around Ismay when Ismay reached her. Bethia led her away and brought her to her chambers, patting her shoulder as if she understood all about it.

Such a man.

Once again, Ismay thought of asking the head chambermaid what she meant by such a comment spoken in a tone that would surely spark Lewis's ire.

"He canna give ye what ye need, gel."

Ismay stopped and stared at her. "What is it ye think I need?"

"The same thing we all need," Bethia answered and opened the door to her chambers. "A tender heart to treat us well."

"The Lochiel has a tender heart," Ismay insisted, letting Bethia lead her to her small sitting chamber.

Bethia did not agree or disagree. She sat Ismay down and then took a seat next to her. "If he is called to battle, he will go. He is a staunch supporter of the exiled king."

"What has that to do with me?" Ismay asked her. "It isna as if he is going to take me as his wife—"

"Och, goodness," the chambermaid threw her hand to her chest and laughed. "I know that!!" She gave another short laugh as if she had never heard of anything so preposterous.

Ismay bristled. This woman surely knew how to insult a soul. "What do ye find so humorous about that?"

Berthia's smile faded and she gave Ismay a pitying look. "Child, he was already a husband."

"Aye, I know."

"Then ye should also know that he still loves her. Can ye fight a beloved ghost?" She did not wait for Ismay to answer but shook her head and continued. "Ye willna secure his heart. He will never give it up again. Ye may have his favor but unfortunately, 'tis temporary."

Ismay held her breath hoping there was no more to hear. It was difficult, almost impossible to take in such hopeless words. But—she did not want a man in her life. Did she? "He is changing me."

She did not realize that she had spoken out loud until Bethia reached over and took her hand. "Do ye want to be changed, Miss Drummond?"

Ismay pondered the question for a moment and then shook her head. "'Tis safer to remain impervious to the Lochiel's wiles."

"His wiles?" Ismay heard the chambermaid ask under her breath.

"Aye, he is charming, all right," Ismay said more to herself than to the older woman, who was still casting her an incredulous look. "He is verra handsome when he smiles. He is handsome when he is scowling too. He is fair and slow to lose his temper."

"Slow to—"

"He cares fer his kin, and everyone at Tor. Aye, his affections run deep, but they are locked behind a wall of stone."

"Aye, and that wall was built fer his wife," Bethia interrupted before Ismay went any further.

"It may have been built fer her and fer the scars of battle. But that wall is doing him harm. He needs to heal."

Even before he knocked, Ismay felt the chief outside her door. An ache in the air, familiar and unspoken.

When the chambermaid pulled open the door, Ismay was not surprised to see Constantine.

Seeing Bethia first, he scowled, making Ismay wonder what happened between them.

"Chief," the older woman said in a low voice. "I was just leaving."

He did not turn to look after her, but kept his gaze on Ismay.

When they were alone, he took a step closer to her.

Ismay wondered if the sitting room was always this small, his shoulders this wide, his legs so long. His presence filled the entire space.

She felt her belly going warm and then remembered him waiting to go home. Away from her.

"Chief," she asked tersely, "what are ye doing here?"

"Come home with me," he said with authority, though his eyes betrayed his unsure heart.

She nodded without hesitation and let a small smile curl her lips. What would Bethia think of this? Ismay did not truly care. "I willna be a bother," she assured him, knowing he liked the silence.

"Who said ye were a bother?" He turned his scowl on the door from which Bethia had left.

"No one," she let him know, tugging his sleeve to regain his attention. "What changed yer mind?"

"What changed yers?" he countered. "Ye let me know on more than one occasion that ye wanted to leave Tor."

"Ye changed my mind, Lochiel. I will still leave if that is what ye want, but it isna what I want anymore."

He stood stock still, staring at her until she began to squirm.

"I told ye because I know ye are not the kind of man who is influenced by anything."

He nodded and looked away.

Ismay had the urge to pull her hair and let out a frustrated scream at his silence. But he had invited her to his home. That meant something, did it not? Did he have to actually say it? She definitely had his favor.

But was Bethia correct? Was his favor temporary?

What if she fell in love with him? The horror of it almost made her shiver. As it was, she liked being with him. She liked it very much. Was it more than that? How should she know? She'd never been in love before.

She let her gaze fasten to his when he looked at her again.

"I have meetin's with the elders fer the next couple of days. After that, I will be free."

She nodded happily. She would question if she were mad or not later. She still hated chiefs and men in power. But she liked Lochiel Constantine Cameron.

She was almost completely sure that he liked her too.

"About Bethia…"

"Hmm?" she urged when he paused.

"She loved Alison very much."

"I am not concerned about that, Chief."

"Yet ye revert to callin' me chief."

She smiled. "'Tis a habit."

Another knock came to the door. The chief went to it and opened it to Geoffry. "A missive has arrived from Chief John MacKintosh." He handed the parchment to Constantine.

The chief read this missive and Ismay felt a surge of pride that he could read. After a moment he crumpled the missive in his fist. "Prepare the men. If he wants to fight, let us go show him how 'tis done."

Geoffry's face lit up with a wide smile. He nodded and then hurried off to alert the others.

"What does the letter say?" she asked Constantine when they were alone.

"The clan chief threatens to attack if I dinna return his cattle along with two of my fingers fer killin' his son."

Horrified, Ismay threw her hands to her mouth. "Ye are not going to—"

"Nae," he assured. "But he is more merciful than I. if 'twere my son, I would settle fer nothin' less than his life."

Ismay paled. Would the MacKintosh chief want Constantine's life?

"Dinna go," she said, doing her best to conceal her fear, but she failed.

"Lass," he said huskily, taking a step toward her. "Are ye worried over me?"

She nodded.

"I should be insulted that ye think the MacKintosh worm can harm me."

She returned his warm smile and let her gaze welcome him closer. "No man is unbeatable, Chief."

"I am," he boasted.

"Do ye promise?" she asked with a thread of demand tainting her voice. "Do ye promise to come back to me?"

She knew it was an unreasonable request, but his smile widened and he nodded. "I promise I will come back."

His neglect of the last two words did not go unnoticed by her. He would come back…but not necessarily to her. Still, at least he promised. After all, she wanted him to live and not only for her selfish desires.

With a smile she suspected affected him more than he would admit, she gave his forearm a pat. "I shall see ye again when ye return."

He suddenly clasped his hands behind his back, gave her half a smile that nearly buckled her kneecaps, then turned to leave.

"Constantine," she called out, stopping him. He turned.

"Will ye be verra long?"

He shook his head, his gaze going soft. "Nae. No' long."

And then he left her chambers. She stared at the door for a few moments, without him for the first time in days.

She realized with a sinking heart that she relied too heavily on him. Were her emotions deepening because her time with him reminded her of the last sixteen years of her life, when she had felt safe and cared for? Did the Lochiel represent a time when she was happy? Was she confusing her feelings of familiarity and happiness with something else?

She thought of his jaw, chiseled with determination to remain loyal to a ghost. His chin, slightly dimpled beneath the shadow of gruff, his nose, mayhap the first perfect thing she noticed about his face. Straight but not sharp, a bit flatter at the soft contoured tip, his lips—oh, even now, the memory of them made her heart flutter. They were decadently full, scandalously plump—almost always set in somber disregard.

Almost always.

When his eyes, her favorite thing about him, settled on her, his mouth softened and went from somber to curious and amused. She liked having the power to bring warmth to his soul. She liked him. She liked a man. A chief. Impossible, she told herself, shaking her head and leaving her chambers. Impossible. But true.

———— ✳ ————

CHAPTER TWELVE

CONSTANTINE SAT ATOP his warhorse with thirty-seven of his men around him, excluding Lachlan, mounted and ready for a fight. Facing them were MacKintoshes, sixty strong, swords polished and ready to stain Glen Loy with blood.

To Constantine's left, Lewis laughed, eager to fight. Constantine also was eager to fight and get back to the castle.

"Lochiel," one from the MacKintosh clan called out. "Where are my cattle? Where is my son?"

This was John MacKintosh, the chief coming forward. Constantine watched him with contempt in his eyes. "Yer son took a woman from my care and meant to rape her. He is with the devil where he belongs. As fer yer cattle, ye were warned no' to bring them through my land. Yet ye sent one of yer sons to the task. What? Did ye no' care if I killed that son?"

"Who is this woman ye claim is in yer care?" MacKintosh shouted, ignoring his question.

Constantine was not about to tell him. There was only reason the MacKintosh chief wanted to know who she was. Constantine frowned at him from across the unseen barrier. Alas, here was the threat he had hoped his enemy would refrain from making.

"Allow yer other sons free rein to go anywhere near her and ye will find oot before ye put them in the ground."

"Ye're a bastard, Cameron!" the chief bellowed and pointed

his sword at him.

Constantine drew his claymore. All around him his kin readied for battle. It was what MacKintosh wanted all along. He knew Constantine well enough to know he would not get the apology he desired. The Lochiel always kept his word. If he said he would take their cattle for herding them through Lochaber, then he would.

Everyone knew the Cameron chief would not hesitate to kill a man if the man was fool enough to try to take what belonged to him.

But Miss Ismay Drummond did not belong to him. The thought of it somehow angered him enough to flick his reins and send his horse into a full gallop.

Though his eyes were fixed on the MacKintosh chief, thanks to years of riding in the middle of stampeding cattle, he was acutely aware of everything going on around him. Lewis and Fionn reached the first of the MacKintoshes and brought down their swords while blocking with their shields.

Blood and splinters flew everywhere from the melee. Constantine took down six opponents, careful not to kill them. He liked fighting. He did not always like killing. Sending men back to the homes wounded and broken was sometimes much more satisfying.

He broke through the small group of men protecting the MacKintosh chief and finally reached him. He brought the flat of his sword down hard across his enemy's belly and almost knocked him out of his saddle. But the MacKintosh held on to his reins and remained seated.

Affording him no time to catch his breath, Constantine flipped his blade in his hand then caught it by the hilt and smashed it into MacKintosh's head.

Finally, the enemy chief fell from his saddle. Constantine leaped the ground beside him, and before any other man could reach them, he pummeled his fist into the MacKintosh's face until blood spewed out.

One of the MacKintosh's sons jumped on Constantine's back, another reached them and swung his sword close to the Lochiel's belly. Constantine whacked his heavy claymore at Will MacKintosh, the chief's third son, then cracked his elbow into the nose of Will's brother Kenneth.

Reaching them, Geoffry sprang from his saddle and sliced the air—and Kenneth's forearm with his already-bloody sword.

Four more men arrived on the MacKintosh side, cutting the air with axe and dirk. Constantine and Geoffrey held them off. He managed to knock two of the chief's sons out cold with fists to their jaws.

He spotted Lewis fighting off his horse, hurling men left and right with his sheathed claymore.

But when Lewis's gaze found him, his eyes went dark, and he ripped his sword free.

Constantine noted the terror in his cousin's expression an instant before he felt the stinging sensation in his belly. He looked down and saw the hilt of a dirk sticking out of his middle.

Damnation, he thought. Miss Drummond may never forgive him for this.

It was his only thought as he sank to his knees.

His eyes took in the vision before him of the MacKintosh chief's youngest son, Hamish's head flying from his shoulders and rolling on the ground.

CONSTANTINE WOKE SEVERAL hours later, but only for a few moments, and only long enough to feel a cool cloth on his head and gentle fingers curled around his much larger hand. He did not know where he was, nor did he care overmuch. At first, he thought he had died and this was his Alison tending to him. but her image did not even form in his mind before Ismay Drummond appeared before him, real or imagined, he was not sure.

She was engulfed in flames around her head, but they didn't harm her. He thought he reached out to touch them, but she still held his hand.

"Ye have finally come back to me."

Leave it to her to remind him of his promise. He was glad he kept it. He smiled—almost chuckled. And then she was gone again. She did not leave him alone though. She visited his dreams, returning over and over into various scenarios. Contrary to him, stubbornly pulling smiles from him, chipping away at the memories that darkened his soul. He started out protecting her, feeling pity for her, then slowly feeling his heart giving over to more.

If any lass had the mettle to keep him alive, 'twas Miss Drummond.

She even infiltrated his guarded thoughts, the ones where he secretly dreamed of kissing…of kissing her.

He saw her so clearly, her eyes so vividly fastened on him. He mustered all his strength to lift his arms and take her by the shoulders. He summoned his strongest resolve to pull her down and press his mouth to her delectable lips.

She pulled away, using hardly any strength and touched her fingers to her lips.

He tasted her, breathed in her slightly lavender scent, and felt her heart beating against him. Had he dreamed of their kiss?

He did not dream again for the next twelve hours.

The first thing he became aware of was the faint aroma of lavender. The second thing was the guilt and shame overwhelming him at the memory of where he had smelled the lavender before.

What kind of husband and father was he that he did not even mourn his family for a full five years before he let another—

"Constantine?" Her lyrical voice played across his ears, shattering his shame and guilt. "Chief? Are ye awake, this time?"

As opposed to another time? he reasoned.

He opened his eyes. Ah, like a kick in the guts, her bonnie

face knocked the breath out of him. "I believe so."

"Do ye remember what happened?" she asked as innocently as a lamb.

"Aye," he lowered his gaze. "I dinna usually behave so—"

"Ye were stabbed," she clarified. Was that a crimson streak shooting across her face? "The wound was deep. Yer castle physician didna know if ye would recover."

"But ye decided I would."

Like the radiance of a summer sunrise, her smile washed him in warmth. "Nae, Lochiel. I never doubted that ye would do what ye said."

He was so relieved that she did not bring up them kissing. It meant it did not happen. Strangely, he was not sure how he felt about it. Had his body betrayed him? Or was it his heart?

He wouldn't bring it up if she didn't.

"Wait," he said and clasped his fingers around her wrist when she moved away from—his bed. In his room. The room no other woman save Alison had even been. "Where are ye goin' already?"

"Hugh wants me to keep him informed when ye awaken."

"Inform him later." He pulled her back while memories of pulling her over him to kiss flooded his thoughts.

He released her. "Fergive me, Miss Drummond, I didna mean to manhandle ye."

Her gleaming eyes widened. "When did ye manhandle me?"

He closed his eyes, grateful to be so forgiven so easily.

When he felt her tug on the sleeve of his tunic, he opened his eyes.

"Were ye falling to sleep again?"

He shook his head gently, careful not to fall into unconsciousness again. "I was feelin' grateful fer bein' fergiven."

"Chief," she began, covering his hand with both of hers. "There is something—"

The door to his bedroom swung open and Geoffry and Fionn came barreling in. When they saw him with his eyes open, looking at them as if they had just interrupted something potentially life threatening, they hurried to the bed.

"The Confederation has declared…" Fionn began and then stopped again when Constantine turned to him. "…they have declared war against the Camerons and the MacDonalds."

Constantine took in the news without changing his expression. Even when Miss Drummond scolded them for barging into his room with such fretful news, he kept his expression stoic, though he wanted to smile at her. Again. God help him.

"Some of the men are concerned that ye willna be able to fight with us," Geoffry let him know.

Now, Constantine turned to them with a dark scowl. "Why are they afraid of such a preposterous thing? Of course, I will fight."

A little sound ripped out of Miss Drummond. "What? Dinna be a fool, Chief! Ye were stabbed. Will ye only cease when ye're dead?"

Fionn and Geoffry cast her angry looks. "Why would ye speak of the Lochiel being dead when he has just recovered?"

Constantine was not surprised when she did not back down. She rested her fist on her hip and glared right back at them. "I want him to stay recovered. I thought ye did as well."

"We do!" Fionn defended.

"Then how could ye tell him this news knowing full well that he would want to fight! Especially when *some of the men are concerned that he will not be able to fight with them?!*"

Constantine wondered how long this slight wisp of a lass had been holding back such a temper? Likely, her whole life. Of all the things he was so ridiculously happy about lately, her confidence in her safety here—enough to argue with his men without fear of consequences, made him happiest.

Fionn, and especially his brother were going from repentant to insulted as she went on. "Are ye the ones so concerned that ye will lose without him? What if he isna ready to fight—and he is not! And he gets killed? Will ye take responsibility fer that?"

Geoffry opened his mouth to speak but shut it again when

Constantine sat up on his elbows and veered him off his angry path.

"Miss Drummond, thank ye fer havin' my well-bein' at heart. I will admit that I am no' against it." He ignored Geoffry and Fionn's quick, startled breaths and stunned expressions at his words and continued. "But bein' the leader here, I dinna have the luxury of remainin' in my sickbed—even if ye are sittin' beside it." He almost smiled when he caught the brothers out of the corner of his eye, turning to stare at each other. If they believed he cared for her, they would be doubly cautious about how they treated her.

At first, he thought her scalding cheeks were enough to keep her from arguing with him in front of his men, but they soon cooled. "I dinna care if ye are the leader. I willna let ye out of this bed."

He felt his gaze go warm, almost as hot as her cheeks had been. "How will ye keep me here?"

With a mumble oath, Geoffry spun around to leave and pulled his brother with him.

The door slamming shut snapped Constantine and Miss Drummond out of their reverie, and they looked away from each other.

"Lass." He returned his attention to her first. He realized while his belly sank and flipped on the way down that he liked looking at her. "I spoke true when I said thank ye fer havin' my well-bein' at heart. But when my kin leave to fight, I will be with them."

"Nae, ye will no'."

His dark gaze hardened. "Ye insult me."

"I dinna care," she let him know, folding her arms across her chest.

He scoffed. "I dinna take orders from ye."

"Should I beg?"

Was she being serious? Did he see a flash of fear in her eyes? Not fear *of* him, but *for* his being.

"Nae!" he rushed to tell her. He could not take it if she—

"Please, dinna go, Constantine."

—begged him. He swallowed and looked into her eyes. "Clever lass."

She did not respond but let him keep looking.

"I shouldna let ye have such dominion over me."

"Why no'?" she asked softly, her voice skipping over his ears like a faerie's laughter.

But he was the one who laughed. "Why not? Because…" He paused, trying to think of a reason to give her. Finally, he came up with one. "Because, if I let ye have me, and I lost ye, it would destroy me. My clan needs me. I canna let myself be destroyed."

Whatever dreamy thoughts she looked like she was having a moment ago, faded into stunned disbelief. "What?"

He offended her. Damn him. "I didna mean it the—"

"Ye didna mean it?" she repeated coolly.

"I refuse to love again."

She clenched her jaw.

Why could he not find the right words to tell her? "I'm no' the hero ye think I am because I protected ye. 'Twouldna be right to let ye lay claim to a heart that barely beats."

"It beats, Chief," she corrected him. "I felt it in yer pulse and felt it pressed against me."

"Hmm?" he asked, his anxious gaze fastened on her. Did she just say…? "Pressed against ye? When was my heart pressed to ye?"

She still appeared serious, but he was sure he saw a spark of fight still left in her.

"When ye kissed me last night, Constantine. I think since ye took yer pleasure in my mouth, ye should at least obey me."

He felt like he could fall through the floor and then continue to burn his way to the earth's core. He had kissed her. It was not a dream. It flooded images through him. Her eyes, closing to receive him, her sweet breath mingling with his. And aye, he had taken his pleasure in her and then doubted it was real.

"Fergive me," he said, fully repentant.

"Do ye mean that?" she asked him, narrowing her eyes. "Truly?"

Constantine somehow sensed that his answer was more important than he realized. "Aye, I took advantage of ye."

She laughed quietly behind her hand. "Ye were the one who was weakened, not I. How could ye take advantage of me? If anyone is guilty, 'tis me. And I am no' sorry."

Constantine did not know if he should laugh or swear allegiance to her. "Then ye are no' angry?"

She shook her head. An auburn curl tumbled down her cheek. He lifted his fingers to it, but she pulled away from his touch. Almost, it seemed, on instinct. He lowered his hand, but he was not offended or hurt by her rejection. Aye, he was sorry he had kissed her when he should understand that she had been hurt and left skittish and untrusting of men. He was not like other men. He did not know why it was so important to him that she knew it.

Of course, he was letting his wounded body fantasize about her, she was not his woman. She was not staying at Tor. If his heart and head were in a better place, he might consider a longer future with her. But, a part of him was angry at himself for letting her into a place where only Alison was allowed.

"I will think aboot yer *request* that I no' fight while I recover."

Her face lit up with joy. "Thank ye, Chief!"

He knew he was in danger of falling hard, but what could he do? What defense did he have against her clever wiles? He would not fight while he recovered. He just had to make certain he recovered quickly.

They ate together in his chambers, after she helped him sit in a chair. His cousins visited him and carefully watched his interactions with his female guest, muttering amongst themselves. Only Lachlan grinned like a fool while they shared ale around Constantine.

Hugh even came to sit among them in the chambers without

any other purpose than to check on the Lochiel's well-being and the well-being of Miss Drummond.

Constantine was glad others felt protective of her. After this afternoon's incident, Geoffry and Fionn seemed to have forgotten her insult. The drunker Fionn became, the more lovingly he stared at Miss Drummond.

Constantine liked having them all around, but he was tired and wanted a few last moments with Miss Drummond before he fell asleep.

None of the men complained or teased him about throwing them out before the darkness of night settled on Tor. Lachlan, the perpetual rogue, winked at him on his way out.

Constantine considered making the lad train more. Since he had time for so many lasses, he could use that time to practice fighting.

"Why are ye scowling?" Miss Drummond asked while she began to clean up the cups and jugs the men had left.

"Because ye are cleanin' instead of sittin' near me."

She stopped and looked at him, then smiled. She put down what was in her hands and came to sit on the chair closest to the bed.

"Miss Drummond—"

"When are ye going to call me Ismay?"

He felt the need to gasp for air looking at her pouting lips. "I…" He swallowed another breath and then took hold of himself. "Ismay is a verra bonnie name."

"My father gave me the name when he took me in," she told him proudly.

"When ye were born—"

"I didna have a name. I was called many things—but none of them are proper."

She spoke as if he'd likely heard the same story from twenty other people. He had never heard such a tale in his life. A child without a name for the first eight years of her life. Who murdered the chief with whom she lived and became a child murderer and a hater of clan chiefs.

"Yer father chose wisely," he said on half a breath. It was not that he pitied her anymore. Now, he could only stare in admiration that she had withstood the most tender ages under torment and survived, and then when her new, better life ended, she still did not give up.

What if he asked her to stay and then he died in battle?

"Ismay, I—" What? What did he want to say to her? "I want ye to sleep in yer bed tonight. Dinna tend to me. Bethia will do so. Ye need rest." No. That was not it. He wanted her to rest, but not yet. He couldn't tell her that now without sounding like an indecisive fool.

She waited a moment, as if she knew there was more he wanted to say and was waiting for it.

When nothing more came, she nodded and left her seat. "Goodnight then, my lord, chief." She smiled and Constantine thought she moved a hair's breath closer to him. Did she want him to pull her down for another kiss? Was he trying to convince himself that she wanted the same as he?

She left without kissing him, and he decided that if he were not so sleepy and his heart were his to do and feel as he chose, he might have gotten up out of bed and gone after her.

In fact, when he fell asleep a moment or two later, he dreamed he did just that.

---❖---

CHAPTER THIRTEEN

"WHATEVER THE REASON, 'tis nice to finally have ye here with us."

Ismay looked up briefly to smile at Hilary while she pulled her needle with dyed saffron thread through a linen kerchief. She was not sure what Hilary meant, as Ismay had been there twice already. She could not help it if she enjoyed being with the Lochiel more than sewing, or anyone else's company. Even Hilary's—and Ismay was quite fond of Geoffry and Fionn's sister.

Hilary's disputable wedding was fast approaching and she was full of excitement about the event. She was also worried about what was to come after the celebration and filled with doubt that she was being selfish and may be the cause of another feud. She was happy one moment and a ball of sobbing tears the next.

Ismay helped her as much as she could, which was not much since she had never been in love. She tried to at least be there with Hilary and listen, but she often felt her thoughts drifting to the Cameron chief.

When she left him in the Great Hall this morning, just a sennight after he was stabbed, he seemed stronger and all his color had returned. But she could not forget the blade the castle physician had to pull from his guts. His body was still a wee bit weak.

Did he need her right now and she was off embroidering

some useless thing? Should she excuse herself from her friend and hurry off to find him?

She scoffed out loud, unknowingly drawing Hilary's attention. She had never chased a man in her life, and she would not begin now.

"What troubles ye, Ismay?" Hilary asked, as Joan stepped into the sewing chamber with refreshments.

"Och, Joan," Ismay dropped her work in her lap. "Did ye happen to see the Lochiel?"

Joan threw a conspiratory glance to Hilary. "Nae, I didna see him, lady."

Ismay smiled and shrugged as if it did not matter to her. No one believed it.

"Anyway," she said pleasantly and picked up her needle and kerchief to continue working, "Hilary, ye know ye are no' to see yer betrothed the day before the wedding."

"The whole day is too long!" Hilary lamented, forgetting Ismay's obvious preoccupation with the chief quickly enough.

Fionn and Geoffry's sister went on for most of the afternoon, drawing Joan into their mostly one-sided conversation.

Ismay liked Joan. The gel's fascination with Lachlan was understandable, for the young Cameron, with his golden halo of curls and pleasant, laid-back nature enchanted many. Joan was not oblivious to his roguish ways. She did not care who he spent time with, if he made time for her. It was an arrangement Ismay could never ascribe to. If she were in love with Constantine—She stuck the needle into her index finger and drew back with a cry.

"Ismay, what did ye do?" Hilary went to her and pulled Ismay's finger out of her mouth.

Joan hurried to get a wet rag.

What had she done? She had been embroidering long enough not to prick her finger.

"This is why ye should come every day to practice," Hilary lamented.

"I will live through it," Ismay assured her.

"Aye, ye will," Hilary agreed. "'Tis the Lochiel I fear ye willna live through."

Ismay pulled her hand from Hilary's grasp. "What are ye saying?"

"I know ye care fer him," her friend clarified. "Ye spend all yer days and many nights at his bedside, nursing him. 'Tis clear yer heart is lost to him." At her side, Joan nodded in agreement.

"I dinna know what ye are talking about," Ismay defended. "And if I did, why would ye say that I will not live through it? What do ye all think is so terrible about him?"

Hilary looked at her as if she had never seen Ismay before. "He is like a dead man. 'Tis frightful. Ye do know that he is a thief, aye? And a cattle raider? He has killed hundreds both in battle and oot of it."

Aye. Ismay was reminded of him kicking in the door of where the MacKintosh's son had taken her. She saw Constantine run him through in one fell strike. She knew he was no hero. He was her guardian angel, always keeping her safe. That's what she knew. And it was enough.

"Aye, his expressions can be subtle," Ismay told them in a quiet, calm tone. "But I think he is letting himself feel more lately."

Her two friends blinked at her.

Joan looked to be thinking about it and then nodded. "I have seen him smiling."

Hilary's wide blue eyes settled on Ismay. "Is it because of ye?"

Ismay shook her head. "I dinna know. But he is the least frightful man I have ever met."

Her friends stared at her for a moment and then both of them burst into laughter. Ismay laughed with them since it felt so good.

"Och, tell us everything, Ismay!" Hilary threw down her embroidery and clamped Ismay's hand.

"Aye, everything!" Joan joined in.

Ismay was not going to at first, but she felt as if she would burst with emotions she had never felt before. She had to tell someone. "Well," she began, "he slept by my door at the Doomsday Inn and Tavern two nights in a row to keep me safe."

She enjoyed their breathless sighs at all she told them about the Lochiel saving her from her kidnapper—and a coyote—and mostly, her fears.

"Lachlan didna mention the Lochiel bein' in love—" Joan told them.

"He is not in love," Ismay quickly corrected.

"Not yet," Hilary said excitedly.

"Now, stop it both of ye," Ismay tried then laughed again with them.

Someone knocked at the door.

Joan leaped up to open it.

When they saw the Lochiel on the other side, they broke into hysterical giggles that held him at the door.

Ismay bounced up from her chair and offered him her most thankful smile. He'd come to her, saving her the mortification of chasing after him.

"What is so amusing about my arrival?" he demanded without any authority.

"Nothing at all," Ismay assured him and led him back out of the embroidery room and into the hall.

"How are ye feeling? Are ye in pain anywhere? Let me have a look at ye."

She grabbed hold of him and started feeling his arms first. She quickly realized what she was doing, and how irresistibly hard his arms were, coiled with muscle and sinew. She lifted herself a bit and pressed her cheek to his chest. His heart sounded strong, beating a rapid litany in her ear. She pushed away, staring up at him with repentance in the curve of her lips.

How had this man managed to pull such unabashed, shameless behavior from her? For twenty-four years she had been content without a man in her life. She had firmly believed it would always be so.

"Do ye need me?" she asked like some kind of blithering fool.

Of course he didn't need her. He appeared absolutely, perfectly fine. Perfectly.

He looked as if he wanted to say something other than what came out of his mouth. "Nae. I thought ye might be needin' me."

She shook her head, mayhap a bit too vehemently. "Nae, I was embroidering." She really wanted to tell him that she might need him more than she would admit. Even here, where she was safe sewing flowers in a kerchief.

"Then, I will leave ye to finish," he said politely and turned to go.

"Chief," she called out, stopping him. "Now that ye are here with me, why dinna we take a walk? Are ye up fer it?"

Thankfully, he nodded, seemingly pleased with the idea, though he did not smile. Since she had known him, he was not the kind of man who bared his emotions for all to see. Like her, he was a master at hiding. Mayhap that was why she noticed the smallest nuances of change in his expressions more often than not lately. She pleased him, and despite once being repulsed by the idea of belonging to a man, she thought it would not be so terrible to belong to Constantine Cameron.

"Let us go to the loch's edge!" she said with an enthusiastic bounce in her step, close beside him. "Show me where ye bathe so I can join ye next time. Och! I mean," she paused and felt her face go up in flames. "Not together! Goodness, what I meant was…"

"Verra well, I'll take ye there now, and then in the mornin', I'll bring ye with Bethia and Joan so ye can bathe. I willna remain while ye bathe but I'll stay close by in case there are any men in the area."

Her cheeks cooled but her heart remained warm. "Do ye mean it?"

He looked a little insulted, even pouting his lips. "I wouldna have said it if I didna mean it."

She ignored his insult and gave him her best, most happy smile. "Thank ye, Chief."

"Constantine," he mumbled and turned to look away. "Ye thank me fer nothin', lass. Why would it be so difficult to please one who makes nae demands?"

"Me?" she asked, a bit surprised. "I make nae demands?"

"Nae." He continued on his way down the stairs.

She followed, then caught up. "What about when I wanted to walk with ye in the mornings?"

"That was no' a demand," he pointed out in a gentle voice.

"When ye refused I followed ye anyway."

He shrugged. "Nae harm came from it."

Was this the Lochiel she was speaking with? What about obedience?

"And did I no' demand that ye no' return to battle while convalescing?"

"'Twas fer my benefit," he defended her.

Well, he was certainly singing a different tune. But she was not complaining. If he wanted to absolve her of her demanding ways, she was grateful. In fact, she was so grateful she considered looping her hand through the crook of his elbow. Not too long ago, she would never have done such a thing. But now…she trusted this man. Like Fraya, his bonnie coo, he was winning her trust more every day.

With a sigh of resolution, she closed her eyes and took his arm, keeping pace with his steps.

He didn't flinch. He didn't seem to mind in the least.

Finally, she stopped clenching her jaw and smiled. He didn't mind her touching him. She felt her face go hot and then remembered to breathe when they ran into Lewis and Geoffry. The Lochiel exchanged words with them and then led her away.

Hugh stopped him to read a missive that had arrived. It was written by Angus MacKintosh, Clan Chief of the Chattan. He was writing in response to his cousin—the troublesome chief John MacKintosh's last correspondence and list of grievances against the Cameron chief. John MacKintosh wanted his cattle, twenty Cameron women, to pay for the death of John's sons, and finally, the return of their land, mainly near Loch Akraig and Glen Lui. The Confederation ordered a battle to end the 360-year feud. No other clans from the Confederation would fight, but they wanted the feud over one way or the other.

"One way or the other?" Ismay asked, drawing his and Hugh's attention. "Does that mean one chief or the other?"

"I willna lose to him," Constantine assured her in a low voice—like a growl.

"The Chattan chief will help him. They are cousins," she argued. "Do ye believe they will stand by while ye beat him?"

Hugh stared agape at her. "Miss Drummond, who taught ye such disrespect?"

"Ye are correct," Constantine said to her as if Hugh had not spoken a word. "It gains them nothin' if I win. They know I will beat him, and if I do, I will be bigger than the Confederation. They willna leave it to chance."

Ismay agreed, relieved that he was strategic and not a prideful oaf that ignored sound advice because it came from a woman.

"Hugh, advise the men to meet me in the Great Hall after supper. There is much to be discussed."

"Where should I tell them if they ask where ye are right now, Lochiel?"

"Tell them I want them all here after supper."

That was all Hugh was getting, and knowing it, he backed up and then turned to do the Lochiel's bidding.

"I dinna want to keep ye from yer duty, Chief…Constantine," Ismay corrected herself with a shy smile.

"What duty? Och!" he exclaimed and pointed in the direction Hugh had taken. "Ye mean that."

Ismay nodded and gave a poor effort to hide her smile. Had he forgotten the Confederation's threat already? Did his absent-mindedness have to do with her?

He waved her concern away. "The Confederation willna dissolve if they dinna hear from me immediately. Unfortunately, they will still exist tomorrow."

Ismay knew enough about them from her father's involvement with them. Her father, being a MacPherson baron, had defended them on a few occasions when penning missives to Oliver Cromwell, commander of the New Model Army of the English Commonwealth. She knew enough about the Chattan Confederation to know MacPhersons stood on their side.

Well, not this MacPherson.

"Shall we go?" she asked, tightening her arm around his elbow.

He led her out without a look back.

"Does this mean ye will postpone yer visit to yer home?"

"Aye. Fer a wee bit."

"Do ye plan on finishing the chief in a quick strike then?"

"The quicker, the better."

He was utterly serious. He had no doubts in his ability to win. She found such confidence attractive and comforting.

"Tell me about yer home," she said, wanting to end the topic of battle.

"It sits at the foot of Ben Nevis. I didna live there long. I was away fightin' more than I was home."

"Still, it holds a deep place in yer heart."

He stared at her while they walked out of the courtyard. "I built it fer my wife and daughter. But they didna get to live in it either. So that she wouldna be alone, Alison remained at Tor with her parents while she carried Katie."

Ismay remained silent while he seemed to relive something that brought shadows to his eyes. Ismay already knew his wife and child had died. But when he spoke again she was stunned by what he told her.

"I didna make it home to see Alison before she left the earth. I also missed welcomin' my daughter into the world despite losing her mother. By the time I arrived, four days after wee Katie died, Alison's kin had her and our babe buried."

Ismay felt as if an arrow just pierced her heart. "I'm grieved that ye didna return to them in time, Constantine."

His dark eyes gleamed with unshed tears. He offered her a smile filled with meaning despite its slight visual appearance. Then he turned away and continued walking.

Keeping pace with him, Ismay understood what had snatched away his happiness. All the amusement she brought him, all the humor in his eyes, and the warmth in his smiles, no matter how scarce, suddenly meant so much more. She wanted to bring more days of happiness to him.

Did she truly intend to remain here with him then? Would he ever want something more permanent with her?

"The loch is just aroond that bend," he told her, pointing straight ahead.

They walked to it together, keeping their conversation lighter, with the somber Lochiel giving up smiles and even a low, almost horrified chuckle when she admitted to things she, Hilary, and Joan talked about in the embroidery room.

"So, ye are all convinced that I favor ye." It was not a question.

She slanted her smoky gaze to him. "Is it so impossible?"

"Aye," he answered in a deep, meaningful tone. "'Twas once, no' too long ago."

She held her breath. Was it possible that a man like him would favor her of all people?

"But…"

"Aye?" she pressed when he remained quiet. "But what?"

"Are ye always so bold, lass?" he said, not bothering to cover up his pleasure in her.

"Aye, my lord," she countered with satisfaction glinting her eyes. "Nothing is gained by being a delicate flower."

"That is true," he agreed, stepping in front of her and walking backward around the bend. "But in the right hands, a delicate flower will thrive and bloom."

That was the instant Ismay knew she could love Constantine Cameron, one of the most powerful clan chiefs in the Highlands. To prove his declaration true, he stepped out of her way and revealed an inlet arrayed in the colors of autumn, with a cascading waterfall, larger than the one at home that flowed into the clear loch.

Her eyes widened on the paradise as she stepped forward. She wanted to go to it and feel the cold water on her toes. "Is it deeper near the waterfall?"

"Aye," she heard him tell her.

Perfect, she thought, moving closer to the edge.

"Miss Drummond…?"

She turned to cast him an anxious glance.

"If ye want to go in now, I willna look until the water covers ye."

When she paused, he continued, "Trust me."

Aye, she wanted to go in now. In a few more days, it would be colder.

She watched him turn away, and then she began to undress. She did not look his way again. He had asked her to trust him. She did.

She gasped and sucked in her breath as she stepped into the water. Exhilaration filled her as she waded deeper, closer to the waterfall. The sound of the water moving all about her was deafening. She dipped beneath the surface then came up to her shoulders and let her eyes search for him.

She found him watching her swim. From where he sat on the stump of a tree, she could see him smiling at her.

Her belly flipped, and her body followed, dipping under, then bobbing back up, soaking her hair and washing away a month of grime, grief, and fear.

When she was done, she motioned to him to turn away while she left the water. He obeyed and her heart swelled when he gave her all the time she needed to dress without turning back to face her—even for a moment. She knew, for she watched him the entire time. Not to test him but because it was difficult to look away from him once her gaze had settled. The back of him was no less virile and appealing than the front. His long legs encased in woolen hose, his slender hips and flare of his shoulders all captivated her. None of the suitors who had tried to win her favor were fashioned like the Cameron Lochiel. Even if they had been, it would not have mattered to her if his heart were rotten or vile.

No one would ever convince her that he was either of those things.

She finished dressing and went to him. When he moved to face her, she turned her back on him and presented him the untied laces of her bodice.

"Tie them please," she said. "I canna reach."

She squeezed her eyes shut when his finger brushed her the nape of her neck. She trembled. Did he feel it? She felt as if her feet might leave the ground. He used gentle pressure to pull the laces tighter. She held her breath as more of his fingers fell against her ribs. She lifted her hand to her brow and wiped the bead of sweat that had gathered there at his touch.

If she were truly bold as he claimed, she would turn around and press her body to his and hope he would respond by taking her into his tender embrace.

But she was not sexually bold—the thought alone made her heart pound.

She stepped away when he finished tying.

"How was it?" he asked about the stream.

"Exhilarating," she replied about his touch. "Thank ye fer keeping yer word."

He nodded, slipping his hands behind his back. "Should we head back?"

"Nae," she said without hesitation. "Let us sit here fer a bit."

He bent his knees and sat back down on the tree stump. Ismay thought he looked like some fabled king on his throne.

She joined him on a nearby rock and ran her fingers through her wet hair. She felt his eyes on her but when she looked, he quickly averted his gaze.

"Ye are the color of autumn," he said, finally giving away his fascination with her.

"And ye are like the winter, thawing in spring."

He grinned from beneath his brows and Ismay was thankful he did not do it often. If the simmering seduction that shaped his lips and sparked his eyes were not enough, he rose from the tree stump and went to her. Without saying a word, he bent again, this time before her and leaned in close enough to kiss her.

He did not kiss her but reached up to touch her hair. "We should return to the castle and let Joan dry yer tresses."

She shook her head. "I want to stay here for a wee bit longer."

"Verra well," he said with tenderness.

"Ismay," he breathed her name. She responded as if he touched her. "May I—"

"There ye are!" Lewis called out with a smile. "I have been looking fer ye since we met in the Great Hall."

Constantine clenched his jaw but said nothing in anger to his cousin.

"Is it true? Are we going to fight the Confederation?"

"'Tis possible if they side with John MacKintosh," the chief told him, to which Lewis let out a boisterous shout of glee.

Constantine didn't say what he had meant to tell her before their interruption. May he what?

They returned to the castle and Constantine left her to meet up with his kin in the Great Hall.

Ismay spent the rest of the afternoon with Hilary and Joan, the former lamenting that her kin were going to battle against the kin of her betrothed. Ismay refused to think about Highlanders coming at Constantine with swords and axes. He had been stabbed once already since she had known him. She prayed he didn't get stabbed again.

Later, when word came the meeting was over, Constantine did not return to her, but Lachlan found her and let her know that the Lochiel waited for the elders to let them know his decision. He would fight.

CHAPTER FOURTEEN

FOR THE FIRST time in years Constantine didn't want to leave for battle.

He sat alone in the Great Hall after his kins' meeting took place. His men had all left and now he waited for the elder council.

In the silence, his thoughts drifted toward things of war. He had been a soldier since he was a boy, though it was not until he was five and ten that his fame began.

Dispatched to Inverlochy by his older brother, Gilbert, Constantine had fought under the Marquis of Montrose against the Campbells. They won a decisive victory and every battle after that. When it became evident that the victories were all due to him. He was promoted to captain and gained several other titles. But the cost had been too high. So high.

It didn't escape Constantine's notice that he had been apart from Ismay Drummond for several hours and thoughts of Alison had returned to haunt him.

He had been called to duty while building their home at the foot of Ben Nevis. He had not wanted to leave her. She was carrying their babe and the thought of her alone had vexed him deeply, so he moved her parents to Tor Castle to be with her. He had left to fight the Battle of the Pass Near Tullich, but after that victory his name became something to be feared and admired for his great strategic mind. He fought, loving making the enemy suffer for supporting Cromwell and killing his kin. He feared no army and won the next three battles.

He had received word that his wife had started her pains of labor. He celebrated with his men and asked for leave to see them. By morning, approval for his leave had been granted but it was too late. His wife and child had perished in the night.

He felt a swell of regret and guilt course through him now.

Fighting and killing took precedence over yer family, Constantine, his father-in-law had rightly accused.

Nae, her mother had spat. *'Tis fame and glory that beguiled his twisted heart.*

We took them away and buried them without ye. Ye didna deserve to be there.

"Constantine."

He opened his eyes to the sound of twinkling bells in his ears and looked into Ismay's eyes.

"Lady, I must have dozed." He sat up straighter.

"Were ye having a bad dream?"

His gaze found hers again. She marred her brow and concern narrowed her eyes as if seeing a glimpse of the truth in his gaze.

He quirked one side of his mouth to reassure her. Also because seeing her made him want to smile. She was like sunshine in the gloom. "Yer concern is unnecessary."

"Is it?" she asked him, staring into his eyes. "I have never seen ye look so afraid before."

He thought he should toss a mocking laugh into the air. But he could not deny that she was correct.

"Who or what is it that brings such fear to ye?"

How could he tell her that he was so afraid of the truths pouring from Alison's parents' mouths? Truths he hated. It had indeed come to a point that he loved the glory he brought to the Camerons. He poured all of himself into studying battlefields and the routes that reached them. He had planned off the field and polished his sword at dawn, hoping his enemies' allies arrived to aid them and give him more to kill.

"I was a monster and I'm haunted by the joy I took in it." He blinked. Did he just speak out loud?

Who was this woman who he was confessing his sins to?

"Ferget I spoke," he said with more command than he intended. "Just push it from yer thoughts. Aye? I spoke a feelin' rather than a fact."

"Why avoid speaking what ye are feeling?" she asked him, slipping into the chair on his right. "I speak about what I am feeling many times. It cleanses ye."

"What?"

"Ye feel better when ye speak about yer feelings."

He chuckled. Good. If she wanted to fixate on speaking her feelings, rather than focusing on his, that was fine with him.

"Chief," she said in her soft, sorceress voice. "Is it possible that two monsters have found each other and have stopped long enough to help the other heal?"

His heart shuddered in his chest. Could they heal each other?

"Perhaps 'tis," he responded with tenderness toward her. "But ye are no' a monster, lass. Ye were a child, battered by a clan chief—a man above reproach. Ye killed to live."

He reached out slowly and wiped the pad of his thumb across a tear pausing on her cheek.

"And ye, Constantine, the past is over. No amount of regret will change anything." She took his hand and pressed it against her cheek. "A monster doesna grieve. It doesna feel anything. 'Tis clear that ye feel much."

He heard the footsteps of men entering the Hall. He looked around Ismay's shoulder and saw the elders. The first few wore looks of stunned apprehension, their eyes fastened on the couple sitting at the table.

Had they heard her declaring that he was not a monster? That he grieved?

Had the elders, or anyone in Lochaber considered the great weight that infected his confidence? They saw a hero, a protector, but his wife and child saw nothing, and his enemies saw the ravenous beast that lived off praise.

But he grieved. She was correct in that. In everything she said about him. Was he so transparent?

"Will she be here fer the meetin', then?" asked old George Cameron, Constantine's second great-uncle.

"Nae," Ismay answered with a warm smile, saving Constantine from having a word with his uncle later about his manners. "I was just leaving."

With one last smile, she moved in close enough to whisper into the Lochiel's ear, "Dinna take any of their heads." Then, she bid him a swift farewell and was gone.

He almost laughed out loud while she walked away. Hearing such a thing would likely cause at least three of the elders to fall down dead.

Turning from her departure to their weathered, weary faces, he let out a silent sigh and began briefing them on the Chattan's missive. After that, he told them his plan. "We will fight at Achnacarry. I want fifty men at the ford on the northern side of the loch ready to attack the rear. Meanwhile, I and a regiment of our kin will march aroond the head of the loch to outflank and attack the MacKintoshes from the east."

"That is an eighteen-mile trck?" Lord Bran of Tilliisburgh pointed out.

"We can make it," Constantine assured him.

"From whom will ye request aid?" asked Marten MacDonald, who fought in the battle of Craig Cailloch and many battles before that.

"I have already sent out messengers to the MacGregors and the MacIans, and of course, the MacMillans."

"Good," most of them muttered amongst themselves. A few narrowed their eyes on him, trying to gauge his confidence in this.

"Do ye think the MacMillans will help us since ye are now estranged from their kin, yer in-laws?"

"We will discover that soon enough," Constantine let them know, then got off the topic of Alison MacMillan's parents. "I anticipate some clans from the Chattan will arrive, possibly to aid MacKintosh. But I would have ye all know, 'tis nothin' that concerns me."

They discussed strategies and minor concerns, and when the meeting ended well into the night, Constantine found himself searching for Ismay.

He found her asleep in his private solar, curled up in an over-sized chair by the hearth, with his plaid covering her. He did not want to wake her. He wanted to crouch before her and simply take his fill in the sight of her, so comfortable and at home in his solar.

So, after adding more wood to the hearthfire, that is what he did. After moving a nearby chair even closer to her, he sat and spread his gaze over her.

He had missed her today. He missed her playful glances and concerned frowns that marred her brow. She worried about him. And though, at times, he thought it a wee bit insulting, he found himself liking her concern. She was not full of bravado, but she carried herself with quiet strength. He considered, letting his gaze trace the delicate steel of her jaw, that she would be a worthy wife to any Highland warrior she chose, if she chose to marry.

The idea of her as another man's wife made his belly knot up, his hands ball into fists.

Aye, he was fond of her. So? Did it mean his demise or hers? Nae. Nae, it did not. Did it mean he was letting go of Alison and Katie? How could he?

He had planned out a future with Alison in his head from the moment he'd met her. And in one day, it was all over. He hadn't had the chance to bid her farewell or promise to find her in heaven.

And now, because of this fiery woman covered in his plaid, he was not certain he wanted to find Alison.

His gaze roved over the sweet contour of Ismay Drummond's lips, the color of ripe peaches. The thought of tasting them to see if they were as sweet as they looked almost overwhelmed him. But he was not one for letting go to his desires. If he were, he would have continued killing enemies like Oliver Cromwell's garrison and the rest of the English and their supporters.

Her small, pert nose reminded him of her challenging tongue and brought a smile to his face. He liked her temper. His woman should not be a—His woman?

He closed his eyes in defense of her, but then, uncharacteristically unable to fight himself and win, he opened them again and set them on her long, black lashes smudging her cheeks.

His resolute heart faltered.

He spoke her name on a whispered breath, agonized by what he was beginning to feel for her.

Her lashes lifted, exposing his admiring gaze on her. He did not look away at being caught. He did not want to look away ever again. Had she not been away from him enough today?

When she offered him a dreamy smile, he felt his mouth go dry and his muscles tighten throughout his body.

"Apologies fer coming in here while ye were away," she began then stopped when he shook his head.

"Nae apologies are necessary, Lady."

"I was thinking of ye and ended up here." Her gray eyes were like turbulent seas he wanted to run to.

He raised his brows and chuckled softly. "Do ye think of me often then?"

When she nodded her bonnie head, he wanted to bolt out of his chair and shout with joy that she shared the same plight as he.

"I am enjoying getting to know ye, Lochiel. I mean Constantine," she whispered the last.

He let his smile on her widen. "I feel the same. Ye are a refreshin' delight."

Her cheeks grew pinker. She gasped a little breath when he leaned in. He should stop. He would stop if she requested or demanded it. He hoped she would allow it.

Her breath was sweet against his lips, proving his first assumption. He breathed her in and reached for her bonnie cheek. Pressing his mouth to hers was the hardest thing Constantine had done. Marching into battle, clothed in mists with bagpipes playing a haunting tune all around him was not as hard as this. Going home to an empty house was not as difficult.

He knew himself then. Kissing Ismay Drummond meant he was changing into someone he didn't know.

Let me be a stranger to myself, he settled it in his head. He took her in the way a starving peasant enjoyed his first meal in days. He did not kiss her harshly or without control. Nae, he took his time, caressing her petal-soft cheek then running his fingers through those bouncy flames and moving her head closer. He savored the scent of her, the feel of her in his hand, the taste of her like sweet fruit off the tree.

He could have continued basking in her for the rest of the night, but when he stroked the inside of her mouth with his tongue, she froze up and backed away.

He was glad. It was better to stop before he did something he would regret—like promise her anything.

"Ye are the first man who kissed me with intimacy," she confessed. "I fear I let it overwhelm me."

He offered her a smile. "I think the solution to that is practicin' more often; gettin' accustomed to it."

"Is that so?" she asked with a playful grin that made his foolish head spin.

"Aye. I am a patient man. I dinna let desire rule over me."

"Desire?" she asked, her eyes widening. "Fer me?"

He nodded and watched her face go up in flames.

"Ismay?"

"Aye?"

He did not release her gaze. "I willna let any desire rule over me. Ye have nothin' to fear from me, aye?"

"I dinna fear ye, Constantine. Ye are the only man in my

world whom I trust."

Now it was his turn to blush. To trust another being in this life was a risk. If one was graced to be the one another trusted, it was an honor. A great one. Knowing Ismay had no one else made his heart break. She had had one man in her life, only one she trusted. Now that her father was gone, she had no one.

Nae. She had him.

It hardened his resolve to protect her, even from himself.

"Come, the hour is late," he urged gently, hesitantly. "Let me escort ye to yer chambers."

"All right," she said, suddenly shyly.

She walked beside him down the hall to her chamber door. When they stopped before it, he leaned across her and opened the door with one hand. His heart thrashed wildly in his chest with the desire to kiss her again. But he had promised to let control lead him.

Before he had a chance to move out of her way, she gave him new things to dream about when she stepped past him and gave his lips a short, bold kiss.

He watched her disappear into the chamber, too surprised and pleased to speak.

She kissed him! He found it so exhilarating he almost knocked on her door to see if she would do it again. He laughed softly. He laughed! Och, what was he to do with her? He would not send her away and return to his dull, dreary days, hearing the same talk about responsibilities, raiding, the troubles of others, some fact he already knew about his enemies.

Ismay Drummond breathed fresh air into his days and he would not be quick to let her go. But would she stay? Or would she choose a holier life hidden in a convent than one with him? He would not force her to stay. He would not force her to do anything she chose not to do. If she left, would his guilt over betraying Alison's memory leave with her?

Would she wait while he went off to fight?

For the second time in his life, he wished he did not have to leave for battle. It would be a fight to the death. The MacKintosh chief would die and Constantine would inherit yet another sorrowful spirit that lived in his head.

He'd been killing for a long time now. The weight of all he had done was slowly destroying him, for he was drowning in the darkness.

But…his smile returned, reigning supreme. He wasn't a monster. He was a soldier. If he had to fight, he would. If he had to kill a man for kidnapping a woman with vile intent, he would. But he would add praying for a way to avoid the upcoming battle to his list of strategies.

The MacKintosh was fortunate, he decided, stepping into his chambers. If this missive from the Chattan had been delivered last month, Constantine's enemy would be dead by now and he would have grieved his deed. Because he was not a monster.

HE WAS NOT a monster, but he still could not sleep longer than three hours. The glorious consolation prize was that he didn't remember dreaming. There were no accusing eyes and wailing babies, no cries from men with whom he'd grown to adulthood dying in his arms. He was sure it all had to do with Ismay. It was as if she had taken on his ghosts and was conquering them all.

Remembering the succulent taste of her drew him from his bed. He slipped on a loose shirt and a pair of breeches, then padded out to her chamber door. He did not knock or seek entry, but pulled a chair closer to the door, sat in it, and protected her from dust motes and castle mice until Bethia and Joan turned up at her door early the next morning.

Seeing them and wishing they had not seen him, he scrambled to his feet. But there was nowhere to run. It riled him that he wanted to hide from these two delicate lasses—who were not so delicate at all.

"What are ye doing here, Lochiel?" Bethia put to him sternly.

He was uncertain, but did she add emphasis on his title, as if he had more important things to see to? He didn't.

With a resigned sigh at being caught, he confessed without any regret. He didn't care if he sounded like a fool. He would not hide behind lies to protect his pride. "I'm standin' watch over Miss Drummond"

"Against whom?"

He shrugged. "Anyone who thinks to breach her door."

At that, Joan stepped away ten paces.

And the door to Ismay's chambers swung open.

She appeared as if from the gates of his dreams, where she stood guard with an array of bonnie smiles, playful grins, and most deadly, her tinkling laughter that sounded like siren songs in his ears. Her sleepy eyes took him in before anyone else, so he knew that it was him who brought such a radiant smile to her face.

"I thought I heard yer voice." The sound of her settled over him like a welcomed blanket. "Ye are here early."

"He has been guarding yer door all night," Bethia informed her a bit stiffly.

"Och, and ye believe him?" Ismay said with a little laugh that reverberated through his blood. "He was being playful. In truth, he has come to bring me to the loch."

"The loch?" Joan asked.

"Playful?" was Bethia's choice of query.

"And of course, ye both will accompany us. Is that not correct, Lochiel?"

"Aye, 'tis."

He didn't have to play along. It was his castle and he was lord of it. He didn't have to make excuses for where he spent the night. If others wished to gossip, let them. But Ismay would not have it. So, for her, he agreed. He even smiled to help drive home, mainly to Bethia, that as astonishing as it was, he could be playful—since for her it was the part of the explanation most unbelievable.

"Well," Ismay sang out, leaving the chambers. "Let us be on our way."

Constantine joined her on her way to the stairs. What other choice did he have? It would be like trying to ignore the melodies of fairies, or the call of the waves.

"Did ye sleep by my door, Lochiel?" she asked in a voice only he could hear.

"Aye."

He did not know what he expected her reaction to be, but it was not gratitude. Still, she offered it to him.

"Once again, I earn yer gratitude fer nothin' but protectin' ye from a mouse."

"All right, then tell me. What do ye think ye were doing at my door? Ye know more than I do what ye were protecting me from."

He stopped for a moment and looked into her eyes. "From bein' alone."

He held out his elbow when they reached the top of the stairs. She curled her wrist through it and let him lead her down.

Did she truly wish to bathe in the loch this morning? "The water will be cold, Lady."

"I imagine so," she replied softly, as if to bewitch him. It was working. "But the thrill is worth the chill, aye, Chief?"

His smile lit the halls and drew Bethia's attention. Her scowl, despite it being a mild one, widened into stunned disbelief when he turned to shine on her. Nothing, neither guilt nor shame would veer him off his path to do as Miss Drummond wished.

On the way out of the castle, he met Hugh and told him to tell the cook to prepare a feast and have it brought to the loch. He also enlisted the aid of Lachlan. He reasoned it would be a wee bit more challenging to protect Ismay if he had to watch over Bethia and Joan as well.

"I brought an extra plaid to keep ye dry and warm," he told Ismay, coming up behind her on the path.

She turned to look at him over her shoulder. "Ye are verra thoughtful, Constantine."

Hearing his name, Bethia pulled a kerchief out of a fold in her skirts and wiped her nose.

"I mean Chief-Lochiel," Ismay stammered.

Constantine's smile faded and he turned to glare at Bethia. "How much longer before the darkness engulfs me and I am lost? Would ye prefer that?"

The older chambermaid gave her nose one last swipe with her kerchief and then ran off. Constantine did not go after her. She was Alison's friend, and to the MacMillans went her loyalties. Nothing would change that.

He didn't care. He wanted to be right where he was with Ismay; making her smile—which in turn, did the same for him— and he hadn't smiled in so damn long.

He would have time on the field, waiting to fight, to consider what everything with her meant, and if he should ask Ismay to stay with him for good. Today was hers.

When they rounded the bend and she saw the small pool and its glistening waterfall, she squealed with delight and hurried toward it.

He watched as Joan rushed to her and began untying the laces of Ismay's stays. He commanded Lachlan to look away if he wanted to keep his eyes.

He did the same and turned toward the trees, then he smiled, pleased at the sound of Ismay's laughter filling the small cove, and all the nooks and spaces of his heart.

---※---

CHAPTER FIFTEEN

I SMAY SHIVERED STEPPING into the frigid water. He'd kept his promise to bring her here this morning. She knew he would, that was why she came prepared, wearing extra petticoats and a shorter leine beneath her longer one, so that when she removed the outer layers before stepping into the water, they would remain dry. Most of all, thanks to the layer underneath she would not be completely indecent in the sight of the Lochiel.

She felt her face burn for the tenth time already since finding him outside her door. All her blushing was born of one thing. His kiss in the solar. Would the memory of it always make her insides, most specifically the place below her navel, burn? She wished she had her fan. Though the air was crisp, her body felt uncomfortably warm.

What if he kissed her again? Would it seal her fate? It was why she chose to come here to the loch this morning. She knew he would not bring her alone.

She wished Joan would accompany her into the water but her friend refused to follow her into the icy depths. She squealed when the water touched her, as if in pain and causing the two men waiting by the trees to come running.

Ismay laughed and swam to the waterfall. The same thrill did not bubble Joan's blood, but her friend did not leave the water's edge while Ismay bathed and swam. Even Lachlan was forgotten while Ismay's new dear friend watched over her as closely as the Lochiel did.

Twice, Ismay lightly splashed her and they laughed, the sound echoed by the men watching.

"Come closer," Ismay invited with a sinister grin.

Her belly flipped when the chief laughed softly, knowing what she was devising.

"I dinna know what ye did with the old Lochiel," Joan said, lowering her voice so only Ismay would hear, "but whatever it is, dinna bring him back. This Lochiel is more pleasant."

Ismay splashed her, not so lightly this time, and then laughed and swam away when Joan vowed to catch her and make her sorry.

Escaping, Ismay let happiness spread its warmth on her. Here she was, in a glorious loch where, if she closed her eyes, the sound of its waterfall reminded her of the waterfall near her father's house. She had a loyal friend in Joan, just as she had in Murrun back home. And she had more. She had what had been missing in all the best scenarios of her life; a man she could allow into her heart, her life, and her bed.

She found him watching her from the close tree line. She waved. Lachlan and Joan waved back. It made Ismay cover her mouth to giggle. She had been accepted at Tor Castle. Every day it felt more familiar, more like home.

The only one who did not seem to want her there was Bethia, though she made it a point to always be the first one to attend Ismay. According to Constantine, Bethia came to Tor with his wife. It was understandable that Bethia was loyal to her lady. Ismay tried not to take it too personally.

Her eyes caught Constantine moving. He was making his way toward a row of twelve men carrying trays of food to the grass and setting down at their chief's direction.

She remained in the water until the men left and then, under Joan's careful guard, she left the water and changed into dry clothes.

When she was dressed, she made her way to him and stepped into the woolen plaid he held open to receive her.

"Did ye enjoy yerself?" His arms closing around her and his breath against her ear filled her with warmth.

She nodded, wanting to invite him in with her next time. She said nothing and closed her eyes as his scent of pine and morning mist covered her, filling every inch of her.

She knew he would be leaving any day now to battle the MacKintoshes once and for all. Would he return?

With a slight shake of her head that made her short tresses sway, she refused to think on such things. Of course, he would return. He was the Lochiel. The most savage man she had ever met.

"Ye're shiverin'," he said huskily and wrapped her up more tightly in the plaid.

"Och, lady!" Joan lamented, standing behind her and at least five safe steps away. "Yer hair is still wet! Why would ye bathe in the freezing lake?"

Ismay moved to smile and reassure her. "I'm well, Joan. Ver-ra well."

Her friend got the message, stopped, and smiled brightly at her, and then at the Lochiel holding her.

Because she decided at that moment to rest her cheek against his chest, her ear heard the sound of deep rumbling from someplace within him. Was it the sound of his resistance to what was clear to Joan?

Taking mercy on him, Ismay stepped back. But he didn't let her go. She couldn't lift her arms to embrace him or push him away, so she simply let him warm her.

She realized it was a vulnerable position to be in—unable to lift her arms in defense. But this was no mere chief. This was the man who had taken her under his protective arms and had not let go.

She trusted him without caring why she offered it to him so easily. He would not hurt her the way others had.

Finally, he bent his head and shoulders back to take a look at her. His dark eyes moved over her wet strands and she struggled a little to instinctively lift her hand to her hair. He lifted his to it instead.

From behind her she heard Joan's startled intake of breath. Ismay worried he might kiss her in front of the others. She wished they were alone so that he would indeed kiss her. He didn't. He pulled the length of the plaid over her head and rubbed it on her head.

When he finally let her go, she felt cold and alone for an instant. But his warm gaze on her was like hot coals heating the deepest cavern of her heart.

They ate a feast of braised duck, and pheasant. Hare stew with turnips, mushrooms, and carrots. This morning's black bread with honey, currant tarts, along with dried and smoked herring, various custards and savory and sweet pies.

While they filled their bellies, she learned from the worshipful words of Lachlan, things Joan could not tell her about the Lochiel because she had not been privy to them. Like how Constantine had saved his men during all six of their major battles against both Cromwellian garrisons making their way into the Highlands, and enemy clans, like the MacKintoshes, MacPhersons, and even sometimes Campbells.

Ismay wasn't surprised by any of it. He had appeared fearless when the MacKintoshes had arrived at the inn. But she wished he did not enjoy fighting so much. One day, his life would catch up with him.

"Do ye have to fight?" she asked, hating herself for it.

He looked up from his cup of water and simply stared at her. Then, with a hint of a smile on his decadent lips, "I will do all I can to avoid it."

She was tempted to gape at him, but fought it, not wishing to appear a hapless dolt. "Ye will?"

"Ye will?" Lachlan almost sprang to his feet. "Do ye jest?"

"I want to give killin' up and live a wee bit, if I can," he told his cousin—who didn't care what he looked like with his mouth hanging open.

"What will we all do withoot ye, Lochiel?"

Constantine let out a sigh and shook his head. "I will fight when I'm needed."

At this, Ismay tossed the younger Cameron a dark glare. She said nothing in front of him, lest she become the enemy before his men even found out she was a MacPherson. She would not make Constantine's decisions for him, unless they might get him killed.

Nae. She quickly shook her head at herself. It was not for her to say. His life was his own. He hadn't pledged it to her.

"Let us not speak of fighting on such a perfect day," she suggested, doing her best not to worry about tomorrow or the day after that.

After they ate, they rode to the Doomsday Tavern and Inn for drinks with Lewis.

While Ismay watched Constantine and his cousins, she marveled that the Lochiel was the same man who had stood with his back against the wall while she wept into her stew. He hadn't laughed then. He hadn't smiled. He looked mildly interested in the goings on around him—except when his dark gaze found hers.

His cousins also appeared surprised but happy at his recent mood.

"Lady Ismay," Lewis turned to her, holding his cup to his lips. "Did ye already mention who was yer father? There was a patron here this mornin' who spoke aboot the daughter of his lord running off in the night."

Her belly tightened into a knot. She felt lightheaded at the table and tried to conceal it from Constantine.

"Did this patron mention who is the lord whose daughter ran off in the night?" he asked.

Lewis shook his head. "He seemed fiercely loyal to his lord— or his lord's daughter. He said only this when I asked him, 'If she left, she likely wants to stay hidden.'"

Ismay sat in silence, fighting to keep her tears at bay. She tried to ask a question twice, and both times a lump in her throat made it almost impossible to speak. Finally, she managed, keeping the quaver that felt as if it were shaking her whole body, out of her voice. "Who was the patron? Did he tell ye that much, at least?"

Lewis shook his head and turned his gaze to Constantine, who was staring at him with a spark in his glaring gaze.

"What?" Lewis asked, sounding hurt.

"Ye upset her," their chief said in a low growl.

Ismay turned to him. Was he angry over such a thing? "Nae, I'm quite all right, Chief."

He didn't look convinced. She turned an apologetic look on Lewis. "Thank ye fer sharing that tale with me, Lewis," she told him letting him—and the chief—know he was forgiven.

"I didna mean to upset ye, Miss Drummond," Lewis told her, dipping his repentant gaze. "Fergive me."

Ismay knew he apologized for Constantine's sake and not for hers. He was always kind and respectful to her because Constantine was fond of her. She didn't mind. The lethal Highlander frightened her a bit with his piercing eyes that seemed to penetrate as deeply as twin swords, but he was fiercely loyal to Constantine and she liked that about him.

"If he returns, send fer me," Constantine told his cousin.

After that, Ismay sat quietly pondering who the patron could be. There had been some kind servants in her father's house. Many of them loved the baron and would likely be on her side. But who? And did she want Constantine to meet him so he could tell the Cameron chief all about his MacPherson lord and his runaway daughter? It couldn't be Chief MacRae, could it? Why would he call her father his lord? Nae. It was not MacRae.

The more she thought about it, the more ill she felt. But she smiled when everyone else did, not wanting to seem anxious or afraid in front of Constantine.

She drank all the wine Lachlan and Fionn set before her. At

one point, Constantine turned from his conversation with Geoffry and looked at her just as she was swigging her fourth cup.

She wiped her hand across her mouth and slammed the cup down, harder than she intended, on the table.

She expected him to say something. Ask her if she was well or not. Tell her to stop drinking. Something. But he was quiet. Indeed, he let his murderous glare on his two younger cousins do the talking for him. When Lachlan set down another cup a little while later, they seemed to warn: *Take it away before ye canna move another thing fer the next year.*

No one offered her another drink. By the time they left, the sun had set and Ismay was a wee bit less drunk than before. She didn't protest when the handsome chief offered to help her to his horse. Though she would admit that when he bent to lift her into his arms to carry her, she doubted she had any wits left to say a word without sounding like a pitifully obsessed admirer.

Cradled against the Lochiel's chest, she wanted to sleep. Och, to sleep without a care safe in his arms. But she couldn't sleep because she had to—be sick. Every time she closed her eyes, the ground spun.

"Put me down," she commanded.

All the men walking close by turned to have a look at her.

"Constantine!"

They all gaped at her calling him with intimate familiarity.

She covered her mouth with her hand. He seemed to understand and set her on her feet. Thankful, she ran the other way, until she realized she couldn't see her hand in front of her face. How could she forget how dark the night could be? Her feeling of being ill disappeared, replaced by fear.

She turned in a circle. The only light came from the lanterns along the inn. There was nothing else in her vision but black. She heard something snap to her right. Another coyote? Chief MacRae?

"Ismay!"

She turned in Constantine's direction and ran into his arms. "I wasna sure…"

"Aye, that is thanks to all the ale inside yer belly. It's gone to yer head." With that, he ran his palm over her head as if she were his favored dog. "Come, now, hold onto me."

He slipped his arm around her waist and dragged her close beside him. She held onto him when he led them to the others, then, into his saddle. She was happy she could not see the men's faces, staring knowingly at her as their Lochiel mounted behind her. Did they dislike her because their untouchable Lochiel suddenly seemed…touchable?

He didn't seem to be bothered by his cousins, if he could see them. Pulling her closer, he flicked the reins of his horse and left for the castle.

She felt queasy being jostled around in the saddle, but she managed to keep her belly quiet.

Though it was past the evening meal, she was not hungry and let Constantine help her to her chambers when they returned to the castle.

She dreamed that he tucked her into her bed and spoke in his low, seductive voice, something she couldn't remember. She dreamed of other things, like swimming with him, laughing with him, and best of all, kissing him.

Morning came too soon and brought with it the stark ugly truth of day. Constantine would be leaving for battle with the MacKintoshes—and whomever else from the Chattan would help them.

She ate with Hilary and Joan in the Great Hall. None of the men were there. They all rode with Constantine to Achnacarry to scout out the territory before the fight. Hilary wept at the possibility of one or both of her brothers not being here for her wedding. Joan admitted she loved Lachlan and if he perished on the field she could not live another day.

Ismay had lived through terrible loss before. It was a good thing she hadn't allowed herself to feel anything more for him than a growing fondness in her heart. She didn't love him. Yet, the thought of him dead brought tears to her eyes and felt like a cold spear through her heart.

She didn't see him all day. She spent most of her hours alone, preferring it that way over spending hours weeping or listening to others weep. She sat beyond the tree line at the loch and remembered his gaze on her while she swam and drying off wrapped in his plaid, warm and safe in his strong arms.

She smiled thinking of how he was single-handedly changing her opinion of chiefs. But was it enough to stay here? When he returned from battle—and he would—would he still care for her. Would it ever be enough to pull him from the arms of a ghost?

If it was, what would he do when he found out the truth about her?

She rubbed her belly and moved to stand. Hugh suddenly was there, blocking her way back.

"Are ye worried fer him, or are ye feeling ill, lass?" Hugh asked with sincere concern shaping his features.

"What are ye doing here, Hugh?" she asked, taking a step to the left and clearing her path, but not going forward.

"I saw ye from the battlements, where I stood watching fer any signs of the Lochiel," he told her.

"And ye followed me because…?"

"Ye shouldna go beyond the gate. It isna safe out in the open."

She realized he was right. Even Constantine had brought Lachlan to help him protect her while she swam.

Repentant, she hung her head. "I was just about to return."

"A wise decision," he said, then stepped completely out of her path. "Let me escort ye back."

She nodded, then lifted her head again to offer him a smile. She guessed Hugh wasn't so bad. He questioned his chief, but some men did, even if just in their hearts. Constantine did not throw him out or have him killed for his opinions. She would put them aside too.

"Ye said ye were watching fer the Lochiel's return," she reminded him. "Is there a reason—"

"He has guests waiting fer his return. I sought to warn him."

She stopped and looked up at him. "Warn him of his guests' arrival? Why?" she added when he nodded his head. "Who are they?"

"His wife's parents."

Ismay swallowed. The knot in her belly tightened. *His wife*...why did hearing those words prick and slice her as if she'd just fallen into shards of glass?

"Why have they come?" she asked with hesitance softening her tone.

"Most likely to remind him that he hadna loved their daughter enough and whatever other things they usually throw at him."

"Do they take pleasure in hurting him?" she demanded.

"I dinna know about that, Miss Drummond, but I know they use the guilt they cause him to squeeze his coffers. He allows it, of course. And in the meantime Tor's coffers will soon run dry."

Ismay stared at Constantine's steward. Were Constantine's in-laws truly here to squeeze his coffers? Did his steward have any sort of loyalty to Constantine, or was it solely to Tor's coffers? She had heard him questioning the chief about draining the coffers the morning she had followed Constantine out into the mists.

Her brow dipped over her eyes creating shadows in their depths, like turbulent seas under a charcoal sky.

"'Tis best if ye do yer best to avoid the MacMillans," the steward told her, "and dinna look at them as if ye have been keeping company with a savage."

She blinked and confusion washed over her. Did the steward like Constantine, or hate him? The chief's own men were not certain, and neither was she.

"Do ye consider the Lochiel a savage?"

He picked up his steps again and didn't look at her when he spoke. "A man who could cut down a regiment of enemy soldiers with nae other help than from his arm has to be a savage. Dinna ye think? Surely ye have been around savages before. Ye are running from one."

How did he know about MacRae? Had Constantine told him? Had she and she didn't remember? Was he even referring to MacRae?

"No' a savage but a soldier with a skilled arm and a strong will to live," she corrected him.

He smiled but there was more mockery in it than merriment. "Does the Lochiel strike ye as a man with a strong will to survive, then? Nae," he answered for her, "ye didna see him when he returned from battle covered from foot to crown in the blood of others."

She shook her head as if to chase away images Hugh conjured in her thoughts. "Should he have laid down his sword and died then?" she challenged, tired of hearing his treacherous talk coated in false compassion. "Hugh, has it not occurred to ye that he suffers? Ye have heard his night terrors, I'm sure. Even the chambermaids have heard him crying out. Ye say he doesna smile or speak much with others, and then ye tell me how his in-laws accuse him of heinous lies. Do ye truly believe he doesna suffer? Is it not enough fer ye?"

The steward did not stop or even slow his pace, but continued on to the castle. He left her side when a silver-haired woman left the Great Hall, saw her, and came nearer to circle her like a cat.

Ismay offered her a slight smile and took a step to leave. The woman's words stopped her. "Are ye the homeless wench who thinks to take my daughter's place?"

Ismay wondered for a moment where she had come up with that notion, but then she spotted Bethia leaving the gGeat Hall next.

"I assure ye," Ismay said slowly, returning her attention to the silver-haired woman, "no one can take yer daughter's place in the Lochiel's heart. He was verra dedicated to her."

She said this because of what Hugh had told her was the

reason they were here: to remind him that he hadn't loved their daughter enough.

The woman raised her brow as she assessed Ismay. She appeared to come to a distasteful conclusion. "Then why did she die alone, Miss Drummond?"

"Because she married a soldier, Lady MacMillan," Ismay said in a soft voice.

It appeared that Lady MacMillan was not able to conceal her ire the way Ismay could and was doing right now. The older woman tightened her lips and balled her hands into fists. "Listen ye trollop. Are ye trying to blame my Alison fer dying alone?" She could barely deliver her question without trembling, and for a moment Ismay thought she might shatter and break.

"My lady, I am truly sorry fer yer loss. I canna imagine—"

"Ye are correct, ye know nothing of the loss my husband and I suffered. I am warning ye now to stay away from my son-in-law."

Watching her storm away, Ismay wanted to say something else, but truly, it wasn't her place. She didn't know if she was anything more to Constantine than his friend…whom he kissed.

She left the hall and heard Joan calling out to her as she ascended the stairs.

"Dinna pay any attention to that old crow," Joan advised her, catching up with her on her way up the stairs.

"I think Bethia sent for her," Ismay let her know her suspicions. "Lady MacMillan accused me of trying to take her daughter's place with Con—" she paused, hating to appear overly close with the chief and hating even more that she believed she needed to hide it—"the chief."

"Well, if ye do take her place, 'twill be a good thing fer the Lochiel. Ye have been nothing but good fer him."

Ismay smiled at her reassurance but inwardly she cringed. She still could not see her future. She thought he was the one man she would like to marry. But she had spoken the truth to Lady MacMillan. No one could take her daughter's place in the

Lochiel's heart.

It was a truth she was going to have to either accept or refuse.

Joan agreed to bring supper to Ismay's chamber to keep Ismay from having to speak to Lady MacMillan again, and left her friend to see to the task.

But after a few moments of thinking it over, Ismay ran her fingers through her unruly hair in an effort to make it a bit less wild, then left her chambers.

CHAPTER SIXTEEN

ISMAY SAT IN the Great Hall at one of the trestle tables with Hilary MacDonald and Glenna Cameron. Supper was almost over, with the last course of honeyed tarts, fig pies, and short-bread with freshly churned butter. There were spiced wines, seasoned with cinnamon or ginger and ale seasoned with cloves to drink.

The MacMillans sat and drank at the Lochiel's table, empty around them, save for Bethia sitting to her lady's left. Hugh could be seen occasionally pacing along the longest table with food set out on it. No doubt, the steward was worried about the coffers.

When Ismay asked, Hilary told her the fine food and wine were offered to the Lochiel's esteemed guests, his in-laws. The menu was Lady MacMillan's doing, not the Lochiel's, who still had not returned from scouting Achnacarry with his men.

Bethia did not come to Ismay's table once the whole night. In fact, she barely looked at Ismay, proving she was the one who told Lady MacMillan about her.

Just after the last course was served, the Great Hall doors swung open. Every eye moved toward the sound, including Ismay's.

Surprised at how deliriously happy she was when she saw Constantine standing beneath the doorway, Ismay almost shot up to her feet. She didn't and she was relieved she didn't. The way she swayed in her spot, her head spinning from the drinks or the sight of him, she would have swooned and tipped over.

His gaze was hard and sharp as steel as it roved over tables, coming to settle on his in-laws. He started toward them, but then his steps paused and he turned his head to look at Ismay. Though his gaze was brief, his eyes seemed to speak to her. *Fergive me.*

She offered him the slightest of smiles in response. Outright fawning over him in the sight of his deceased wife's parents would have been tactless.

Ismay did her best to find interest in anything besides him reaching them. Hilary, on the other hand, did not take her eyes off them.

"He appears verra angry," Hilary observed.

"He always appears angry," Glenna Cameron, Lewis's younger sister pointed out, then narrowed her eyes on the Lochiel and his guests. "Who in all the Highlands wouldna be angry if they had a past with those two MacMillans in it?"

They all agreed. Ismay finally let her gaze drift back to him. He stood over his in-laws' chairs, and Hilary was correct, he appeared angry indeed. He said a few more words then bowed and turned in Ismay's direction.

She blinked away from him, mortified that she'd been caught admiring him.

He reached her in four long strides and stood before her. "I had no knowledge they were comin'," he said apologetically. "I have requested that they leave in the morning."

Her friends stared in surprise at his tender tone.

"Och, Lochiel," Joan said in a pleading voice. "Is Lachlan not with ye?"

"The men have gone to bed," he told Joan. "We have been in the saddle since sunrise. They were exhausted."

"What about ye?" Ismay asked him. "Are ye not weary? Go on to bed, then—"

"I'm quite all right," he assured her and requested Hilary's seat beside her.

His MacDonald cousin moved over and gave him her seat.

Plates and bowls were immediately set before him, along with spiced wine, which he asked be replaced with water.

"The battle begins tomorrow. I must keep my head free of spirits."

Tomorrow. Her throat began to burn. "Ye should truly get some sleep, Chief. I want ye to be strong and return to—" She stopped, and bit her tongue. Not with his mother-in-law watching them with hellfire in her eyes. "—to return to yer clan. They need ye."

He stared into her eyes as if he knew she was speaking of herself when she mentioned his clan.

"Verra well," he gave in. "After I eat, and if ye allow me to escort ye to yer chambers. I dinna want to give Lady MacMillan any more opportunity to harass ye."

She smiled at his thoughtfulness. She was sleepy anyway, so she agreed.

He ate while Hilary spoke on endlessly about this thing or that. It gave Ismay the opportunity to watch him bite into his bread and chew his food, his tongue darting out around his lips every so often.

He cut his glance to her a few times and smiled so briefly she thought she had imagined it. How could the mere slant of a man's mouth and the flash of something warm in his eyes make her kneecaps turn to puddles? How could it make her want something she had never wanted before?

When he was finished eating, he rose up and held his hand out to her. "Ready?"

She looked around, but the MacMillans had left the Hall, so she rested her fingers onto the Lochiel's palm and rose to leave with him.

"They will be gone by the time I leave," he told her, escorting her up the stairs.

She said nothing about his leaving. She had no right, but she would pray for his safe return. They may not have made commitments to each other but she wanted, no, she needed his safe return. Constantine Cameron had changed everything in her life. Especially the way she felt about men. She still did not trust or like them, but now she knew there were at least two good men out there—and if there were two, there were likely more.

But she still didn't want to marry.

Did she?

"Miss Drummond," he said in a soft, heavy voice when they reached the doors to her chambers. "Dinna leave while I'm away. Ye are safe here. Ye know that now, aye?" He waited while she nodded, then he continued. "Twenty men from the surrounding towns and villages usually stay behind to protect the women when I'm away. I'll be leaving ten more from the castle to stay and watch over ye."

Ismay's eyes burned and her belly flipped and fluttered at his words. Who was she for him to assign extra men to watch over her? She always felt safe in her father's care, but even he hadn't made plans or provisions to keep her safe in his absence.

"Constantine, I dinna know what to say, save that I would prefer those extra ten men to guard and protect *ye*."

He gave her a warm, slightly indulgent smile. "Ye have nae need to worry over me, lass."

His deep voice melted her bones and singed her blood with fire. "A regimen of wild men led by Oliver Cromwell himself couldna keep me away."

She couldn't help but smile lovingly at him. "Will ye give me yer word?"

"I give it," he gave in easily. "I vow to return to ye."

She looked into his eyes and wondered if he would ever kiss her again. Then she thought, *why should I wait?* She took one tentative step forward, closer to him and rose up on the tips of her toes. For an instant, she felt his warm breath against her lips, his dark eyes boring into hers before they began to close.

She was about to kiss him. Was she mad? Aye. Aye, she was and she didn't care.

She lifted her hands to clutch fistfuls of his plaid. Did she mean to stop him if he moved away from her eager mouth?

He didn't pull away, or step back, even when another tiny step brought her body up against his. Was that his thrashing heartbeat she felt, or her own?

Her lips touched his. She made a slight sound, a stifled gasp as if she were stunned by her own boldness—or by the thrill of kissing him. His arms coiled around her waist and pulled her closer, molding her into all his slopes and valleys.

His lips covered hers, tasted her, reveled in her. He was more than curious, more than hungry for the taste of a woman. His kiss was needful, as if she were air and he must breathe or he would die.

She brought her arms up around his neck and clung to him while he took his fill of her. She only resisted for an instant when his tongue gently coaxed her lips open and then swept into her mouth. But she quickly went weak against him as his tongue explored and branded her like a red-hot iron.

Finally, as his breath came harder and her body yielded to him fully, he broke away—but hesitantly. He didn't go far but gazed down into her eyes.

Even in the dimming candlelight along the walls in the corridor, Ismay was certain she saw in his eyes the things he wanted to say.

"I will return soon."

And then he stepped away and disappeared into his chambers down the hall.

Ismay stood where he left her, staring after him, bringing her fingertips to her lips. Would they think her mad if she sat by his door all night so that she could see him again when he left to fight?

She smiled at herself and then wiped a tear that escaped her eye. He would live through and return. He gave her his word, and he did not go back on his word. That was what she told herself when she let herself into her room and went to bed.

Ismay woke to a quiet morning. The air felt thick. It was hard to swallow. The chief had left Tor Castle. No one was outside in the halls hurrying throughout the castle to see this chore done, or that. Void from the corridors were the sounds of vibrant young men calling to a fair maid or bursting into laughter at something his cousins said. Empty was the big, heavy chair outside her door.

Her bedchamber door opened and Joan entered, downcast and somber. At least she pushed open the curtains on the two small windows to let the sunshine in. Hilary entered a moment later and pulled the heavy fabric closed again.

"I didna get a wink of sleep last night," she lamented, falling on Ismay's bed. "What if my John is called to fight with the Chattan? What if one of my brothers kills him?"

Ismay knew Hilary had a valid fear. The Chattan would no doubt send other clans to the fight to kill Constantine. And if Hilary's betrothed ran into Geoffry and Fionn, he would not have a chance against them.

"Try no' to dwell on the worst that can happen," Ismay told her, lifting her friend's head into her lap. "They will all return. Let us think of that day. The day we see smiles on their faces again."

Hilary and Joan shared a knowing glance.

"Do ye love him, Ismay?" Joan asked her, hurrying to sit near them on Ismay's bed.

"Aye, do ye?" Hilary echoed.

"I dinna think I do," she told them, thoughtfully considering her own answer. "I have loved but one man in my life, and it doesna feel the same with the chief."

"Yer father doesna count, Ismay!" Hilary slapped her arm playfully.

Hilary and Joan knew about Ismay's father, Baron of Raigmore, Lord John Drummond. Of course, she hadn't told them her father was a MacPherson. The same one who rescued Chief MacDonald's wee murderer years ago.

"How can he not count?" Ismay demanded. "If not—"

"For goodness sake!" Hilary sat up and gave her an impatient look. "Do ye truly not know the difference?"

When she shook her head, Joan took her hand and held it as if Ismay were the sorriest, most pathetic being to ever live.

"Ismay," Joan began breathlessly. "Being in love is unlike anything else in our lives. Being in love makes ye feel consumed by the other person. Thoughts of him haunt and overwhelm ye while ye go aboot yer day. Ye dinna care aboot food or sleep. When ye are with him, the sight of him could fill the rest of yer days. The sound of him is like the familiar sound of bagpipes when ye have been lost and finally found yer way home. Would ye do anything fer the Lochiel, Ismay?"

"Aye," Ismay told her without any hesitation.

Her two friends offered her knowing smiles.

Ismay's eyes opened wide. "I'm in love?"

Hilary nodded. "With the Lochiel."

"Nae, I canna be."

"Why not?" they both asked.

"I have stayed here too long. If I dinna keep moving, I will be found."

"Found by who?"

She told them bits about Chief MacRae and how he chopped off her hair.

"The Lochiel will kill him if he comes near ye!" Joan assured her.

"I dinna want him or my mother to find me. Who knows what they will do? What if they bring MacRae soldiers and they hurt ye or Hilary? I never planned on staying at Tor Castle. The Lochiel knows as much."

"Nonsense!" Hilary finally huffed after staring at Ismay as if she had gone mad. "Ye canna leave us to the Lochiel after he has lost another woman he loved."

"Hilary, ye are overreaching," Ismay assured her. "He doesna love me." Even when she said it, she didn't believe it. Still, what did she know about being in love? It was already proven. She knew nothing.

"Enough of this," she told them, scrambling off the bed. Once out of it, she yanked open the window curtains and pulled her friends out of her bed.

In love or not, she was not going to spend days pining as if he were already dead.

He wasn't. He promised.

CONSTANTINE WAITED ALONG the river at the Fords of Arkaig on the Achnacarry side, securing the only ford on the river with about a thousand men. They waited for the MacKintoshes to arrive. Word had already reached the southern end of Achnacarry that, as he and Miss Drummond had suspected, some of the other clans of the Chattan had pledged their arms to the MacKintoshes.

When the MacGregors of Breadalbane had arrived to pledge their aid to the Camerons, Constantine was happy to welcome them. They were allies and had fought together at Glen Fruin. The MacGregors were mostly outlaws—like him. The difference being, the MacGregors had all the English laws against them. Because they were always fighting for their lives, or their names, they were known for their passionate fighting and terrifying swords. Constantine was glad to have them on his side.

While he hunkered down to wait, he thought about Alison's parents. He hoped his in-laws had left the castle as promised. He didn't want Ismay's ears to hear the things the MacMillans spewed about him. He didn't want to think of them now. In fact, it had been some time since their accusing, hateful eyes haunted his wakeful thoughts. Since he met Miss Drummond, he hardly thought of anyone else.

"Lochiel!" Geoffry ran toward him from across the glen. His face was red and his breath, short. "MacKintosh must have discovered that we blocked the ford. He has moved his men, aboot a thousand strong, two miles west of here."

"Gather the men," Constantine ordered. "Tell Rauf MacDonald to remain here with fifty of his best men to keep the ford secured." He looked around for his messenger and called him over. "Find Ennis Cameron of Erracht. Tell him to take a number of his men, via boats, to the northern side of Loch Arkaig. They are to take down the MacKintosh's rear force."

"What of us?" Geoffry asked, ready to gather the men.

Constantine couldn't deny that his blood rushed through his blood like liquid fire bursting through a mountaintop. He might not enjoy taking lives, but he was born for battle. "We will make the eighteen-mile march around the head of Loch Arkaig. There, we will outflank the enemy and attack from the west. We will have him covered on every side."

Geoffry smiled. "A good plan, Lochiel."

Lachlan appeared hurrying toward them before Geoffry set off to his task. "Lochiel, the Baron of Argyll has arrived in the camps, bringing with him about three hundred Campbells. He seeks a word with ye."

What the hell were the Campbells doing here? They were rumored to be part of the Chattan. If they had come to fight for the MacKintoshes, Constantine would put the MacGregors to the enemy's arses. The two clans were fierce enemies. Even more so than the Camerons and MacKintoshes. The Campbells tried to have the MacGregor name abolished in the proscriptive acts of the MacGregors fifty-four years ago under King Charles 1. If the baron saw even a trace of the MacGregors here, on the side of the Camerons, war would break out and it would take him longer to get back to Tor Castle.

He would soon find out why they were here by granting the Campbell lord an audience. Only Geoffry and Lewis went with him. If the Campbells committed any treachery after calling for an audience, his two cousins were all he needed.

When they arrived in the Campbell camp, the baron promptly informed him why he was there. A good thing too, it gave Constantine time to call off his forces.

"I have arrived with three hundred of my most skilled men," the baron boasted. "I advise ye, as I will advise the MacKintosh chief, that I will add my forces to the battle and fight against whomever initiates this fight."

Aye, Constantine was born for war. And he'd fought his share. He was also born to love Ismay Drummond and he wanted to do that in peace. "Why?" he asked Campbell.

"Why question it. Just agree to peaceful terms and this feud will end."

"What terms?"

"The MacKintoshes must agree to sell the disputed territory. Ye must agree to purchase it."

Constantine didn't flinch. If the terms weren't fair, he wouldn't agree to them. "Purchase what is already mine?"

The baron cast him a sly smile. "The land was never yers. Yer kin took it. Aye, it had been seemingly abandoned by the MacKintoshes. But they have the deeds. They own the land."

"How much?" Constantine asked, wanting to be done here and either fight or go home.

"Pay MacKintosh 25,000 merks."

Constantine was a bit surprised by the fair amount. He narrowed his eyes on the Campbell. "What of his sons and his cattle? He made demands that I will never agree to."

The baron smiled and nodded. "Aye, I've heard aboot his sons and his cattle. His first son is dead due to consequences he brought upon himself. His second son stabbed ye with a dirk. And the cattle...well, seeing we are in Lochaber, ye have protection and there is nothing he can do about his herd." He stopped for a moment and looked Constantine over. "Ye are a formidable enemy, Cameron."

Constantine nodded. "An enemy neither John MacKintosh nor ye wants opposin' ye."

Campbell let out a boisterous laugh but nodded. "Ye agree then?"

"I do," Constantine let him know.

"Verra well. I am certain MacKintosh will agree, as well. He doesna want to face my men." Campbell motioned one of his men forward and instructed him to send for John MacKintosh. "The exchange will take place in Clunes," he advised Constantine. "Three days from now the Cameron/MacKintosh feud will end."

They wouldn't be fighting. A sense of relief washed over Constantine. He didn't want to pay for the land the MacKintoshes had practically given up. But if it ended the long feud, he would buy the land and shut them all up.

CONSTANTINE SENT MOST of his men back to their homes, and rode toward Clunes with his four cousins by his side. He would rather be heading home to Tor and…to Miss Drummond. Ismay. He'd kept her kiss from his thoughts all day, else the memory of her soft sweet lips would consume him and compel him to think on nothing else. Which would not have gone well with the Baron of Argyll.

But now, riding in silence, he let himself remember the sight of her, the scent of her coming close, stretching upward to kiss him. His heart crashed against his ribs like a fishing boat caught on the tumultuous sea, shattering from a power against which he was helpless.

When she had clutched his plaid and pulled him down, he felt the power of lightning go through him, stilling his blood flowing through his veins and turning it into liquid fire.

He'd held her in his arms. Mayhap, he shouldn't have, but he had. He had never wanted to let her go. He'd felt every inhalation of her breath against him. Her heart thumping, same as his. He wanted to relish seemingly winning her heart. Was that what he wanted? To win her heart? Mayhap. Mayhap he hadn't known it was what he wanted until the notion of it felt so real.

Pushing Alison and his daughter out of his thoughts when

they would have come to plague him was easier than he'd expected. As he neared Clunes with the real possibility of an end to the Cameron/MacKintosh feud in sight, and a bonnie lass waiting for him in his castle—a lass he wanted to kiss again, he finally felt a touch of peace within him.

That peace didn't last long.

Signing the agreement between the clans in the witness of the Chattan Confederation went peaceably enough—if one didn't count Ronald MacKintosh muttering an oath when Constantine dipped his quill into the inkwell and Geoffry muttering back that he was going to hack Ronald into pieces and feed him to the wild animals if he made another sound.

Constantine's peace was still held firmly intact after he paid MacKintosh 25,000 merks and then drank to peace with his men in a tavern a half league from Gairlochy.

It ended with a patron who sat at a wooden table stained with rings from hundreds of cups. He wore a thick woolen plaid in shades of blue and green and a blue bonnet atop his oily yellow hair. The cup from which he drank contributed to the stained table when he set it down.

When they were done having a drink, Constantine and his cousins rose to leave. Following behind them, Constantine was the last one to reach the door.

"Tastes like piss," the stranger complained, swiping his knuckles across his thick lips. He looked at Constantine watching him from the door and chuckled, exposing a row of yellowed teeth. "There is nothing else aroond, so 'twill have to do, aye?"

Constantine turned away. He didn't care who this stranger was. He preferred to let Miss Drummond flit around in his head over talking to a man with airs about him that reminded Constantine of a few Cromwellians who wished they hadn't met Lochiel of Lochaber.

"Alistair MacRae," the stranger introduced himself. "Clan Chief of the MacRaes of Beauly."

Constantine set his hand on the door. MacRaes. He thought

hard about whether the Camerons and MacRaes were enemies. He couldn't recall any battles with them. He was sure he remembered hearing that the MacRaes were staunch supporters of the MacKenzies.

Constantine looked over his shoulder at him. If he didn't need to kill or maim the man, there was nothing else to say to him, so without reciprocating the introduction, he pushed open the door to the tavern. He saw his cousins waiting for him outside.

"I'm stopping in every burgh, nae matter how small, to find her. Mayhap ye have seen her?"

Constantine halted his steps and returned his attention to him. "Who?"

"My betrothed."

"Yer betrothed fled from ye?" Could this be...? Constantine took a step closer to him, his dark gaze locked onto the stranger.

The man's lips grew tight belying the friendliness of his smile. "I didna say she fled, good friend."

"I said nothin' to give ye the impression that we are good friends," Constantine countered with a warning thread in his tone.

"Ah," the man laughed without any mirth. "Fergive me, ye surely didna say anything of the sort."

"What aboot yer betrothed?" Constantine steered him back to the previous topic.

"Alas, my dear Ismay disappeared from her home and I fear she may have been abducted."

Constantine's world rocked back and forth. He put his fingers to his head as if that might still him. Was he moving? Did this bastard say Ismay? He was the *cruel* betrothed from whom she'd fled. She was correct about him searching for her. He had come as close as Gairlochy?

"I'm heading back to Beauly, but I'm asking everyone I meet...so tell me, I beg ye, have ye mayhap seen her passing this way? She has hair the color of autumn leaves."

Constantine thought he might be ill if he had to listen to this swine speak of her another instant. He had to get home to her. MacRae was close. Constantine had to reach her first.

"She has the face of a goddess," the fool continued, taking his life into his own hands. "And the tongue of a viper." Did he realize he was scowling while he spoke of her? "She's bewitching and if a man is no' careful he will find himself charmed beyond good reason."

Constantine did his best to conceal his trembling muscles. "Is that what ye're tellin' everyone ye meet?" he asked him through his ground jaw. "That she is dangerous?"

"Och, she is," MacRae insisted.

Constantine wanted to kill him for trying to force Ismay to marry him. But he didn't have to kill him. The bastard was heading to his home in Beauly. Still, before Constantine leaped for MacRae's throat, he stormed out of the tavern.

He needed to get back to the castle...back to Ismay Drummond.

✳

CHAPTER SEVENTEEN

"THISTLE, MISS DRUMMOND?" Lady MacMillan sneered at the embroidered flower on Ismay's handkerchief. "Can you not think of a more delicate flower?"

Ismay looked at it and sighed. She was weary of contending with this woman.

The MacMillans were supposed to leave the same morning Constantine left, but Baron MacMillan, Alison's father had fallen ill in the night. The castle healer insisted the baron stay at Tor and recuperate. So, five days later, they were still there.

Five days may not be overly long, but in that time, Lady MacMillan had taken over the embroidery room, scrutinizing the ladies' sewing, especially Ismay's. When she wasn't sucking her teeth at Ismay's sewing skill, or her taste in what she sewed—like thistle instead of the primroses everyone else sewed—she followed wherever Ismay went and always found something about Ismay to criticize.

"Delicate flowers die too easily," Ismay told her, without looking up. "I prefer something more hearty that will live through the winters of its life."

For a moment, Lady MacMillan looked about to faint.

Ismay leaped from her chair and reached for her. "Are ye all right, my lady?"

Lady MacMillan, with cheeks as red as a summer sunrise,

hauled back her hand and slapped Ismay across the face. "How dare you liken my Alison to something weak and pitiful!"

Ismay furrowed her brow at her. "What? What are ye talking about? I was speaking of flowers!"

But Alison's mother didn't want an answer, nor did she wait for one. Taking a step closer to Ismay, she spoke through clenched teeth. "I will see to it that you never step into my daughter's shoes."

Hilary, who bolted to her feet when Ismay was struck, stepped forward. "And how will ye do that, my lady? The Lochiel willna listen to ye. He already cares fer her! Quit holding my cousin hostage to yer guilt. Yer daughter died giving birth. I'm sorry to say it happens all the time. Alison was not weak because she died. Ye know that isna what Ismay was saying. Ye simply want to hate her because the Lochiel likes her."

As usual, Hilary said too much.

Lady MacMillan gasped in a succession of three deep breaths that Ismay thought might make the older woman faint for certain. And then she left the embroidery room.

Alone with the other women of Tor, Ismay covered her face. She wasn't embarrassed by being slapped. It wasn't the first time. But she had never fought a ghost's mother before. It felt terrible, weighing more on Ismay's shoulders every day.

Where was Constantine? Was he fighting or on his way back? She missed his face, always so impassive, softening into humor or fondness at the sight of her. She was becoming the only thing soft about him. She liked that most, being his soft spot. But wasn't a warrior's soft spot his most vulnerable, most valuable possession?

Just how dangerous would it be for the Lochiel if she owned his heart? Hurting her would be the easiest way to hurt him.

Contemplating leaving Tor was becoming easier with each day Constantine wasn't there. There were so many reasons she should continue on her path to the safety of a convent. She wasn't made to be a wife. What if he was abusive toward her after time passed? What if he stopped loving her, or even grew to hate her?

What if he ordered her about and forbade her look askew at any man but him or he would take a knife to her tresses?

She shook her head. Could she avoid what she feared so many times in her life? Aye, but it was only guaranteed if she left.

But Constantine Cameron laid all her doubts to ruin. He would not physically hurt her. He was soft and thoughtful.

"I'm not hurt," she said looking up at the other women there, including Bethia. "She is in worse pain than I. Imagine losing yer child and yer grandchild hours apart?"

"Ismay, ye're a better person than I am," Hilary told her with a slight blush across her cheeks. "I wouldna fergive her fer striking me."

Ismay wondered painfully if Hilary would forgive her when she discovered she'd murdered a MacDonald chief.

"It looks to be a beautiful day," she remarked looking toward the window and needing some fresh air. "Let us go out."

"All right!" Hilary exclaimed and clapped her hands. "We can read!" She leaned in closer to Ismay's ear. "I'm in possession of banned books in support of the monarchy under King Charles ll."

Ismay was in support of the monarchy, so she agreed happily and looped her arm through Hilary's to leave.

They invited Joan to join them under the great oak tree but before long, reading became giggles about the Lochiel, Lachlan, and Hilary's betrothed, John.

The afternoon passed without incident with Lady MacMillan.

Ismay thought she might like to spend the rest of her days with Constantine resting under this tree.

A voice calling her name shattered her pleasant thoughts. She looked toward a lass she recognized as one of the servers at the Doomsday Inn and Tavern. Coleen! Ismay smiled and waved at her as she hurried closer.

"Coleen, is everything well with ye?" she asked after seeing the gel's anxious gaze.

"I remembered his name, my lady."

"Who, Coleen?"

"The patron at the tavern who asked about ye," Coleen let her know.

Aye, the man of mystery who—

"He said he was called MacRae, Alistair MacRae. From where, I canna recall," Coleen said regretfully.

Ismay stumbled back. Joan hurried to catch her. It was Chief MacRae. Ismay knew it. She knew if she stopped or slowed down he would catch up to her.

"Och, my lady," Coleen lamented seeing Ismay's reaction to the news. "Who is he? He didna seem unfriendly or dangerous at the tavern. Is he not a friend?"

A friend. Why had he pretended to be a friend looking for her? So as not to rouse her suspicions if she found out he was close by, she told herself. And it had worked.

She cast a nervous glance around the perimeter of the back garden. Was he near? Och, Constantine, where are ye?

"We should go inside," she suggested to the others and herded them in, looking over her shoulder as she went.

She gave Coleen a brief explanation about why she did not want him to find her. To Joan and Hilary, she said even less. They knew who Alistar MacRae was. She'd told them just last night.

What if he showed up here? Would he hurt these women without the young men here to save them? She knew what she had to do. If he hurt Joan or Hilary, or any of her other friends…she couldn't think of it. She had put them all in danger by coming here.

If Constantine were here—but he wasn't.

"Joan, please tell Hugh not to let in any strangers, no matter who they say they are, until the men return."

"Ismay," her friend began, reaching for her.

"I'm fine, Joan. I just need to think. Alone." She looked from Joan to Hilary.

"If no one lets him in," Hilary noted, "there's no way fer him to know ye're here."

Ismay shook her head. With each passing moment, her heart

beat faster. "Someone may tell him. The baker and the tanner come and go. One of them could mention me if he describes me. I have to think," she added when her two friends gave no rebuttal but stared at her.

"I'm going to my chambers. Joan, please dinna ferget to tell Hugh."

When the chambermaid nodded, Hilary took both their hands in hers. "We will keep ye safe, Ismay. I will kill him if he somehow finds ye."

Ismay could almost hear Constantine's voice promising to keep her safe. She wanted to throw her arms around her braw friend and thank her, but she also wanted to scold her. Ismay could not live with herself if Hilary was hurt...or worse, because of her.

After sending them on their way, she nearly collapsed while she ascended the stairs as thoughts of running overwhelmed her. She didn't want to run away. She liked it at Tor Castle. She liked her friends and she liked the Lochiel—very much. But she had always known that her stay here was temporary. It was best for everyone, even without the threat of Alistar MacRae. Hadn't she already decided that?

Aye. It was time to stop being idle and indecisive. It was time to leave.

She didn't mention her plans to Joan or Hilary when they visited her chambers later that evening. She wanted their last night together to be spent smiling and laughing together. She also didn't want anyone to try to change her mind, which her friends would no doubt do. Her resolve was too weak. She would never leave if they wept over her. But the threat had become very real.

"What was the Lochiel like in his youth?" she asked Hilary, since Hilary was his cousin and they had all grown up together.

"Och, he was mayhem with a heart."

Ismay laughed at such a description. "Explain, if ye please."

"When he was just eleven summers old," Hilary began with a furtive grin, "he robbed the chicken pens of almost every

MacKintosh clan from Lochiel to Inverness. Him and his wee accomplices—my brothers and some of the other lads—werena caught fer a year and half a year after that. But what was Gilbert to do aboot it? He loved his brother and wouldna punish him, and I think he secretly admired his little brother's courage.

"When his chicken thieving days were over, he was always away fighting or raiding cattle. He even took to robbing others on the road. Whether on horse or in their fancy carriages, Constantine took everything they carried with them. But he left them alive. He was trouble away from home, but the moment he stepped back inside Tor, his heart was restored. He was good-natured and he smiled often."

"And he changed so much after Alison and his babe died?" Ismay asked, knowing by now what it had done to his heart to lose them.

"Och, nae, he changed after Gilbert sent him off to fight in Scotland's wars. It had only taken a sennight to realize what a skilled fighter and brilliant strategist Constantine was. He remained a soldier fer a long time. He started changing after that. He smiled less when he came home. He barely slept and grew agitated often. But the lasses still loved him. He met Alison and they eventually wed."

Ismay held up her hand. She knew most of the rest from Constantine telling her.

"What kind of child were ye, Ismay?" Joan asked, appearing completely engrossed by learning what kind of children they were.

But Ismay couldn't tell her. She couldn't tell her that she'd been a filthy waif who needed the mercy of a stranger to keep her alive.

So, she just smiled and shook her head at herself. "I was a quiet child. I kept to myself most of the time. When I met Alistar MacRae I knew he wasna the man fer me. When he cut off my hair at my mother's dining table, I was frightened of what he might do after we were wed. So I ran away. 'Twas cowardly."

"Cowardly?" Hilary asked incredulously. "I would say 'twas quite a courageous thing ye did to protect yerself! I am certain he would have hurt ye. Best that ye left before he did."

"I put myself and possibly others in grave danger," she insisted quietly.

"Mayhap," Joan said, hesitantly, "ye should have let Hugh send word to the Lochiel."

"And distract him on the battlefield?" Ismay gave her a horrified look. "Nae! I am certain there is nae reason fer our alarm. If MacRae meant to come here, he would have been here already. The tavern isna far."

The others agreed with her, and soon they were laughing once again about this silly thing or that. They all agreed, it was better than weeping over the men they missed.

Ismay had to push them out of her chambers toward midnight, blaming her sleepy eyes for sending them away.

Alone, she wiped those same eyes as tears spilled from them the instant the door closed. Then she set about packing. She didn't have much more than what she arrived with: a few more dresses which she would take to sell and the trinkets her father had given her. She donned her old breeches and coat and a man's tattered plaid.

Tucking her hair under her bonnet, she left her chambers a little after the second hour past midnight. She stayed close to the wall as she descended the stairs, afraid someone might be awake and see her. Hugh and Bethia did not usually stay awake too long after dark. But she would hate to run into either of them. She tiptoed and scurried in the shadows like a thief in the night, there to rob the inhabitants of their safety. Not her. Nae. She was getting out before they were threatened any further.

She left Tor Castle the way she left her father's house in Raigmore. But tonight she wasn't escaping for her safety. She was going for the safety of others.

With each silent step she took, her heart broke a little more. She didn't even get to bid farewell to Constantine or thank him for everything he had done for her, especially heal her heart. Mayhap, she would return one day. MacRae wouldn't look for her twice in the same place, would he?

She left the castle and began to run. Darkness overtook her, sounds of nocturnal wildlife filled her ears. She remembered this lonely feeling from her journey to Lochaber. Like being the only person left in the world. The thought had become comforting to her in her three months alone, but not anymore.

Now, she felt cold, besides the drop in the fall weather. The world had changed in a short time. She had discovered that there was a man alive out there who could help her love instead of feeding her hatred and hurt. Was she wrong to want a life for decades more with a man like that?

She had to stop twice to lean against a tree and cry her eyes out. She cried harder and shed more tears for having to leave Tor than she had shed into her stew at Lewis's tavern and inn.

But fear kept her going, farther away from the place she was starting to feel was home.

She hadn't slept when the sun began its lazy ascent. Her feet were blistered as she traveled. Ah, she remembered that too. Her feet were a testament to becoming harder after struggle. Staying still had weakened her.

The worst thing was the food she had saved from the night before. It smelled rotten. She put it away as her belly grumbled. She had become spoiled by eating a rich breakfast in the morning.

Thankfully, by noon she found a small inn near the town of Torlundy. She was able to pay for a meal and a room for the night with one of her silk dresses.

After eating delicious hare stew with turnips and carrots and freshly baked black bread, Ismay went to her room and slept until the darkness settled over the inn.

She dreamed of Constantine and when she woke, she missed him more than ever. Would she ever see him again? Aye. Aye, she would. Someday.

She wept in the darkness outside the inn. She knew she

wasn't safe out there all alone. It was a terrible feeling, and one she'd lived with every day after she ran away from her mother and her betrothed.

Her betrothed. Ha! She almost laughed through her tears as she made her way southeast in the darkness. She would never marry Alistar MacRae. She would die first—or keep running.

Horrifyingly, she thought it possible that she could even kill him in order to save herself from becoming his property. She remembered his crass words in front of her mother, his condescending smirk when he vowed that she would be his, his contorted, angry face before he stepped behind her and sawed off her curls with his dirty dagger. If possible, she hated him more now than she had. For now, she knew what a true man, a good man, was like. Constantine's radiance made Alistar all the more dark.

A forest spread out before her. Rather than walk through it, she traveled the extra distance around it until morning. She kept going, ignoring her painful feet and empty stomach.

A small sign on the road indicated that she was approaching Inverlochy Castle. She went the opposite way, not knowing it had been abandoned over a decade ago, but only thinking of avoiding another castle likely owned by a clan chief. She headed toward the hills and glens until early evening, when she came to a vast glen covered in a lush carpet of purple thistle.

She stopped in her tracks and lifted her hands to her chest. She had seen late blooming thistles in Constantine's misty hills, but she had never seen anything like this, with thistle growing through the early frost, vibrant and hearty, surviving where other flora would die.

She stepped forward into the prickly flowers and smiled. Like the thistle, she would survive just to see him again.

"A good eve to ye, young lord!"

Ismay whirled around and saw a man stand to his feet among the thistles. His face was dirty and his hair stood up in various directions as spindly as the plants around him.

He grinned, revealing several blackened or missing teeth.

"Where are ye headin?" he asked.

Ismay looked around. There was nothing but purple flowers. It didn't matter. She had no choice but to take off running. She ran until she had no air left in her lungs. Finally, she cleared the thistles and reached a dirt path.

Bending to grip her knees, she let her breathing slow a bit. She turned around to see if he was still chasing her. She was thankful that it seemed she had outrun him. She decided she was going to need a weapon of some sort. For now, she reached down and picked up a stick.

She didn't see anyone again until she came to the second inn, the Trapped Deer.

She paid for a meal of bread and porridge and a small room behind the tavern with silk petticoats and matching stays.

She barred herself in but barely had closed her eyes when someone broke through the barricaded door to her room and came at her in the bed. She screamed and reached for her stick but he reached her first. He didn't rape her but covered her face in a cloth soaked with something wet but odorless. Her struggle was brief, for with each breath she took she sank deeper into an endless black pit.

She woke up a few hours later feeling as if her head had been smashed in with an anvil. Her body shook and rolled a little. She thought she was dying. A moment later she realized she was in the back of a moving covered carriage. Every time the wheels rolled over a stone or a dip in the road, she wanted to cry out at the pain. Others were crying or moaning around her. Women. When she tested opening her eyes she saw a dozen other women around her.

Someone had kidnapped them! Where were they taking her and the others?

Instead of being afraid, she felt angry. Enraged. How dare any man kidnap women and enslave them? Even animals deserved better.

But there were other kinds of men.

The thought of Constantine filled her thoughts just long enough to help her think clearly. He was fond of her. She knew it by the way he kissed her, the way his gaze spread over her, as if he were burning her into his memory. If she died, like his first wife, it would break his heart. She was determined not to let that happen.

Wherever they were headed, she had other plans that didn't include being a servant to anyone ever again. Whether it was MacRae or some other kidnapper, they were the same. Her promise to herself still stood. She would escape or die trying.

Looking up and around at the heavy covering, she could see that it was tied to strips of wood, and in one corner, the laces that tied the covering to the wood had come undone. Her hands were tied behind her back, but she scrambled her way to the corner and tried to fit herself out of the hole. It was too small.

Using nothing but her teeth, she pulled the next knot loose and looked out of the carriage. The land moving by her didn't look familiar. She didn't know where they were. But that wouldn't stop her.

Looking back at the other women, she whispered for them to follow her. They all shook their heads. They were too afraid and refused to follow her.

Without another word, Ismay crouched and tossed herself out of the carriage.

She hit the ground hard and rolled before she smashed her head against a rock. Then the world, wherever she was, grew black.

"Lady! Lady, wake up!"

Someone shook her and shouted at her until she opened her eyes. Och, her head. She reached for it.

"Hugh?"

"Lady, och thank the good Lord. Come now, let us get ye out of the middle of the road."

"Hugh," she managed while he lifted her in his arms. "How

did ye find me?"

"I followed ye when ye slipped out of the castle. I'm ashamed to admit that I lost ye twice."

He was still speaking when she closed her eyes again.

It was Hugh. She was safe now.

Wasn't she?

CHAPTER EIGHTEEN

CONSTANTINE NEARED TOR Castle and threw off his unused weapons and travel bags and quickened his steps the rest of the way to the doors. He no longer cared about the warnings blaring through his head that he should not care again. Nor did he care about what others thought of him offering his heart to another.

He had waited long enough to see her and to see that she was safe. The man her mother had promised her would come after her. Now was more important than ever to make certain Ismay was safe. He could not get home quickly enough.

But before he reached the doors, Hilary MacDonald burst from the castle. After she made certain her betrothed still lived, she cried to Constantine that Ismay had left.

At first, he was certain he didn't hear her right. Then he prayed he hadn't.

"What did ye say?" he asked numbly.

"She's gone, Lochiel."

Before she said another word, Alison's parents left the castle to meet him.

When he saw them, Constantine assumed if Ismay had any reason to leave, it had to do with these two, who were supposed to have left days ago.

He stormed toward them with rage in his eyes. Lady MacMillan stepped back and covered her neck as if he meant to rip it out. "What did ye say to her to make her leave?

"Lochiel," Lady MacMillan dared to bite out. "Yer dear Miss Drummond didna run away because of us. She left because she got wind of a man searching for her close by. Ye were not here once again to protect the woman in yer life."

For just an instant his eyes darkened on her. Leave it to her to point out another failure. He felt something rise up in his belly. Lady MacMillan hated him. He didn't blame her, but he was sick and tired of the enormous weight of guilt he carried. If Alison's mother had such hatred in her heart against him, there was no longer any reason for her or her husband to visit.

"I told ye both to leave Tor. If ye are not gone by the time I return, I will use force to evict ye." He slipped his hard gaze to Bethia next. "Ye go with them."

Without another word, he turned to cast his cousin a glare only slightly less dark. "What happened, Hilary? Where did she go?"

"I dinna know where she went, cousin. She found out that bastard MacRae had been at the Doomsday Tavern. We planned on not letting him inside the castle, but she ran away in the night."

Constantine felt his knees quake beneath him. *She left in the night.* He covered his face with his hand. "Did anyone go with her?"

"Not that I am aware of," Hilary told him. "But Hugh seems to have disappeared the same night."

Hugh? Constantine's guts seared inside him. If the steward hurt her, he would kill him. "What night was it? How long ago?"

"Three nights now."

Constantine thought he was going to be sick. They were three nights ahead of him. According to Hilary, no one knew in which direction she traveled.

She'd found out that MacRae was at Lewis's tavern. So then, Constantine reasoned, it was definitely MacRae he had met near

Clumes. But that meant MacRae was moving farther away. Still, Ismay didn't know. She was afraid and she ran. Rather than leap on his horse and guess the way she went, he thought about it for a quarter of an hour, fighting off Lady MacMillan's words in his head. He hadn't been here for Ismay just as he hadn't been here for Alison.

The urgent need to find her helped him battle the guilt. Where was the nearest convent? Did Ismay know about it?

After thinking on it, he saddled his fastest horse and took off, riding northeast. He didn't go far when he suddenly stopped short. Dangling from a low branch before him was a parchment waving in the cool breeze. He rode closer and looked at the writing.

L,

Go southeast.

H

Constantine read it again. It had to be from Hugh. The steward was one of the few living at Tor Castle who could read and write. Still, it could have been written by some other traveler. But the *L* it was addressed to had to be Lochiel, and southeast was the way Ismay was traveling.

Constantine turned his head to look that way. It was the direction of Ben Nevis—and his house. Was Ismay heading to the house he'd built? Was she mad to try to go alone? She knew the man she almost married was on her tail. How did she know he wasn't also going that way?

He whirled his horse around and flicked the reins. Just let her have arrived there safe and sound, he prayed as his mount's hooves tore up the dirt behind him.

He stopped at the first inn he came to, near Torlundy and asked the innkeeper if he'd seen a lad with burnished autumn hair. He didn't want to waste time traveling the wrong way because he was wrong about a missive he'd found. The innkeep had in fact given a lad of that description a meal and a room.

So then, Constantine's heart rejoiced, she had come this way, for certain.

Without wasting any time, he started out again, traveling around the forest without stopping, until he came to the abandoned ruins of Inverlochy Castle. Would she stop here on her way to his house? Was Hugh traveling with her?

"Well then!" a man's voice called out on the road just outside the castle. "Look who it is!"

Constantine turned and set his eyes on Alistar MacRae. He was searching for Ismay.

"Has yer search led ye here?"

"It has," MacRae confessed with a smile. "The wench would come running to the shelter of a castle—even an empty one."

Constantine disagreed. He should thank MacRae, for he was reminded that Ismay would never trust the chief of any castle. He recalled how much persuading it took to get her to go to Tor with him. She hadn't stopped here.

"I thought ye were returnin' to Beauly?" Constantine asked him.

"I received word that my Ismay was seen farther south. What brings ye here, Lochiel?"

He knew who Constantine was. That meant he'd asked about him. "My steward robbed me while I was away fightin'. I'm told he was seen in Inverlochy."

MacRae frowned. "He deserves fifty lashes fer robbing ye. 'Tis what I will give my betrothed."

Constantine stared at him long enough to make the Beauly chief tremble in his plaid. "Should I deliver her to ye if I find her first?"

"I would be in yer debt," MacRae managed. "Remember, ye will know her by her fiery hair. Careful she doesna bewitch ye with her tresses. I myself had to cut them off, before I lost the ability of my good senses."

"Ye cut off her hair?" Constantine asked him in a low, steady voice as memories of her autumn-hued hair falling over her eyes or pinned up with bonnie pearl clips.

But by social standards, short hair for women was their shame. Constantine would kick out anyone's teeth who dared shame Ismay, starting with this worm.

Constantine would deal with him before he crossed into Ben Nevis territory.

"As any man has the right to do to his betrothed."

She was not his betrothed. Not as long as Constantine lived. He smiled, controlling himself—just barely—to keep his hands off MacRae's throat.

"Though..." MacRae looked off and away, as if he was remembering her. ... "it didna stop her from flicking her viperous tongue."

Constantine fought the urge to smile, proud of her and her viperous tongue.

Where are ye headin' now?" Constantine asked him, eager to follow him until he had him in a secluded area.

"South."

"Well then," Constantine turned his horse toward the open gate.

But after an hour of following MacRae southwest, he caught up with him again.

"Lochiel." MacRae looked sincerely startled to see him.

Constantine dismounted, then walked around his horse and yanked MacRae out of his saddle. "Ismay is nae longer anythin' to ye. Do ye understand? Ye cut off her hair. Ye were so cruel to her that runnin' into a world completely unknown to her was better than stayin' with ye. And here ye are chasin' her still, as if she were an animal. I'm goin' to end it all fer good. I'm goin' to repay ye fer everythin'."

His fist cracking MacRae's jaw was satisfying. But it wasn't enough. Clutching MacRae's plaid with one fist, he slammed the other into flesh and bone over and over until MacRae was barely recognizable.

When he was done, he leaned down, his lips close to MacRae's ear. "If ye ever go near her again I will kill ye. I vow it."

He left the chief of Beauly bleeding in the dirt and started on the road back home toward Ben Nevis.

"Aye, I saw him," confessed a red-cheeked patron at the Trapped Deer tavern. He grinned at the merk in Constantine's hand. "But they dinna take lads, so I'm guessin' he was a she."

Constantine heard only four words. His tongue felt like it was swelling up when he spoke. "They dinna take lads? They take lasses?"

The patron nodded, keeping his eyes on the shiny merk. "Aye, lasses. They carried her off and put her in the carriage."

This couldn't be! She'd been kidnapped? Nae! Nae! He had to find her. "Where did they take her?"

The patron shrugged his shoulders. "I canna be certain, but I think they were headed south."

Constantine paid the patron and sprang from his seat. He stopped before he hurried out. "Who is the proprietor of this establishment where women are absconded in the night and taken away?"

"Ewen Campbell. I am told."

Constantine nodded. "Thank ye."

The patron looked into his hand and smiled. "Nae. Thank ye."

Constantine searched for her day and night, hoping, praying she was safe in his house.

Once, he was haunted by Alison but now Ismay alone invaded his thoughts. Her smile and her laughter. The way she hadn't let her childhood keep her in some prison of her own making. As he had done. She was understandably mistrusting. But she trusted him, and it made him feel important and worthy again.

When he slept, he dreamed of her. He laughed in his dreams. He loved her in them and relished in the freedom of it.

He finally reached the home that he'd built below Ben Nevis. He wasted no time leaping from his moving horse and running toward the door.

He went through every room. She wasn't there. Hugh wasn't there. There was no sign of them. He ran his hand down his face and tried to think clearly. Was he ahead of her? Should he wait? What if she wasn't coming here specifically? He rose up, not thinking about his weary body or his even wearier thoughts.

He'd been so busy trying to run from her and from what he was beginning to feel for her, that he hadn't realized how much he enjoyed having her in his life. He wanted her back in it. He would tell her that he didn't want her to leave. His kin already loved her.

Hugh was with her. His steward wouldn't hurt her. He was helping her. Constantine didn't care why. He was glad Hugh was watching over her.

He got back up in his saddle. He didn't care what it took. He would find her and he would make certain she never felt the need to run again.

But first, he had to find her.

SOMETHING COLD HIT her face. Ismay opened her eyes and gasped at the icy water up her nose.

"Wake up, wench!" A man's voice commanded. His tattered boots crunched the dry hay under his feet.

The dry hay that poked her in the back since she'd been thrown into it the night before. She tried to remember what happened. She had been kidnapped. She had jumped from a moving carriage. The memory of it pulled a moan from her lips and her hand to her head.

"I said up!" the oaf, whom she noted was bald when she sat up, shouted at her.

"Who are ye?" she asked him quietly. She realized with a sickening twist in her belly that she was still afraid of them.

"What do ye want?"

He stormed toward her. She gritted her teeth not to cower before him.

"Who do ye think ye are to ask me questions?" He raised his hand behind his head to strike her.

Nae. She was sick and tired of fearing men. Constantine and his cousins were not like these bad ones. And why should she be afraid? Didn't she have two hands and decent enough wits in her head to fight back? She did when she was eight.

Dipping her eyes, Ismay saw what she needed. She reached out and snatched the hilt of a dirk sticking out from under his belt.

Instead of his palm hitting her face, it met the steel of his dirk. He screamed, staring in horror at his blade going through his palm and coming out the other side. She scrambled under him as he fell to his knees.

She looked around for another weapon to use against him. She was in a barn. There was lots of hay.

"Ye bitch!" he screamed at her.

She remembered her few lessons with Constantine and stepped to the right to grab a pitchfork. She held it like a spear and when he reached for her with his bloody hand, she jabbed the points of metal into his forearm and drove him to the ground.

She looked around while he screamed like an alarm to whoever was outside.

And then she did what she'd learned to do best. She ran.

When she burst out of the stable doors, she paused to let her eyes adjust to the night. She moved to continue running but a memory stopped her. She had been quite ill. She reached up to touch her head. It was still sore. A man had been with her. He took her to a small cottage to have her wound seen to by an old healer. Men had broken into the cottage to get to her. She'd recognize their voices as the same who had kidnapped her at the inn. Had they followed her? Who was the man who'd carried her to the healer? Hugh!

Where was Hugh?

To her left was a small village aglow in the moonlight. To her right, a large wood house with a single window lit by a candle from inside. Where was she?

Ahead of her was pitch black. She could run into it and disappear, but she couldn't leave Hugh.

She turned around to face the house and ran toward it. Reaching it, she crouched in the shadows and scurried along to the lit window on the ground floor.

She had to stand on a rock to reach, but she looked inside. Her brow knit together and her breath felt short in her body.

Seated at the back of a desk, across from a man who looked more like a high-ranking soldier than a Highlander, was Hugh.

A hundred reasons why Constantine's steward was here assailed Ismay's thoughts. None of them were in his favor. Was he fraternizing with the people who had thrown her into a haystack?

She cursed the steward and whirled on her heel to start running, when she hit a wall made of lean, hard muscle and a throbbing heart.

Her eyes adjusted to the dim light and when she saw him, she threw herself into his arms. "Constantine," she cried against his chest. "I knew ye would find me. I just had to stay alive until ye did."

His arms closed around her and pulled her closer, as if she were his most precious possession. But he hadn't tried to possess her. He had agreed to her freedom. She could leave Tor whenever she wished. It made her want to stay forever. He thought it his inherent duty to protect her, and he always would.

"Ismay," he whispered after quickly looking through the window, "dinna make a sound."

He broke away from her and disappeared inside the house. Should she follow?

Immediately, she heard things crashing to the floor inside. Fighting. She chanced a peek in the window. She saw Constantine tossing a man across the room and into the wall. It was the man in the military uniform. She looked around but didn't see Hugh.

Where was Hugh?

$$\text{---}\ \text{✳}\ \text{---}$$

CHAPTER NINETEEN

THE WORLD AROUND Ismay was dark, but she wasn't afraid to lie beneath the canopy of shedding branches. How could she be afraid held tightly in the embrace of the most lethal chief in the Highlands? She didn't doubt for an instant that Constantine couldn't keep her safe.

His body was slightly harder than the ground and immensely warmer.

They didn't sleep, but that wasn't because either of them were afraid.

"It would have served no purpose to tell ye MacRae cut my hair," Ismay told him drowsily.

Instead of answering, he ran his palm over her head, down to her shoulder where her tresses stopped. "As much as it angers me, I dinna think killin' him fer his crime is deservin' of death. I take so much pleasure in the sight of yer throat and yer earlobes thanks to yer short hair."

He made her smile. Anyone who dared suggest the Lochiel was a melancholy tyrant would answer to her!

They ended up speaking about Alistar MacRae. She had finally told Constantine his name. "I thought he might hurt the others if I was there."

"Ye dinna need to run anymore," he whispered into her hair.

"While MacRae is alive, I should be worried. Ye see that he

was at the Doomsday Inn. Think of how close he was."

"He willna look fer ye anymore, Ismay."

She picked up the sharp edge in his voice and looked up at him. "What do ye mean?"

He was quiet for a moment. "I met him in Inverlochy."

He met MacRae? Ismay blinked her eyes. "What? Ye met him?"

Did MacRae tell him who she was guilty of killing? That she was a MacPherson?

"What did he tell ye?"

"He told me ye had a viperous tongue and that ye beguiled men oot of their senses."

Was that all? MacRae didn't tell him she was a MacPherson?

She pouted her lips. "Ye didna believe those things, did ye?"

"I believed every word," he replied succinctly.

She lifted her head off his chest and stared at him in the dark. "What is that supposed to mean?"

"My precious flower," he elaborated softly, deeply. "Ye have indeed bewitched my logic—"

She sat up and took a swipe at him. "What is the matter with yer logic now?"

"It has abandoned me and set ye in the place of everythin' else."

She felt her hackles settling. Was he telling her she came before everything else?

"In that case," she told him, leaning in close to his lips, "ye have bewitched me, as well. "But, Constantine, he didna tell ye anything else?"

"What else is there?" he asked.

If the MacDonalds at Tor found out the truth about her, they would likely want to kill her.

"Nothing else," she lied.

"Dinna fret over him any longer," he reassured in his deliciously deep voice.

Trusting him, she snuggled close against him and listened to the sound of his heartbeat in her ear.

He stroked her hair and back until she grew too tired to keep her eyes open. But she wasn't asleep. Her mind was too fixated on what was happening to her heart. Even now in this moment of listening to his breathing coming slow and steady, her heart was swelling with affection for him. How was it possible that he had infiltrated all her defenses, tore down walls she had erected beginning when she was almost too young to remember why she needed them?

Despite her father rescuing her from the MacDonalds, it had taken her years to learn to trust him. Nae, it had not happened overnight. She trusted Constantine early on though. Was it because he had passed her father's test and kept his word? There were other signs her father taught her to recognize a good man. Did Constantine have good people around him? People who loved him?

His kin loved him for certain. They gave him their respect— not a meager offering coming from a Highlander. And why shouldn't they respect him? He had made them rich with cattle. No one in the entire region wanted for anything. He kept them all fed, housed, and busy with work. He made the Camerons of Lochaber a name to be revered.

She hadn't let a villain into her heart, but a good man, who knew how to water it and keep it blooming. She smiled against him and whispered into his chest.

"Thank ye fer finding me, Constantine."

CONSTANTINE LAY AWAKE in rays of filtered sunlight coming through the trees. Beside him, Ismay slept, set aflame in the dawn. She took his breath away. He was ready to die for her, but he would rather live with her.

He pulled his plaid up around her delicate shoulders. Delicate but strong enough to drive a pitchfork through a man's arm.

His heart warmed on her for the dozenth time this morning. She was soft on the outside and so strong on the inside. She was fashioned for the Highlands. Fashioned for him. What was he going to do about it? He didn't want to think about the future but this moment. When she slept in his arms, treasured in his eyes.

But it was time for them to go. Until Hugh was found and questioned, being out in the open wasn't wise.

He knew how he wanted to wake her, and so leaning in, he pressed his lips to hers and kissed her briefly, then moving on, he kissed her closed eyes, her temples, and buried his face in her tresses.

He felt her awaken in his embrace and smiled when she clung to him more tightly.

"There were so many times I thought I lost ye."

"Ye will never lose me," she reassured him, the strength in her eyes proof of her bold claim.

They kissed a little more. Constantine wanted more. His body felt feverish with his need.

Not here. "Let us go home."

She sprang up smiling and putting the sun to shame. "Home?"

"Aye," he said with a quiet, knowing smile. "That is where ye were headin' was it no'?"

"I didna know it until I was halfway here," she admitted with a slight laugh. "I think in my heart I hoped ye would know where to look fer me."

He sat up with her and shook his head. Confusion knit his brow remembering his steward's missive. "We have Hugh to thank fer that."

"He carried me off the road after I jumped from a slaver's carriage."

Constantine let the rage that boiled beneath the surface cool. He rose to his feet and took her hand to help her up.

"Ye jumped from a *movin'* carriage?"

Her eyes searched his, and finding the furious beast crouching in the shadows, she smiled as if her action was of no importance. She was incorrect.

"What else could I do, Constantine? I couldna stay with them, aye?"

He gazed into her eyes, as sunshine and stars restored his heart to life. He was in love with her. He almost sighed, thinking what a challenge she was going to be. He smiled instead.

When she took a step away from him. He took her hand and pulled her back.

"Ismay, take me as yer husband."

She grew serious, staring at him in disbelief. "Why?"

"Why?" he echoed. He was hoping for an *aye*, not expecting a *why*.

"Why have ye changed yer mind? A sennight ago ye couldna let go of yer past. Now ye're eager to race into another?"

He could have been offended at her criticism, but she was correct to question him. The change in him surprised him, as well.

He told her the truth. "'Tis as if I were in the darkness and I didna know it until ye shined yer light. Now, I never want to go back."

Her bonnie eyes opencd wide and her smile grew. "In that case, my answer is aye."

He surprised her—and himself by the elation he felt. Swooping down, he lifted her off her feet and carried her laughing and cradled in his arms to his horse.

They shared his mount for a short way. The horse wasn't built for two and Constantine would not push the beast.

With the reins in one hand and her hand in the other, he led her to the home he'd built.

He looked around at the hills darkened in the shadow of the high mountain range of Ben Nevis in the distance.

"I had to position my house where the shadows didna reach. It took two months to get it precisely correct, but being washed in the radiance of sunlight is worth any struggle to find it."

She blushed and smiled knowing he was referring to her.

When the house finally came into view, Constantine remembered how much he loved it here, in his little sunlit glade beneath the great Nevis. He could do nothing but smile when Ismay broke away from him and ran forward.

He hadna had the chance to live here happily yet. He planned on doing it now.

Dropping the reins of his horse, he raced after Ismay. He caught up to her quickly, laughing with her as they entered the house together.

He showed her every room, as she requested, lighting candles in each room they entered and apologizing when he realized there was no food or ingredients in the larder.

"I wanted to prepare fer when ye came here," he told her.

"'Tis perfect," she said, coming up behind him and closing her arms around him. "I need nothing but ye."

He turned in her arms and aimed his smile on her. "Ye have me, lass."

"Even here in this house?"

He looked around and nodded. "Everywhere," he promised.

When he leaned in closer, she closed her eyes, readying for his kiss.

While his tongue stole over hers, he lifted her off her feet and carried her upstairs to his bedroom.

ISMAY OPENED HER eyes and looked at the side of the bed where Constantine had slept in the night. The space was empty now. She thought about rising, but she didn't want to leave his bed. Not ever.

She sighed then smiled, then giggled at the scandalous memories rushing into her head. She had no idea he could make her feel the way he had. What man was like him? None, that was who!

She squealed with delight at all the new sensations he had awakened in her. She had trusted him not to hurt her, and he hadn't. He was gentle, though restraint tightened his jaw and made his muscles tremble.

She'd known from the moment she came awake that she was in love with him. Her! In love! Och, her father would not have believed it. If he had tried to wed her to Constantine, she would have agreed wholeheartedly.

Where was he? Getting them something to eat, mayhap? Had he gone hunting? She waited a little longer, humming as memories played through her thoughts, leaving her smiling.

Finally, she left his bed and swung her legs off the bed. Immediately, pain assaulted her. She put her hand between her thighs, over her chemise. She was sore there. For some mad reason, it made her smile again. Would she ever be able to stop? Would she feel this happy waking up with him every day? Aye! Every day.

Now that Constantine had dealt with Chief MacRae, she was no longer worried about him finding her. Besides that, after traveling alone and fighting for her freedom and her life, she trusted herself more.

She would never be so afraid of any man again.

She left the room and called out his name. Silence replied. She knew he wouldn't go too far, so she took the opportunity to look around in the daylight streaming through the windows.

There was a carved staircase leading to the landing below. She vaguely remembered being carried up them last eve. She blushed and then spun around in a circle.

She felt reborn, renewed. Her world and everything she believed about herself had changed. She loved Clan Chief Constantine Cameron of Lochaber.

Walking past the stairway, she continued down one of two large corridors with three doors on each side. One way led to a library, a study, and another bedroom. The other, when she traipsed down it and swung open doors, led to two solars. One was decorated in darker wood and bigger furniture while the other was just as spacious with more delicate furniture and lighter wood. It would have belonged to another woman he'd loved had she lived. The third room was smaller than the rest, with a smaller bed.

"Even here?" she asked, stepping into the room.

Everywhere. She heard his deep voice in her thoughts.

Looking around his daughter's room, Ismay couldn't help but lose her heart to him even more—if that were possible. He had handed his broken heart to her and let her heal him. It was no small offering to accept. This house proved it. He'd loved. He healed. Now, she prayed he was ready to love again. She would be by his side if he did and she would make certain she lived so his heart never broke again.

"Katie's room."

She turned around hearing his voice at the door. She offered him a comforting smile, knowing how difficult this likely was for him. But mayhap, it was part of his healing.

"She never spent a day here," he went on, entering the room and sitting on the bed. "I dinna know what else to do with it."

"Why do anything yet?" she asked, sitting beside him. "Though her life was brief, she was yer daughter. Ye shouldna' ferget her or her mother."

He was quiet for a moment, staring at the floor. Then he looked up at her and smiled. "There is room in my heart fer all of ye...and more to come."

"More?"

He aimed a slanted smile at her and nodded.

Her heart flipped behind her bones and made her spring to her feet and head for the door.

He followed and caught up with her. He was still smiling.

"Where were ye?" she asked and patted her forehead with the back of her hand.

"Fishin' fer breakfast."

"Och!" she gasped with excitement lighting her eyes. "Is there a loch nearby?"

"A stream."

"That will do."

"Fer what?"

"Fer a quick wash."

"'Tis a cold mornin', lass." he told her.

"A wee bit of cold never killed anyone."

"Aye, actually, it has," he corrected to no avail when she snatched his hand and pulled him with her down the stairs.

He wrapped her in two plaids and then kissed her forehead before stepping outside with her.

She was surprised and delighted to find the ribbon stream glistening in the sun, not ten steps away from the back of the house. When she saw it, she hurried toward it.

She hurried to the edge and dipped her feet into the water. She squeaked with delight and turned to him. "'Tis freezing!"

He laughed behind her, but not too far behind. "Shall we head back then?"

"Nonsense," she told him, grabbing fistfuls of her skirts and stepping into the steam up to her calves.

He was quiet so she turned to find him. He was there, removing his boots and rolling up his pants.

"What are ye doing?" she asked and laughed when he entered the water.

"Ye said ye needed to wash." He moved closer, his voice grew huskier. "I'm here to help."

She blushed at the thought, but her blood also felt hot, like liquid fire. Did men do such things as bathe their women? She found the idea of it quite pleasing.

But it felt so much better than she could have ever imagined. His hands explored her with curious fingers that felt like fiery brands on her skin.

Her flesh reacted, growing tight and needful. She wanted to

tell him she loved him, but at a time like this—when passion reigned—her heart was likely not on his mind. She could understand why not. Her body was reacting because she wanted more with him physically. What if he thought she was mistaking love for mere passion? Though, in truth, there was nothing *mere* about it.

He gave in to her every whim, and she gave in to his.

Later, he carried her back to the house and set her in the sitting room before a roaring hearth and covered her in a wool blanket. She snuggled in the blanket, seeking more warmth and felt him behind her. She closed her eyes and sighed in satisfied delight when he began rubbing her hair with another, smaller cloth.

When he leaned down and kissed her temple, she wanted to weep with how much she loved him. He was like water to her thirsty soul. Every moment with him made her love bloom and grow more.

"Constantine?"

"Aye," he whispered, going down her check.

"I love ye." There she said it. She told him.

He went still, setting her heart to ruin. He said nothing, making her want to run and never stop.

"Ye dinna have to reciprocate telling me," she told him, wanting to crawl away. "I understand."

He moved and came to sit before her, affording her a view of the face she never wanted to forget. "Ismay," he said, taking her hands in his and staring into her eyes. "Understand this. I love ye more than I ever dreamed. My heart was dead and dried up, but ye came and ye rescued me, lass. I canna bear to be away from ye and when ye're near, I feel at peace. 'Tis somethin' I havena felt in a verra long time." He smiled when a tear fell down her cheek. "Do ye want me to tell ye every day?"

She nodded. "Aye, promise me ye will."

"I promise to tell ye that I love ye every day. And I promise to show ye."

She didn't doubt him. She never had so far—and he hadn't let her down.

He cooked her breakfast of fish stew with mushrooms and turnips, seasoned to perfection with the spices in glass jars on a shelf in the kitchen.

"Ye're fierce and fearless," Ismay told him while she considered him sitting across from her. "Ye're handsome and ye kiss quite well. On top of all that ye can cook!"

He gave her a surprised look with a smoldering smile. "Ye think I kiss quite well?"

She laughed with him across the table. "Is that all ye heard?"

"What is more important than that?"

She thought about telling him that they could live without kissing each other. They couldn't live without food. But she wasn't convinced she could live with not kissing him.

"Nothing, my darling," she said and rose from the table to step around it and go to him. "There is nothing more important."

$$\ast$$

CHAPTER TWENTY

LADY MARJORIE MACPHERSON sat at the long, polished table in her dining hall, clicking her fingernails on the wood. Seated across from her, beaten and broken, was Chief Alistar MacRae. Good-for-nothing sot that he was. Why, he hadn't even seen Ismay in the month he'd been gone! Marjorie found it difficult to believe that Ismay was so clever to continue to elude her betrothed.

"How do you know the Lochiel of Lochaber has her?"

"I already told ye," MacRae said with frustration tainting his tone.

"Tell me again." Majorie knew MacRae would do as she demanded. Their agreement provided her immediate monetary aid, while providing him Ismay's inheritance when she died. And seeing the chief's temper, Marjorie doubted Ismay would live much longer after the pig wed her. Marjorie didn't care. She'd often wished the wee waif her husband had brought home with him sixteen years ago had died before John had found her.

"The basthard ambushed me. He broke my jaw and knocked out eleven of my teeth."

Aye, Marjorie did all she could to hide her amusement at the way he spoke without his teeth and his jaw held by a tightly wound bandage. He could not pronounce *s* at all, trading the consonant to *th*. It was positively hilarious. She'd wanted to hear it again.

"He told me never to go near her again or he would kill me.

Marjorie sighed in boredom. Some of his words sounded more amusing than others.

"You must defy him. She is yours," she snapped at him. "Do ye know how much she is worth? My husband left everything to her. But 'tis mine. Remember our agreement, Chief. You pay me a dowry and when she dies, her inheritance will go to you. You agreed to pay me eighty percent, keeping twenty for yourself. 'Tis a binding agreement, Chief. If ye try to break it and take the full inheritance fer yerself, ye will be hunted down and killed."

"The gel ith too much trouble," MacRae remarked.

"Aye, she has been trouble fer me since the day she stepped foot in this house. 'Tis time fer her to go so I can get what is rightfully mine. If ye have changed yer mind, I will find someone else."

"I have nae doubt he will kill me," MacRae tried to explain.

She shook her head. "I know something. Something that will make the Lochiel throw her out of Tor. Mayhap, he will kill her himself. The best part, Chief, is that ye dinna have to show yerself at all. All ye have to do is go to the Chattan chief and tell him what I am about to tell ye. Simple, hmm?"

The MacRae chief nodded. "What ith it that will make the Lochiel throw her out?"

Marjorie smiled and wound her finger around one of her chestnut curls. "Will ye agree to do what I tell ye?"

"Tell me."

She gave out a little sigh. The instant she didn't need MacRae anymore she would have him killed. "I found a letter she wrote to my husband." She looked around conspiratorially. "In it she is utterly repentant fer killing a man."

The oaf didn't seem surprised. But he was curious. "Whom did she kill?"

"Roderick MacDonald, Clan Chief of the MacDonalds of Glencoe."

He thought about it for a moment and then his face drained of color. "The mighty chief Roderick MacDonald who wath felled by a mere gel? Talth are still told about that child. She ith hailed by many to be more of a hero than a murderer."

"Not a hero to any MacDonald," Marjorie assured him. "Remember the Camerons and the MacDonalds are kin. So anyone who kills a MacDonald is the Camerons' enemy. Tell the Chattan about Ismay and her whereabouts. Tell them how much danger she is in from the Camerons. They will try to rescue her. Ye are to let them so ye can marry her. If ye canna wait fer the money and want to see her dead, ye have to marry her first in front of witnesses. Do ye understand? That is the only way to get the inheritance."

"I underthand." MacRae lifted his hands in surrender. "Ath long ath I dinna have to be near him."

Marjorie looked him over with his purple, swollen face and wanted to laugh at him. "Do ye truly think he would kill ye? Another Highland chief? Would he risk another feud fer her?"

"I've nae doubt he would kill me," MacRae told her and shivered as if a cold breeze blew through him. "I felt hith affection fer her with every punch." He stopped for a moment, then smiled. "And if hith heart ith gone to her, I may wed her and then have her and make him watch."

Marjorie wanted to scorn him openly. He was such an unpleasant, rash young man. She covered her mouth with her hand and laughed at how he sounded without his teeth and a broken jaw. "Ye are too eager, Chief," she said to cover her amusement at how the Lochiel had left him. The Lochiel. Marjorie ground her jaw. Why him? She'd heard of him, everyone had. He was a deadly ghost, killing without mercy or remorse. He did all to keep his kin fed and protected. He was a dreaded enemy, leaving Oliver Cromwell's army rotting dead on the fields where they fought, or left alive at various castles they had taken hold of just so the Cameron chief had enemies to fight when the mood struck him.

And this complete fool before her thought nothing of making the Lochiel his enemy…and hers, as well.

"Chief, if ye intend to torture her in the sight of such a man as Constantine 'the Ghost' Cameron, best make certain to kill him if he cares fer her as ye say he does. Be prepared to kill all his men as well. Everyone at Tor Castle, in fact. I'm told he is well-loved among his kin. Ye would be wise to wed her quickly and take her away. Forget him. Use her fer yer pleasure until she perishes, I dinna care. Just procure that purse."

The fool seemed to be thinking about it. Marjorie rolled her eyes heavenward. "Chief, if ye are going to visit the Confederation, ye should be on yer way."

She didn't offer him a smile when he rose and left. Och, had he truly been her only option in searching for a husband for Ismay? She sighed and climbed the stairs to her rooms. Thanks to her dead husband telling her suitors lies, no eligible man, young or old, wanted a wife who didn't cook or clean, had a vile temper, and sores that sometimes broke out over her body. John was clever—and eager to make his wee Ismay happy. If she didn't want to marry, he made sure she was rejected by all.

MacRae hadn't wanted her either until Marjorie told him her plans for Ismay's inheritance. She didn't worry if he refused to give Marjorie her share. He would be dead before then.

Inside her sitting room, she paced before a bench facing the hearth. Hanging on the wall above it was a painting of her and John standing behind a chair, where a little fire-haired gel sat like a queen on her throne.

Marjorie reached for an empty goblet on the table beside the bench and threw it as hard as she could at the little brat.

John never told her the child he brought into their home was a murderer. She could have killed Marjorie at any time. "I will never fergive ye fer that, John. I will never fergive ye fer leaving everything to her!" she seethed at the painting. "I'm happy ye are finally dead. If that brat of yers ever steps into this house…*my house*, I will kill her, just as I killed ye."

CONSTANTINE STOOD BEFORE Father Langley MacDonald, Tor's resident priest and cousin to almost everyone living there. He repeated what the priest asked him to say. But he barely heard his own words. He was marrying again. He wasn't mad, nor was he riddled with guilt. He was too in love with Ismay Drummond to think of anything else. He didn't need a priest to tell him he was Ismay's husband. The night he had first claimed her, he was hers. Aye, only death could separate them, and even then he would fight without ceasing to stay by her side.

He became aware of her delicate voice. She was declaring her heart to him.

"I promise to love only ye."

He slid his gaze to her. His heart quickened inside him. It made him cough. It helped keep tears from filling his eyes. At the thought of tears, he scowled.

His beloved Ismay immediately appeared upset by his expression. He realized what he was doing and slew his scowl. "I promise to love only ye," he let her know with a tender smile.

She giggled. "Ye already promised that. Are ye paying attention?"

He laughed with her and shook his head. "I'm too stunned that ye have agreed to never leave me."

"Until death do ye part," his cousin, Father Langley tossed in.

"We will never be parted," Constantine told her in his most needful voice.

Ismay smiled at him as if she didn't hear the messenger running, breathless, into the inner court shouting he had news from the Chattan Confederation.

Constantine watched her smile fade as she finally turned toward the messenger. He wanted to reach out and touch her mouth, make her smile return. Whatever the messenger had to tell him, Constantine didn't care. Not now. Not today. He wanted to shout for everyone to get out and leave him alone with his bride.

"Lochiel, I have word from the chief of Chattan." The messenger unrolled the missive he carried and began to read. *"Lochiel, be hereby advised that it has come to our attention that ye have in yer custody Lady Ismay MacPherson, daughter of Baron John MacPherson of Raigmore and his wife Marjorie. We dinna care how she came to be in yer possession, we demand ye let her go.*

We know why ye might refuse to release her, but she is our kin and we willna stand idly by while ye punish the woman. She was, at the time of her killing Chief Roderick MacDonald of Glencoe, just a wee child. The death was an accident, we are certain. If ye harm a single hair on her head, we will go to battle with all of ye. Release her or we will come take her from ye."

When the messenger finished, Constantine understood why some kings killed their messengers. This one before him couldn't be speaking the truth. She was a MacPherson? Daughter of Baron John MacPherson, the man rumored to have harbored the Chief MacDonald's murderer? He turned to her, as her words echoed in his head.

I became a murderer.

She was the wee gel in the stories told around the fires about the mighty Chief MacDonald.

She'd lied to him all along. Why? Fear most likely. She was a Highlander. She knew Highlanders held long grudges. For killing their chief, they might demand her blood as payment.

She had lied to him about her name. She knew MacPhersons were part of the Chattan and enemies to the Camerons. He could understand her deceit in it all.

Still, hadn't she claimed to trust him?

Her deceit proved she didn't.

He wanted to tell her he didn't believe it, but her face was drained of color. He thought she might fall to the ground and took a step closer to her.

She moved away, breaking his heart.

It was true then.

He turned to look around at his kin. Empty stares, void of any emotions met his gaze. Then, as the truth dawned on them the way it had on him, anger, betrayal, and silent accusations filled the void.

She was an enemy of his clan. She had deceived them, pretending to be a Drummond. What should he say? He hadn't known the truth either.

Surely, they would not turn on her just because she bore the name of the man who adopted her. It wasn't that she was born a MacPherson.

He snatched up her hand and pulled her forward to the castle. "Come with me."

This couldn't be, he thought while pulling her along. So, she was a MacPherson in name only. But she was not just any MacPherson. She was the MacPherson lass who had killed Roderick MacDonald.

Constantine knew the chief had abused her. He knew she had been a child, but his kin, or at least some of them, would not forgive her for killing one of their chiefs.

When they entered the castle, Constantine still didn't say a word to her. He held her hand while he climbed the stairs and then led her to his private solar.

"Ye killed Roderick MacDonald," he said after he closed the door.

"I didna know that was his full name. I knew him only as 'Chief MacDonald.'"

"Why did ye no' tell me the man ye killed was a MacDonald?" he pressed. He kept his voice neutral, despite the fear of his kin's revenge. He'd vowed to protect her, but could he end any one of his kins' lives?

"I would likely have been killed if yer kin found out," she defended. "At the verra least, I would have been thrown out of Tor Castle."

"I thought ye wanted to leave all along."

She wrung her hands together and didn't answer right away.

He wanted to go to her and take her in his arms. He wanted to tell her not to fear. He would speak to his kin. All would be well. But he wasn't sure of it.

"Ye deceived me, lass," he said softer, more quietly than he intended. It was the worst part of it all. He thought she trusted him. It was the light that pushed everything else forward. "Did ye believe I would harm ye?"

"Fergive me fer deceiving ye, Constantine. I didna know ye well enough to assume how ye would react.

"Whatever I wanted before is no' the same anymore," she went on. "I want to stay here. With ye. I dinna want to have to run anymore, or lose someone I love again."

He wanted to go to her, but his feet would not let him. Was there anything else she hadn't told him?

Someone rapped on the door. Before Constantine could give entry, his cousin Hilary threw open the door. When her eager gaze found Ismay, her expression darkened.

"Is it true, then?" she demanded. "Did ye kill my great uncle Roderick MacDonald?"

Ismay's color drained again, and it was like seeing the sun through a cloak of charcoal clouds.

"Hil," Constantine warned her in a low voice.

His cousin threw him a stunned glare. "Does it not matter to ye, Cousin?"

"Do ye know what 'twill do to everyone when they find out ye have sold yer soul to the enemy?"

"Hilary," Ismay interrupted quietly, her voice tainted with guilt. "I dinna want to be yer enemy. I—"

"Are friends deceitful to each other, Ismay?" Hilary snapped at her. "Aye, we are enemies—no matter what my traitor cousin feels fer ye." She turned for the door, giving up her fight and leaving in a hurry.

"Roderick MacDonald's servants took me in when I was two summers old," Ismay's words stopped her. "I was raised in the kitchens with the other scullery maids."

"Why did ye not tell me before this?" Hilary asked her, sounding less angry.

"The chief began striking me when I was four," Ismay told her, continuing on. "If I was slow to a task, I was punished. Many times I had to eat a taste of his food before he did to ensure that I would die rather than him if 'twas poisoned. If I refused, I was punished. I only refused once. Most times I wished 'twas poisoned. I was punished fer everything. I grew wishing I would die."

Hilary turned her stricken gaze to her cousin, but Constantine was quiet, hearing the full weight of Ismay's tale.

"When I was eight years old, he dragged me to his room, but he didna hit me. I would have rathered he killed me. He threw me to his bed and when he came near, I took hold of his dirk and sliced it across his neck. When I fled his room covered in blood, it was quickly discovered what I had done. I was promptly dragged outside and tossed into the square. More and more people were hearing of what happened and they gathered with the rest until there was a crowd. A few picked up stones, and then the rest followed, shouting that I was a murderer. They were going to kill me. But no rock was thrown. I was rescued by a man passing through the burgh. He took me away from my would-be executioners and raised me as his own. His name was John MacPherson, Baron of Raigmore. He left the earth and his bereaved daughter four months ago.

"After being promised to another cruel man, I fled my father's home and my betrothed. And ended up here."

Hilary wiped her eyes and sniffed deeply. "Och, Ismay, I didna know yer life had been so…"

"'Tis better now," Constantine's bride told her.

"Fergive me fer being so cruel and cold to ye," Hilary cried and ran into Ismay's arms.

Watching them, Constantine prayed the rest of his kin would be so forgiving.

He quickly got rid of his cousin by practically pushing her out the door. Locking the door behind him, he turned to Ismay and motioned for her to have a seat on one of the carved chairs facing the hearth. He poured them both a cup of spiced mead from the clay jug on the small table behind her chair.

"If ye hadna killed him, I would have ridden oot to do it myself," he told her, coming around her and handing her a cup. "He didna deserve…" He stopped himself, biting down on his teeth. His Creator knew what kind of man Constantine could be. Constantine preferred that Ismay remain ignorant of it.

"I intend to help ye ferget those days," he promised, debating whether or not he should fall on his knees before her or sit in the chair facing hers.

"Ye already have," she told him softly and with warmth spreading to the depths of her eyes while he sat. "I could never love ye as I do if ye didna make me ferget the past. Ye brought yer radiance and lit up those dark corners, exposing them, and helping me vanquish them."

Hearing this, he slipped out of his chair and bent his knees before her.

"Bonnie Ismay, we may be facin' difficult days ahead from some of my kin. But I will protect ye from all. I will stay by ye and destroy anyone who tries to take ye from me."

She nodded and he knew she believed him. It made his desire to protect her even more passionate.

"What shall we do about everyone out there?"

His gaze revealed another promise. One more inviting and intimate. "Let them wait."

He moved up her body until their lips met in an eager, urgent kiss that left them both breathless.

ISMAY STOOD AT the door to Constantine's solar, ready, after tidying her appearance and blushing when Constantine cast her scandalous smile. She smoothed her skirts and patted her hair, then nodded. Whatever was to come from the Camerons and the MacDonalds, she would face head on.

When he opened the door, she stepped out with him close behind. Would he protect her from his kin? She didn't want him to have to.

Joan appeared on the other side of her when she stepped into the hall. Her friend did not say anything. She simply smiled and gave Ismay more courage to continue on.

Ismay was thankful that Hilary had forgiven her, and more thankful for Joan's silence. She cut her glance to Constantine walking on her right. His first reaction was quiet rage—the kind that made so many of his enemies drop their weapons and run. His subsequent reaction was vowing to continue to protect her.

She loved him. There was no point in denying or doubting it. She loved how he felt like a mountain—her Ben Nevis, mayhap— beside her, and how his shapely mouth relaxed when he set his dark mahogany eyes on her.

He flicked his gaze to her now and grinned at her appraisal.

She giggled into her hand like a milkmaid who had attracted the most handsome man in the village.

When they stepped into the Great Hall, Ismay's gaze fell to Constantine's table. There, Geoffry and Fionn MacDonald sat drinking as they usually did. Lachlan's smile widened on Joan when he saw her. Lewis eyed her narrowly, and then, seeming to come to some conclusion in his head, he dipped his chin in repentance.

Hilary was there, sitting across from Geoffry. Her eyes were red and puffy when she waved at Ismay and beckoned her forward.

Almost everyone who set eyes on her offered her a pitying look. Hilary must have told them about their dear relative, Roderick MacDonald.

If it helped them forgive her, then good. Let them all know. But they did, and some of them glared at her as if she were an unwelcome intruder. But their Lochiel's glare was darker and more dangerous, so they looked away.

She was happy to see Father Langley there and agreed with a joyful heart when he offered to finish their wedding ceremony.

That night, when the food and drinks stopped flowing and laughter turned to silence, Lewis asked if she was truly only eight when the incident took place.

She answered all their questions having nothing more to hide. They were her kin now and she loved the ones at her table.

"No one there came to yer aid?" Geoffry asked her with a distasteful slant of his lips.

"And find themselves at the end of his sword?" She shook her head. "Nae, no one came to my aid."

Constantine let the others ask her questions because he knew she could take it. They had a right to know.

Twice, she met his gaze and smiled as if he were the only man in the world. He was the only one who mattered. She couldn't wait for the night to be over so she could be alone with him and promise to love until thistles no longer bloomed.

But before they all retired and Constantine took his wife to bed, a guest appeared at the castle doors.

When Hilary saw her betrothed, John MacBain she ran to him, elated. "Darling, what brings ye here at this time of night?"

"May I enter?" he asked before coming inside.

Constantine took a step forward. John MacBain paled and stepped back. Almost out of the castle, but Ismay stayed his hand. This was the one Hilary loved. For that, Constantine needed to hear him.

"Fergive me, my love," MacBain said softly to Hilary.

"What should I fergive, John?"

He pushed on the open door and pulled it wide. Immediately, two hundred men came rushing inside, weapons drawn. They were MacPhersons, MacKintoshes, and others from the Chattan Confederation.

Just as quickly, Ismay was pushed behind Constantine. They both looked up at the long sword descending on them.

CHAPTER TWENTY-ONE

ONSTANTINE'S CLAYMORE FLASHED above her and stopped the enemy sword's descent in a clashing blow that rained sparks down on her head. In less than an instant her eyes took in everything going on around her. There were men everywhere, slicing, jabbing, and chopping with their swords. Blood spewed, and Hilary was whisked away by her betrothed.

The bastard whose sword had come down on them crumbled to the ground and lay in a bloody heap at her feet. The smell of blood seeped into her nostrils and then filled her lungs. She would have gagged, but Constantine grasped her by the wrist and pulled her to the stairs.

"I will come fer ye," he promised, urging her up the steps. "There is a trapdoor in my solar, beneath the west window."

She shook her head frantically while men all around her cried out or swore vengeance as they died. "I willna leave ye, Constantine."

He pushed her up another stair. "Go to the loch." He paused to offer her a brief smile in the midst of the chaos. "The loch where ye like to swim. I will come fer ye, my love."

A look of horror passed over her features as a stranger came up behind him and lifted his blade. She didn't have time to scream before Constantine turned and in a split second sliced his blade across the stranger's belly.

Before this opponent hit the floor, another was upon him. He spared her a worried glance then fought his new opponent.

Ismay knew she was distracting Constantine by being there, so, with almost crippling reluctance, she hurried up the stairs, afraid to look back lest she see him fallen on the stairs where he had carried her to his room. If he died, she would drown herself in the loch.

She made it to the second landing and was met by John Mac-Bain and Hilary.

"My kin will never fergive ye, John!" Hilary shouted at him. "Nor will I. Do ye understand? I will never—" Hilary's words were cut short when she turned and saw Ismay at the top of the stairs.

She hurried to her. "Ismay! Are ye hurt?"

Ismay shook her head and turned to MacBain. "What is the meaning of this?"

He came forward and pulled a dirk from a hilt hanging at his side. "Hilary tells me ye are happy here. That is no' fer me to decide. Our chief wants ye set free to be kept safe in our care."

"In yer care?" Ismay echoed.

"The Chattan."

Ismay backed away. "Nae! I winna come with ye."

"Lass, the chief doesna care if we kill the Lochiel," MacBain told her. "In fact, he wants us to kill him. But I can promise ye that if ye come with me, he willna be hurt."

Go with him? Nae! She couldn't. She heard someone's voice from below stairs where the men were fighting. The voice shouted "Lochiel!" It was Geoffry. She turned to run back down the stairs to see what was going on. MacBain took her arm and stepped close to her.

"Come with me and the Lochiel willna be harmed," he said against her ear.

Her eyes opened wide. If going with him was the only way to save Constantine from two hundred men, she would obey.

"John, I beg ye, dinna take her," Hilary cried. "Constantine was the one who agreed to our union. The elders denied us."

"I must obey my orders, my lady." With that, he ended the conversation and still holding Ismay by her arm, pulled her down the stairs.

Ismay struggled to be free to run to where she saw Geoffry. Her eyes scanned the myriad of faces for Constantine. Where was he? There wasn't much time to gain her freedom before the gaping doors appeared before them.

"Constantine!" she screamed out.

Geoffry's wide gaze met hers for an instant, and then he looked down, toward his feet.

Ismay couldn't see what it was at first. But then there came a free space between the legs of a dozen men. She stopped, never wanting to move again at the sight of Constantine's body lying limp at Geoffry's feet.

Should she scream his name again? She didn't have the strength. It drained from her more and more with each passing moment. Her knees gave out beneath her. MacBain lifted her over his shoulder and as he hurried out of the castle, she finally screamed her husband's name.

ISMAY'S EYES OPENED with the shock of what happened flashing across her dreams.

Constantine was dead. Even her nostrils attested to it, burning from the dank odor decay.

She buried her head into the bed and wept.

Bed? She lifted her head and looked around. The room was small and empty save for the bed and a chair. The walls were empty, as well. Where was she? She looked down at herself in her clothes. Who brought her here? Immediately, Hilary's contorted face appeared before her. John MacBain! Where had MacBain brought her?

Her heart jolted. She wanted to forget, but her heart wouldn't allow it.

Constantine was dead.

A chill creeped down her spine. How was she supposed to live another day without him in the world? Why should she care about living or dying? She didn't. But she did want to face her captor. MacBain had not kept his promise to keep Constantine safe. Their bargain was broken.

She had strength enough to throw back her head and scream. Why had he brought his men to Tor Castle? MacBain had mentioned his chief wanting her. Was she the reason they attacked Tor?

"MacBain!" she bellowed. She leaped from the bed and hurried to the door. She struggled to open it but it was locked. She hurried for the chair, intending to pick it up and throw it next.

She paused hearing footsteps coming closer to her door.

She still had strength to throw the chair at him directly. She readied herself as the door creaked open.

When she saw who was on the other side, she let go of the chair and looked around for a place to run.

"What are ye doing here, MacRae?" Her voice shook with fear and anger.

"I have come to help ye," he smiled and took a seat in a heavy chair by the window.

Did he think himself her protector? She quickly rejected him in her own head. She didn't need his protection. She needed an escape route. "Save it, MacRae," she said scathingly. "I dinna know how I came to be in yer possession, but I demand ye release me."

He laughed. "What a filthy tongue. Ye're a treasure to potheth. Other men will envy and admire my ability to tame the wild wench."

Och, how could it be that after all the running and hiding, for all the blisters on her feet, and the nights she'd gone to sleep hungry, he caught her.

"Let me go. I am the wife of—"

"Yer marriage to that unholy Highland outlaw will be annulled," MacRae advised, rubbing his purple jaw. "Then I will wed ye, ath planned. Though now that I have caught ye, ye are nae longer appetizing."

"Good!" she exclaimed, sick to her stomach by him. "By the way, ye sound like the blithering fool ye truly are." She wanted to weep but she wouldn't show MacRae any weakness. How long could she go on without screaming until she never stopped?

What if Constantine was dead? How could he leave her?

Wait. If Constantine had died, MacRae wouldn't need to have the marriage annulled.

He hadn't left her, she told herself with a sudden burst of strength coursing through her. He was alive! He had to be. "He promised to come fer me."

"What?" MacRae looked up from his fingers.

"He is going to come fer me, MacRae. And when he does, he is going to kill ye."

The chief paled and swallowed. "He wath fatally injured. He willna be coming fer anyone."

Constantine was fatally wounded? How long ago had it been since she saw him lifeless on the floor? Did she dare believe MacRae? She shook her head and swallowed back her tears. "He will kill ye whether he is dead or alive."

He laughed but it sounded forced to Ismay's ears. He was afraid, and he should be. If Constantine was truly gone, she would do the killing.

"Where is MacBain?" she demanded. "Did he deliver me to ye? Was my mother involved in this?"

MacRae shrugged his beefy shoulder. "I heard the Camerons were looking fer him." He smiled at his last words and shrugged again. "Dead or alive, he did hith duty."

So, Ismay told herself, reading him easily, MacBain had, in fact, delivered her to him. But by whose order? MacRae wasn't powerful enough to order an army to invade Tor. She asked him.

"Yer rescue wath ordered by the Clan Chief Chattan. Ye are a MacPherthon by yer own dear mother's oath. She wanted ye out of the hands of the outlaw Cameron."

"She told them I was a MacPherson?"

"I did, actually, with her mark on a document of yer identity."

Ismay swore quietly. This just kept getting more mad! "So, my *mother* informed the Confederation of my identity to get me out of the hands of the Cameron, and into yers?"

"Aye." MacRae nodded with a satisfied grin. "We did ye a great favor, Ithmay. Once the Lochiel discovered who ye are, he would have likely raped ye. Now we know he forced ye to marry him."

"He didna force me," she told him woodenly.

He scoffed as if he knew all her family secrets. "We know how ye refuthed every other man that courted ye fer yer hand."

He didn't believe her. She didn't care. She wasn't here to prove anything to him.

"What do ye gain by doing her bidding?" she asked instead.

He curled his lips up. "Yer inheritance when ye leave the earth."

Ismay laughed into her hands. "Once ye kill me, are ye fool enough to believe she willna kill ye?"

He was quiet. It either just dawned on the dimwit, or he suspected Lady MacPherson and planned to kill her first.

Let them destroy each other.

Ismay turned her storm-filled eyes on him. "Where are we?"

"We are thill in Lochaber," he provided, then narrowed his eyes on her. "But we will be moving in the morning. Be ready." With that, he rose up and went for the door.

"The Lochiel will likely be here before sunset."

MacRae stopped and stared at her as if he were waiting for her to laugh and confess to jesting.

"He's coming even now," she warned. "I'm sure of it."

He left her, quickening his steps. Ismay watched him leave and shut and locked the door behind him.

Was she mad? Was Constantine on his way? Was he alive? She prayed that he was and then began to cry because she didn't know. Even if he was alive, how would he find her? She hurried to the window, but the shutters were locked. What should she do? There was no way out. She would have to wait until they left. She would escape him once they left. She would run back to Tor or to the house below the great mountain. Aye, she would hide there.

CONSTANTINE TIGHTENED THE leather strap crossing one shoulder and then did the same on the other side as he stormed toward the stable.

The sound of Ismay's voice screaming his name before she was taken away would forever haunt his memory. He'd heard her as if she were in another time or place. He hadn't been able to move or even wake up as the knife wound in his belly had gushed forth his lifeblood.

"It has been less than a full day since ye were wounded, Chief," Lewis said, keeping up with him.

Constantine gritted his teeth wondering if Lewis thought he was too simpleminded to know how long it had been since that bastard Ewen MacKintosh stabbed him. Why was his cousin trying to stop him anyway? Didn't Lewis know—didn't they all know that he loved Ismay MacPherson enough not to care about her name, her deeds, her kin, or his life? Hadn't killing MacKintosh's son when he tried to abduct her proven it? Would killing every MacKintosh left alive prove it? How about Alistar MacRae? John MacBain? The Chattan chief? Would killing them all bring her back?

Thanks to Hilary, he'd learned, through buckets of tears, that her betrothed, John MacBain had taken Ismay under orders from the Chattan chief, who ordered the attack on his castle on the advice of Lady Majorie MacPherson, Ismay's mother. Which meant, the man he was going to kill, Chief of the MacRaes of Beauly had her.

But where had he taken her? Back toward Beauly, most likely.

"Let us accompany ye," Lewis practically begged. "Geoffry is oot of his mind because ye are goin', and goin' alone."

"Nae," Constantine ground out. He tried to sound more angry than in pain. If Lewis knew how badly his wound pained him, he would lock him inside and not let him go. "I want Fionn to stay here and look after Lachlan."

Aye, MacBain would pay for getting Lachlan run through. According to the castle physician and a local healer, young Lachlan was close to meeting his Maker.

Constantine couldn't let himself think on it overmuch. If he did, he might be tempted not to leave his cousin's side. Joan had promised to stay by his bedside. Constantine had to trust her to look after his cousin. He had to find Ismay.

"Ye and Geoffry are to find MacBain. I dinna care what it takes or how many men ye bring with ye. Find him. If Lachlan dies, then MacBain dies, as well. Do ye understand?"

"Aye, Lochiel, but—"

Just before he entered the stable, Constantine stopped walking and turned to face him. "Lewis, I need to do this. I have to find her. If I bring anyone else and MacRae gets wind that we are close, he might harm her. I can find him and get right on top of him before he knows what has hit him."

Lewis's lips curled into a smile. "The Ghost Cameron."

Constantine mustered up a slight smile and nodded, then gave him a hefty pat on the shoulder and continued into the stable.

He thought of all the men from the Confederation lying dead behind the castle, dragged outside by the Camerons and MacDonalds when the fight was over. Angus MacKintosh, the Chattan chief was a fool to think he would see victory after attacking Tor. Constantine had taken down twenty men before he'd fallen.

He knew riding would be risky. His wound was stitched, wrapped, and repaired as much as it could be in so short a time. If it reopened and bled, he might not make it.

As his horse came charging out of the stable, Constantine didn't think about dying. He'd been wounded before, close to death, and he'd lived. This time, more than any other, he would not allow himself to die. At least, not until he found her and she was safe from MacRae for good.

He would travel toward Beauly and catch up with MacRae along the way. In the meantime, he tried not to think about her screaming his name in terror. Instead, he remembered how his name sounded in her breathy whisper while he made love to her. Her meaningful, bonnie smile eased his fierce heartbeat and helped him think clearly.

A night had passed since she'd been taken from the castle over the shoulder of John MacBain. He pushed thoughts of Hilary sobbing out of his mind. MacBain was going to pay—with his life if Lachlan died.

Even with that terrible thought, memories of Ismay's saucy temper brought a smile to his lips as the wind snapped his hair behind him like a war pennant. *Och, Almighty. She makes me happy. Dinna let her be taken from me,* he prayed silently. Aye, not even Alison had made him so constantly happy and good-natured. He'd been younger and more battle-hardened, with war coursing through his veins.

He was older now, twenty and seven. He had seen the terrible consequences of battle until it had turned his blood cold. Now, he wanted peace, and not just from war, but from the weight of shame and guilt. He was afraid though, that when it came completely, he wouldn't know how to live in it.

Ismay made him want it though. She helped him understand that he no longer deserved to walk in regret. A new beginning was here.

Please, please let her live.

He rode alongside the River Lochy northeast until he came to the outskirts of Gairlochy on the southern shores of Loch Lochy.

Constantine was from Lochiel and almost everyone in Lochaber knew him. That included people in Gairlochy, so when he questioned them about a stranger traveling with a lass with fiery-red hair, many had claimed to see her.

He started off toward the Gairlochy Inn, where they believed she was, but with the inn in his vision, he felt his blood escaping through his wound. He looked down at it dripping into the earth and then felt himself falling. He slipped from his saddle and landed with a *thunk* on the hard ground. Nae! He raged as the dark threatened to overtake him. He had to get up. He had to protect Ismay!

"There, now, Lochiel…"

A familiar voice sounded in Constantine's ears. One of his men at Tor? Nae, he told himself as he was hefted up and carried away.

"Let's be off, then."

CHAPTER TWENTY-TWO

CONSTANTINE CAME TO with the coming of dawn a day later. Beneath him, a soft bed cushioned his back. *Ismay!* He opened his eyes and leaned up on one elbow to have a look around.

The room was rustic, more like the room of an inn but with ceiling rafters of oak and spider webs. He tried to move and leave the bed, but pain shot up his side and through his belly.

He didn't give a damn about the pain. Every moment that Ismay was with MacRae, the danger to her increased. Clenching his teeth, he slid his legs off the bed. The wooden floor was cold on his bare feet.

Who took his boots off?

He closed his eyes against the pain and stood to his feet.

The door to the room opened. Molly Frazier, one of the elder villagers from Gairlochy entered the room carrying a tray. When she saw Constantine awake and standing, she nearly dropped the food she carried.

"Lochiel! Return to yer bed this instant!" she ordered—but gently. "Do ye want to pass oot again?" She hurried inside, set the tray on the wide seat of a nearby chair, and then went to him.

"How did I get here?" he asked her while she tugged on his shirt.

"Ye should be worried about yer wound opening again. The

good Lord was surely on yer side when old Andrew the healer crossed the loch on his way to Craigmor Hamlet and stopped here. He was able to patch ye up, but he worries ye will tear it open again."

"I canna stay here—"

"But ye must, Lochiel," she insisted and gave him a gentle push down.

"Molly, I have known ye fer over two decades," he said on a warning growl. "Let me up or I will push ye oot of my way."

She moved aside immediately, and Constantine secretly felt terrible about frightening her.

"I have to find her."

"Ismay Drummond?" Molly asked.

Word hadn't reached Gairlochy that Ismay was the famous child who slew the mighty chief MacDonald. If MacRae didn't hurt her, someone else taking revenge would.

"He went to search fer her. Ye are to stay here and recover some. Please, Lochaber needs ye."

Constantine gritted his teeth. Then, finally, shook his head. "I have to—*Who* went to find her?"

"Och, Lochiel," she admonished, finding her courage to place her hands on his shoulders to push him back down. "Ye were in such a poor state. We all thought we lost ye. But he...."

Constantine hated himself for passing out again.

Who in blazes went to find his wife?

"Ismay," his voice echoed in the darkest chamber of his heart. *Where are ye, my love. Please...*"Come back to me."

The silence of his dream drove him mad until—he opened his eyes. Golden firelight softened the blare of his solemn wakefulness. Outside the window, moonlight shone into the room.

Ismay.

He felt someone's presence and looked into the shadowed corner. He put his hand to his side, where he usually carried his dirk. It wasn't there. "Step forward," he commanded like a king from his bed.

A man stepped into the candlelight.

When Constantine saw his steward, confusion fogged his sleepy thoughts. All but one. "Did ye find her?"

Hugh shook his head. "Not yet."

"How hard are ye lookin'?"

His steward came closer and pulled a chair with him. "I am only able to travel as far as it takes to be able to return here to ye at night and make certain ye live."

"Dinna worry over me, Hugh!" Constantine couldn't believe what he was hearing. Didn't Hugh dislike him? "Go and find her. We are losing her trail by letting time pass by while we do nothin'!"

He swung his legs off the bed and ignoring a wave of dizziness, stood to his feet. "I will find her myself."

"Lochiel—"

"What is it with ye, hmm, Hugh? What were ye doin' in that house the night Ismay escaped with her life from the nearby barn? If ye were innocent, why did ye run?"

Hugh frowned at what he was hearing. "I left the study after an argument with the man at the desk. I didna even see ye until I spotted ye and Ismay on the road. I knew she was safe, so I left."

"What were ye doin' there?"

Hugh squirmed in the chair and looked up at the rafters. "Lochiel...the owner of that house is my uncle, Padrig MacDonald."

"Why does that cause ye such affliction?" Constantine asked him.

His steward sighed and continued. "He wanted me to bring her to him, so I did. But then...I regretted my decision. I was trying to talk him out of his plans, but he wouldna listen. That's when ye showed up."

"What were his plans?"

"To kill her. Stone her at dawn *as she should have been stoned the first time*, to be precise."

Constantine stopped wrapping his plaid around himself. His

heart stopped. He was sure of it. His thoughts faded. They knew. The MacDonalds knew who she was. He stared at Hugh wanting to kill him. "I should have killed him," he said of Hugh's uncle Padrig.

"Aye, ye should have."

"I should kill ye fer tellin' him who she is." Constantine's threat was spoken on a clenched growl.

"Aye, ye should," Hugh agreed. "But I plead with ye fer my life, Lochiel. I cared fer ye and yer brother fer sixteen years. I am not so much older than ye, but I was always loyal to ye. When ye wed Lady Alison, I loved her as I loved ye. I never even thought about my kin in other parts of the Highlands. But when I first saw Ismay, I knew who she was. I knew my clan had never stopped looking fer her. I thought I was doing the right thing by delivering her to them."

"What?" Constantine asked, in stunned disbelief. "Ye knew who she was? How would ye know that?" he demanded, then continued with a clenched jaw. "Ye expect me to believe ye willna hand her over this time?"

"I already had the chance," Hugh said with remorse lining his voice. "I have come to care fer her well-being. She is kindhearted and she smiles often and with ease. I willna let anyone or anything hurt her. But...ye are here in dire straits and I find myself caring fer ye too much to leave to go find her."

Constantine wasn't sure what he should say or how he should react to such words. Aye, she smiled often and with ease.

He almost lost his senses completely for a moment when he wanted to smile thinking of her. He could decide what to do about Hugh later. For now, he had one purpose and as long as he was breathing nothing would stop him.

"I have to find her."

"I will find her," Hugh tried to assure him.

But Constantine already started for the door, albeit grimacing as he went. "Ye are here and we are wastin' time."

ISMAY SAT PROPPED in the saddle of MacRae's horse while they traveled closer to Beauly.

Where was Constantine? She thought, looking up. What was taking him so long to come to her? Mayhap he was dead, after all. Tears blurred the stars and she wiped her eyes quickly. She wouldn't let such terrible thoughts fill her head. Constantine was alive. He was coming.

MacRae was terrified of him. It enraged him that he should run like a frightened rat in the dark and in his rage, he often struck her. She didn't care. His terror was the one thing that made Ismay happy in the last few days. She made sure to remind him that the Lochiel was coming for him.

They traveled mostly at night to avoid being spotted by the "cursed Camerons." But Ismay left something small behind every time they stopped. Yesterday, when her captor saw that one of her shoes was missing he slapped her hard in the face. He promised to strip her naked and bury her clothes if she tried it again. She didn't. At least, not with her clothes.

An hour later, just before the sun came up and MacRae was busy looking out for the Golden Crow Inn, or an abandoned stable—or a certain Cameron, she saw a large patch of thistles growing in the middle of the early winter frost. She stopped the horse and slid out of the saddle, then hurried towards the vivid purple flower heads. Fancifully, she told herself the thistle was always there to remind her how strong she was.

"What do ye think ye are doing running away from me?" MacRae demanded, catching up with her. "Why are ye smiling?"

She couldn't keep her smile from deepening. She knew he would get angry that she was happy. She was counting on it.

Without answering him, she bent and started plucking the stems from the earth. She was sorry for not leaving the thistle alone, but she needed help. When she held a small bouquet in her hands and lifted them to her nose, he smacked them away. They went sprawling to the ground.

"Get back on the horse," he commanded, giving her a shove between her shoulder blades. "I dinna trust ye not to drop yer under garments as a means to guide him on our path. If ye do," she heard the smile in his voice behind her, "I will be sure to freely take what ye exposed."

"I can assure ye," she said under her breath, "'twillna be free."

"What?"

"Hmm?" She looked at him over her shoulder, and then a hair's breadth passed him to the thistle scattered on the ground.

Dolt.

Find me, Constantine.

They entered Cannich, a village a little over eight leagues west of Beauly and stopped at the Golden Crow Inn to sleep for the day.

So far, the dolt hadn't tried to have her in his bed. She suspected it was because she warned him if tried to have his way with her, the Lochiel would likely cut him to pieces—if she didn't snatch one of his knives and do it herself.

The MacRae chief didn't get a room or share one with her. Instead, he set up a chair outside her door and slept there. Unlike Constantine, he didn't guard her door to keep others out, but to keep her in. The only window in the room had shutters that were nailed shut.

She didn't sleep long when the sound of the lock keeping her captive opened. She sat up, struggling to see through her tired eyes. But she didn't need eyes to recognize the delicate footfall of her mother.

"Ismay, ye look ghastly," Marjorie MacPherson remarked, entering the room. MacRae was behind her, but she slammed the door shut in his face.

"Is it true ye freely wed the outlaw Lochiel of Lochaber? Is that what ye always wanted when yer poor father tried to find suitable suitors fer ye? An outlaw? Did ye know, I wonder, dearest, he can be hanged the instant he leaves the sanctuary of that region?"

Ismay's heart halted, taking with it, her breath. "That was the plan all along." she said, feeling faint.

"My plan," Marjorie MacPherson corrected. "MacRae is too simpleminded to plan an hour ahead."

Ismay breathed and closed her eyes remembering every time she threatened MacRae with the Lochiel's imminent arrival. It was what they wanted—for him to leave Lochaber so they could have him hanged for his crimes of raiding and robbing.

Ismay felt terror creeping up her spine. He would come. She had left him ways to track her. If he found her it was her fault.

"Why are ye doing this?" Ismay asked her on a slight cry. She couldn't help it. She was weak and tired, and she had always wanted this cruel woman to love her. "Why do ye hate me so much?"

Marjorie stared at her, her emerald eyes as sharp as multifaceted shards of glass. "Ye had his devotion, though ye did nothing to earn it. Whilst I toiled fer nine years fer the same from him—and never got it. He left ye everything. Ye, a murderous waif, who would always be as filthy as the cursed day he brought ye home." Her smile curled into something dark and deadly. "There. Does that satisfy yer curiosity?"

"Aye," Ismay said and wiped her eyes. She swung her legs over the side of the bed and stood up. "Ye said it yerself, I was deserving of nothing, yet he gave me everything—as a loving father would. He was my father, and that is enough. I dinna need a mother. It makes me feel pity fer ye, and relief fer any unborn children ye might have borne him."

She took the slap Marjorie shot out at her and ignored the sting. "If 'tis my inheritance ye want so badly, ye can have it."

Marjorie backed up and laughed. "Do ye expect me to believe ye would give it up so easily?"

"I've lived without it all this time. I dinna need it, and if it might make me even a little like ye, I want nothing to do with it."

Marjorie took a step toward her. Ismay wouldn't let her slap her again.

"He spoiled ye by letting ye speak freely. MacRae willna be so generous."

"If ye dinna report the Lochiel fer coming here, I will sign over my inheritance to ye. Otherwise, I can assure ye, MacRae willna kill me. I will certainly kill him first and ye will finally get what ye deserve. Nothing."

Marjorie stared at her in disbelief for a moment then scoffed and looked heavenward. "What would ye have me do with that imbecile out there?"

"I would have ye do nothing," Ismay let her know. "The Lochiel will take care of him."

Ismay didn't miss the slight upward turn of Marjorie's malevolent smile.

"What will ye sign?" she asked Ismay.

"Write up whatever ye wish about the inheritance. I will sign it when I know the Lochiel is safe."

"Ye love the savage," her mother mocked.

"The savage is outside that door, Alistar MacRae," Ismay told her. *And ye, Mother.*

"I will consider it," Marjorie told her and left the room.

Ismay gritted her teeth when she heard the key locking her in again. "Let me out!" she shouted.

"So ye can run?" Marjorie answered through the door. "It willna be much longer."

Ismay wondered what she meant. Did she know where Constantine was? Was he here in Cannich? Had her mother already reported him to authorities? She had to get out of here and warn him if he was close by. She didn't trust Marjorie to keep her word. Ismay had to save him!

She ran to the window and examined the nails driven into the wood of the shutters. They creaked when she pushed. So she pushed harder until she saw the slightest movement of one of the nails loosening. She leaned her shoulder against the wood, thankful they weren't in a castle. She should be on the ground floor.

An hour and three splinters later, the shutters opened enough to let in the sun. Her heart beat frantically. She had to hurry before her mother returned. She gave the shutters one last long, hard nudge with her shoulder. The nails tore from the wood and fell outside the window. Ismay looked out. It was about two feet to the ground. Without another thought, she pulled up her skirts then her leg over the sill. One and then the other. She sat on the edge for just a moment to look over her shoulder at the door. Nae! She wouldn't shed a tear over the woman who practically raised and who only cared about her father's money.

Then she jumped down and took off running.

She didn't make it far when she was caught, scooped up into Chief Alistar MacRae's arms. She struggled and kicked, but his grip held steady.

"I came out to hunt and look at the hellcat I caught," he said, sounding like a purring cat.

"Let me go!" she screamed.

He slapped her in the face. She slapped him back, twice as hard. Why had she cowered to him? Why hadn't she snatched his dirk while he cut her hair off and stabbed him with it?

Without waiting to find out what he would hit next, she hauled her leg back and then let her knee fly into his groan. He went down to his knees clutching himself.

Ismay didn't wait to see if he gave chase. She ran. She spotted the tree line and headed toward it.

Something came bursting out of the trees—too fast for her to make out what it was. Nae. *Who* it was. A rider on a horse, both as dark as death. She slowed, unsure of—

The rider became clear as he neared. Constantine! She ran faster to reach him. The closer she became, she noticed his horror-ridden expression. Was he screaming her name? She wanted to scream his name back to him, but she turned to see what he was seeing.

MacRae was aiming an arrow at her. She turned back to her rescuer—she never doubted he would come. She almost flew into his arms when an arrow shot into her from behind.

———————— ✳ ————————

CHAPTER TWENTY-THREE

CONSTANTINE OPENED HIS eyes and looked at a ceiling he'd never seen before. He was in a room at the Golden Crow Inn. He sat up as memories invaded his thoughts. His bandaged side blazed with pain. He ignored it. Ismay. They had found her in Cannich, running from Alistar MacRae. She'd been shot! His head ached and heart ached and made him feel ill. He'd leaped from his horse and ran to her. His steward raced to MacRae.

"Ismay!" he cried out. She'd been lifeless in his arms. Her preciously adored face turned up to the sun, as if she were returning from whence she came.

But she wasn't dead! She had opened her eyes and smiled at him.

Constantine had been torn about whether to carry her to his horse and race to a town with a physician, or going to MacRae and killing him, *and then* carrying her to his horse.

He had to leave the bastard to Hugh and get Ismay help. Lifting her in his arms, he'd held her gently in his embrace while his heart beat hard and fast against her.

But—he remembered the hot sensation of his blood seeping through his bandages. He wouldn't die. Not until he helped her. He'd managed to mount his horse and sat in the saddle behind her.

Hugh, stained with blood that wasn't his own, had caught up

to them and led them here.

Did she live? He was afraid of the answer. Terrified, he wasn't ashamed to admit.

"Ismay!" he called out, gripping his side.

The door opened to Hugh entering the room with a tray of food in his hands. "Do ye truly want to open that up again? I willna be able to sew ye again, Lochiel."

"Hugh, where—?" Could he withstand the answer?

"In a room down the hall. She will be well, fear not. The healer here says the arrow entered closer to her shoulder and didna hit anything vital. She sleeps but she will recover. I am more worried about ye!"

"Dinna be," Constantine ordered, getting out of his bed.

"Lochiel, she will live!" Hugh shouted at him, nearing the door. "What do ye think she will do without ye because ye were too stubborn to tend to yer wound and died? Would ye leave her here alone?"

Constantine stopped. It was all that could have stopped him from going to her. The worst thing he could do was leave her here alone.

"Verra well," he pouted, stalking back to bed. "But I want reports on her every quarter of an hour."

Hugh screwed up his face. "Do ye not remember that I was never in yer army? What is this every quarter of an hour? Ye will run me ragged."

"Then I will be gettin' up to see her fer myself."

Hugh mumbled something under his breath, set the tray down with more force than was necessary, then left the room, still mumbling.

Constantine leaned back in the bed. She would recover. He was able to breathe again. He wanted to be with her. His body, spirit, and mind needed her. He pulled his shift up and had a look at his dry bandage, then at the door.

He recalled his steward's question about leaving Ismay here alone in this world. He would stay put no matter how badly he wanted to get to his beloved.

Hugh must have stitched him up again. He was thankful for his steward. For so long, he thought Hugh didn't like him, since he seemed to always try to get others to agree that they didn't like him either. But his longtime steward had explained on their first night together, it was the best way to find out who was the Lochiel's secret enemy. And he had them at Tor, according to his steward. Bethia was one. The old cook from two years ago, who disappeared not long after his talk with Hugh. There were several others, all of whom no longer lived at Tor—or no longer lived at all. Constantine wasn't certain. His steward was a mystery.

He returned a quarter of an hour later and stood at the foot of his bed. "The lady is recovering. Nothing has changed."

"How long has she been sleeping?" Constantine demanded. When Hugh didn't answer right away, he swung his legs off the bed.

"She hasna woken up," his steward admitted quietly.

Constantine leaped from the bed and went to the door. "Ye deceived me, Hugh."

"Because I knew ye would do exactly what ye are doing," Hugh said, keeping up with his steps when Constantine left the room. "Ye need to recover."

"I'll recover when I know she will recover as well." He followed Hugh's finger to where his steward pointed down the hall. When he reached her door he was overcome with relief and pressed his forehead to the cool wood.

He had opened his heart to her the day he first saw her—or *him*, as he had first thought. He had allowed her to go where only Alison lived and she stepped in and set up her belongings. He smiled despite his new worries over her. He became aware that Hugh was stepping away.

Constantine breathed and knocked.

When no reply came, he opened the door. His eyes fell to the bed, where she lay asleep. "Ismay, my love," he said softly, entering the room. She didn't stir. He went to the bed and gazed down at her. He never thought he could love again. But he loved this lass. Och, how he loved her.

"My love, wake up. I am already oot of my mind withoot ye. Wake up."

Standing at the side of the bed, he leaned down and resting his elbow on the thin pillow under her head, he whispered close to her ear. "Ismay, I canna go on withoot ye in my life. Ye have made everything fresh and new to me again. Ye promised to stay with me. Someone once told me that a person who gives her word and keeps it can be trusted. Keep yer word to me, lass."

He gazed as one utterly captivated by the beauty she possessed. He ran the tip of his index finger along her nose, the shape of her lips. "Wake up fer me, my light, my love." His whisper became a plea against her temple. "I'll wait right here fer ye."

He waited for two more days, barely leaving her side except to use the garderobe. Hugh saw that his meals were served in her room, and finally accepted the fact that Constantine was not returning to his bed.

The same healer who gave them no new news about Ismay's condition, advised Constantine that in the absence of fighting or bouncing in the saddle, his wound was healing nicely. But what did it matter as long as his wife remained asleep?

He had the urge to grab the healer by the throat and demand he find out why she wasn't waking up. But that kind of behavior would disappoint Ismay. She saw him as more than brawn and battle skill. She saw a man—a chief, who was trustworthy not to hurt her. No use in beating up the healer.

He sighed and sat in the chair beside her bed. He looked at her and didn't move his gaze when Hugh showed the healer out.

"I dinna want to be a soldier any longer, love," he told her while she slept. "I want to settle doun with ye and father our bairns. Aye, seven of them." He smiled at the thought of his sons and daughters: wee May, their first lass, Arailt, their first son. He imagined them all sitting around their mother and father.

"Seven?"

Constantine leaped from his chair and almost landed in bed with her. "My love!"

She stared at him as if he had sprouted another eye. "Seven babies?"

His smile was wide and eager when he nodded. "I'll make the house bigger, but not yet. First, I want to enjoy living there with ye and makin' our brood."

The storms in her glorious gray eyes had finally settled and were like glass seas when they fastened on him. "Fergive me fer frightening ye, husband."

Her voice fell like jingling bells in his ears, his soul. He gathered her hands in his and held them to his lips. "Ye kept yer word and came back to me,"

"I dreamed of ye," she told him with the remnants of sleep in her voice. "Well, not *ye* precisely. 'Twas more like...I sensed yer presence against the door like a shadow that had found its light. I wanted to wake and greet ye, hold ye, kiss ye"—she paused to blush—"but I couldna wake up. I made ye wait, and fer that I am sorry."

He held a finger to her lips. "I love ye, Ismay. Thank ye fer comin' back to me."

He waited a little while before he called Hugh and gave him the good news. He wanted more time alone with Ismay.

"How do ye feel?" he asked. "Does yer back hurt? Yer chest? Anything?"

"My back—MacRae!" she exclaimed as if remembering her wound brought the culprit back to her thoughts.

"Hugh took care of him," Constantine let her know. "He left him fer dead so he doesna know if he made it or no'."

"Hugh?"

He nodded and recalled how much the steward had done.

"I'll decide about him myself when I hear his reasons," she let him know.

"Aye, my love," Constantine let her have her way. He always had and he always would.

He leaned in, fixing his gaze on her mouth as he moved closer to it. This close, he could see the fading bruise on her jaw that had made him vow to find MacRae and if he was alive, make certain he never hurt her again.

He bent his head a little more and ran his nose over her cheek, breathing in the sweet scent of her. He closed his eyes, unable to stop himself from kissing her. Just once.

Hugh opened the door, a familiar habit he'd picked up of not knocking first. When he saw Ismay awake and trying to sit up, he raced to the bed and aided her before Constantine could reach his arm out for her.

Constantine's glare on him went unnoticed as the steward propped her pillow behind her and asked her a dozen questions about if she felt well.

"Why did ye not send fer me to let me know she had awakened?" the steward demanded, turning to aim his own fiery glare at the Lochiel.

Constantine stared at him for another moment and then ended it with a growl and got up from his chair. He offered it to Hugh so that the steward would stop leaning over her.

Luckily, the steward accepted the seat. "Ye had us in a bad way, lady," Hugh told her.

"Hugh," Constantine said to stop him. Why was he trying to make her feel guilty for making them worry?

But Hugh did not catch on. "I thought ye dead several times. Yer breath seemed as if it had stopped."

How did his steward know how softly her breath came? "How close did ye get?"

Ismay heard him and switched her attention to him. She smiled, but beneath a few layers of affection, was a warning for him to watch his temper.

Wasn't it she who said, and only moments ago, that she would decide for herself whether he was a friend or foe? Had she made her decision already?

"Fergive me," she repented to the steward.

Standing a wee bit away, Constantine huffed and looked heavenward.

"As I explained to the Lochiel, I tried to wake up but I coulnda."

Constantine smacked his hand on his thigh. She had just woken up. She needed rest, not someone sitting next to her, pestering her.

"Ismay," he began.

She gave him a look that asked him not to interfere.

Had he refused her since he'd known her? Damn him, he did what she silently asked and kept quiet.

"I'm afraid I've been mistrusting of ye, Hugh," she went on. "Ye have proven yer loyalty to the Lochiel."

Why was she not calling him Constantine, or my darling husband? What was this formal *Lochiel* nonsense?

"And to ye, lady."

"Me?"

Constantine inched closer to his steward to hear what he was saying.

"Ye dinna remember me."

"Hmm? Remember ye from when?" She smiled, setting Constantine's pitiful heart to complete ruin. "Of course I remember ye from being at the castle—"

"Befer that, lass," Hugh corrected with a tender smile.

Constantine listened—harder than he'd ever listened to anything before.

"I was a lad of seven when ye were brought into the castle to serve my father," he told her in a voice meant only for her ears, but Constantine heard him. "Ye were a wee thing of two—"

Wait! Constantine took another step forward.

"Hugh. Roderick MacDonald was yer father?"

"Aye," Hugh confessed. "My mother was one of the servants there." He looked at Constantine. "I wasna treated any better than any other serving boy."

"How come I never knew this aboot ye?" Constantine asked

him.

"Ye were a young lad when I came to live at Tor."

"Hugh?"

They both turned to Ismay, sitting up straighter.

"Ye knew 'twas me who killed yer father," she said quietly, with fear lacing her voice.

Constantine wanted to drag his steward outside and beat him senseless.

"My love," Constantine said reassuringly. "Ye have nothin' to fear. No one will ever harm ye again."

"Aye, but they might try. We must train harder."

Constantine didn't want any more fighting but if anyone came for Ismay, he would kill them all. For now, though, he would love it if she grew strong enough again to train with him. "Aye, love."

Hugh coughed into his hand and rolled his eyes heavenward until he got Ismay's attention. "My kin didna see yer face. No one will tell them yer true name."

Ismay shook her head and let Constantine take her hand when he came near. "Nae. I want everyone to know the truth. I willna hide my father's name any longer. Whatever sins the MacPhersons committed before this had nothing to do with Lord John MacPherson, Baron of Raigmore. He rescued me from life in servitude to an unholy man and asked nothing in return."

"I know my father was unholy and ruthless," Hugh let her know. "He was void of compassion and demanded that his sons, bastards or not, followed his example. But my heart broke fer ye. In the beginning it did. Ye were whipped behind the legs often. I saw his gaze change when ye entered the hall carrying a jug of his ale."

"Ye will stop there," Constantine told him.

"I couldna help her," Hugh went on. "I tried twice and was beaten."

"Dinna tell it to me," Constantine said, coolly. "Tell yer kin, and then be an example to them by pleadin' her forgiveness fer lettin' the bastard hurt her fer so long."

Hugh nodded and then set his eyes on her. "I will live my life helping ye understand how I regret the past. I think I cared fer Gilbert and Constantine so much because I didna care fer ye enough."

"Then ye dinna hate me fer killing yer father?" she asked quietly.

"Nae, lass. I often wanted to do it when he was mistreating my mother, but I was a coward. Ye have more courage than I."

"Nae, I was terrified. I acted out of pure instinct to keep him away from me."

Hugh lowered his gaze.

"There now," Ismay comforted him! "'Twas a long time ago. Since then I have been rescued by two wonderful men, and I have developed friendships with others."

Constantine marveled at her and soon asked his steward to leave so she could rest—and he could be alone with her.

"I dinna remember him," she admitted to Constantine when Hugh left.

"He's not memorable," he teased lightly.

"If it were ye, I would never forget," she told him. Smiling as he neared.

"Of course, ye wouldna," was all he said and she giggled and let him kiss her.

He would have more with her, but now she was recovering. He would let her sleep—but he didn't leave her bedside.

Even when Lady Marjorie MacPherson arrived at the inn.

"I DINNA CARE what state she is in!" Constantine heard her shrill voice permeating the wooden door to Ismay's room. "Step aside or I will have ye removed," she continued, likely speaking to Hugh—the only one who would be guarding the door. "Are ye not aware of my men outside that door?"

"Ye should have bought fifty with ye, woman." On the other side of the door, Constantine smiled at Hugh's warning. Hell, his steward was unexpected as a summer storm. "I'll take down twenty easily. It willna even be a fight."

Constantine went to the door and opened it. He stepped out and shut the door behind him. He set his stare on the woman who tried to cast her stepdaughter back into the kind of life that haunted her eyes.

"Miss MacPherson willna see ye," he let her know with anger tightening his jaw. "Get oot before I drag ye oot."

She gasped and threw her hands to her chest. "Do ye know who I am, ye pagan miscreant? I demand—"

He stepped forward, grasped her wrist, and commenced dragging her out. When he had her outside, he didn't bother looking around at her men. Hugh held them all back with a glare.

"Lady MacPherson, ye will remove Ismay from yer memory. Ye will never see her again unless she wills it."

"Who will stop me? She is my—"

"I will," he promised without a doubt in his voice. "She is no' yer aythin'. Do ye understand?"

"She is to be wed!" she argued.

"Ye speak of Chief MacRae," he said. "That brute rid Ismay of him and yer vow."

For a moment, she merely sputtered her disbelief. Apparently, she had not seen or heard from the rat.

"He willna be gettin' her, and ye willna be gettin' her inheritance. I wed her. I am her husband."

Her eyes opened wide and she threw back her head to let out a scream that finally got her men moving, despite Hugh's death stare warning them not to come near.

They attacked. Constantine held her wrist while he watched his steward put down twenty men. Hugh hadn't lied when he told her it would not even be a fight. It was over all too soon, leaving Lady MacPherson's men lifeless in the dirt around the inn.

"Hmm," Constantine said more to himself than to Lady MacPherson, who was also watching, horrified by seeing all her men fall. "I'll have to make him more than my steward."

"He is yer steward?" his captive asked as her last man went down and Hugh turned to her. "He is a monster."

"Och, he's tame compared to the rest of my kin," Constantine let her know, turning back to her. "Anythin' ye try to do against her willna work. She has been fergiven by me fer killin' her torturer, Roderick MacDonald. She will heal and bloom in my care. My kin and I will kill anyone who tries to harm her again."

"I should get his riches! I was married to him fer over twenty years!"

"Over twenty years and he didna believe ye deserved a pence of his riches. I wonder why that is?"

He didn't wait for her to reply but motioned to her horse.

"Remember," he said as she pulled herself up on her horse, "if ye want to live, ferget her."

He watched her ride away, alone and then returned to the inn.

LADY MARJORIE CURSED under her breath as she led her horse away. How dare an outlaw threaten her? Was he truly Ismay's husband? It couldn't be true!

No matter. No lowborn Highland cretin would threaten her twice. She would never forget that Ismay had her money. She would see everyone dead before she gave up.

Bastard.

CHAPTER TWENTY-FOUR

I SMAY STOOD ON the battlements of Tor Castle and drew her arisaid closer around herself.

With a deep inhale, she filled herself with the fresh clean scent of the earth bathed in snow. She looked out over the white hills and glens stretching out around her and thought about the first time she had stepped into this place. She'd had no idea what she was in for, temporarily living with a clan chieftain again. She had followed that chief—or Lochiel as the Cameron chief was called—into the unknown on the sheer basis of him keeping his word about one thing. But her father was correct about there being a single thing needed to know if a man was trustworthy or not. Her Cameron chief had kept every word he made to her.

The last vow he had made to her was that they would visit the house at Ben Nevis in the spring and live there for a few months, without the pressures and responsibilities of being chief. His most trusted kin would handle them all until Constantine returned.

She loved him for the freedom he presented to her, but she didn't care where they lived or what they did, she would be happy. She would love only him for the rest of her days on the earth and beyond.

She almost wept thinking about him, so tall and lean, built and fashioned by swinging a sword. Thinking of his countenance, she felt herself go flush in the wind.

She fanned herself and giggled inwardly. It was extraordinary the way another person could make her perspire in the winter. He was thoughtful and always filled with compassion with those who were important to him. But it was her eyes that saw passionate love and steadfast devotion in his gaze when he looked at her.

She heard the door to the stairs creak open. She wasn't worried about being alone anywhere in this castle, Constantine had not lied when he told her his men were safe.

They had forgiven her for killing chief MacDonald and even still protected her when they thought she was in jeopardy. Like when Fionn and Lachlan tried to stop her from going to bathe in the loch, or when Geoffry followed her every step for a fortnight until she spun on her heel and snapped at him. She never complained about them to Constantine. He had more serious gripes to settle. She also did not want to get them in trouble with him, and for that, they had told her they would consider her a sister.

Ismay liked that idea. She'd never had siblings. Now she had dozens, including brothers who frustrated her and made her laugh moments in between. She owed Hilary much for losing her betrothed thanks to her, among other things. But Hilary treated her as a sister too—a close sister in whom one confides. And Joan, her dearest friend, who never once turned her loyalties away from Ismay.

They were all invited to visit the house at Ben Nevis when she and their Lochiel left Tor.

When his arms snaked around her, she didn't leap away, afraid of who it was. She knew the rhythm of his breath against her neck when he dipped his warm lips to her.

"What are ye doin' up here, my love?" he asked into her ear.

Ismay closed her eyes to relish the warmth spreading through her from his body.

"I was remembering how I followed ye through the doors of

this castle fer the first time. My fearful thoughts told me the worst about ye, but ye turned those thoughts on their heads and reached gently for my heart. I am so happily yers that I feel as if I have wings and I can soar right off these battlements, on this wind."

He laughed behind her, reverberating through her. When he spoke, his breath was warm against her temple, the cadence of his voice like a fire in the cold. "Then mayhap to keep ye here with me, I should make ye unhappy."

She shook her head and covered his arms with hers. "I dinna think ye can make me unhappy, husband."

His arms drew her in deeper. "I never want to be the cause of yer unhappiness—so tell me what you think about this, Bethia has returned from the MacMillans. She wants me to fergive her fer her disloyalty and let her live here again. I told her she had my fergiveness—"

Of course she had it. That was who Constantine was. Hard and unforgiving on the outside, but soft and inviting on the inside.

"—but I dinna think she should return here to live. She was Alison's close friend and Alison is gone from here."

Alison was gone from here. Ismay didn't know whether to be happy about it or sad for Constantine. "My love," she said softly, tilting her head up to him, "Alison was part of yer life. I dinna expect ye to ferget her."

"I willna ferget her or Katie, but although they will live forever in my heart, they were. Ye are. Ye are everything to me, Ismay. My life is yers. I love ye more than I can say."

She smiled, though he couldn't see it. "Then dinna say anything. Just show me."

Without any more provocation, he took her hand and tugged, leading her to the stairs.

She giggled and hurried along with him. Was this bold seductress truly her? Had she ever—even on her best day—imagined teasing her husband? He freed her from her fears and taught her how to fight a stronger enemy, should one ever come upon her again.

It had only been a short pair of months since she found him—or he found her—she wasn't sure which. It didn't matter. They had found each other. It did not feel as if they had known each other all their lives. It felt as if they had just met, awakened as one struck by lightning. One who had stopped living. Part of Constantine had died when he lost his wife and babe. Part of Ismay had died twice. Once as a child when she lost a huge block of who she was, or who she could be. Then again when her father had died.

She and Constantine had been brought back to life in each other's embrace, in each other's intimate smile, soft words. She still felt those cracks of lightning go through her when he touched her or told her he loved her—which he did often, at night, in his deep, purring voice when they were alone.

"There ye are!" Hugh met them on the stairs. "Ye have unexpected guests waiting fer ye in the Great Hall."

Constantine waved him away. Ismay wasn't sure why Hugh was still caring for the castle and the duties that came with being a steward when his Lochiel made him his lieutenant commander.

"Tell whoever 'tis that I canna meet with them—"

"'Tis General Monck's emissaries from France."

Constantine stopped. So did Ismay. Why had the Royalist general sent his emissaries here? Did it have something to do with the exiled king?

Constantine would be a fool to refuse them, and her husband was no fool.

Turning to her, he offered her an apologetic smile as if he needed to. He didn't. She would have sent him off if he didn't go on his own.

"I will see ye tonight, wife," he promised.

She nodded, happy because she knew he would keep his word.

She watched him hurry off and prayed silently for peace to

reign. She would go sew with Hilary and Joan while she waited for him.

Her friends already knew who was there, thanks to Lachlan telling Joan. "Imagine if the king returns?" Hilary set down her needle to exclaim with enthusiasm. "Och, there will be dancing in the glens."

"Not everyone is a Royalist, Hilary," Ismay reminded her. In fact, there were other Camerons outside of Lochaber who sided with the Presbyterians. "I'm thankful my father sided with the Stuart monarchy."

"Aye, 'tis a good thing to have in common, Cousin."

Ismay glanced up at her and smiled.

Poor Hilary was still unwed, and it seemed as if she would remain that way for a time. She didn't blame Ismay though.

"Whyever would it be yer fault?" Hilary had told her. "John MacBain chose to go against my cousin, and thereby me as well. Why would I want a man like that?"

Ismay didn't know why any woman would, but still, Hilary often looked away and smiled warmly while something crossed her thoughts. Ismay guessed it was John MacBain by the way Hilary scowled just as darkly a moment later.

"Och!" Joan slammed her sewing into her lap. "I canna sit here another moment waiting to find out if our men will have to go back into battle fer the king."

Ismay paled. She did her best not to think along those lines, but Joan was correct. The men of Lochaber would be called to fight for the king to whom they swore such staunch support.

Constantine didn't want to fight. What would his heart be like this time when he returned from the battlefield?

"Let us take a walk," Hilary suggested.

Joan gave her an incredulous look. "I wasna speaking of venturing oot. 'Tis freezing oot there, Hilary."

"Come." Ismay set down her sewing and stood up. "The brisk air will do us good."

"Lady!" Joan looked up at her, betrayal staining her eyes.

"Do ye think 'tis too cold for a quick swim?

Now Hilary and Joan shared the same look of disbelief. Hilary was about to stand but rethought her position and stayed seated.

Ismay laughed quietly and shrugged her shoulders at them, then left.

As she suspected—and hoped—she heard the lasses' footsteps hurrying after her. She rolled her eyes heavenward though when Joan shouted out to Lachlan and Hilary did the same to Fionn and Geoffry, that Ismay was off to swim in the icy loch!

She wasn't going to actually do it. She wasn't mad in the head, risking freezing to death. She simply was trying to lure her friends outside so the three of them could talk. But Lachlan joined them and wasted no time telling her that he would never let her freeze to death. Geoffry (surprisingly) was next, threatening to toss her over his shoulder and bring her back if she didn't listen to him and stop this instant. He wouldn't dare touch her. None of them would. She was the Lochiel's woman and none of them were ignorant of the possible consequences if she were hurt by them.

She continued out of the castle using the kitchen's back door, walking in the direction of the loch and causing an uproar behind her.

"Lady," Geoffry said, hurrying in front of her. "I canna let ye enter the water. Ye will—"

"Of course, I am not going to enter the water, dear Geoffry." He turned red when she called him that. It made her smile go warm on him. "Ye know how I like to rile things up."

He sighed with relief just as an arrow flew between them. Even faster than she could take in, he pulled her under his arm and whisked her away behind a nearby tree. He set her down and then was gone an instant later, racing to the others. Lachlan was shooting arrow after arrow into the trees. Ismay had never seen arrows nocked and fired in a row so fast. But then she saw something else. Someone running toward them from the castle as if his life depended on reaching her. It was Constantine, gaining on them fast.

Suddenly, he detoured and ran into the trees.

"Lachlan stop!" she screamed.

He turned and looked at her and an enemy arrow whistled by him and landed with a *thunk* into the tree trunk where she hid.

Lachlan hadn't seen where the shot came from, but Ismay had. She could see Constantine fighting someone through the bare branches. Was that…MacRae?

He went down as Constantine slammed his body into him. Lachlan and Geoffry took off running to the trees. Ismay ran to her two friends.

A moment or two later Constantine and Lachlan returned to the women. Geoffry dragged a hogtied MacRae back to the castle, where he would be dealt with.

When he saw her, Constantine hurried to her and pulled her into his arms. "Are ye hurt at all?" he asked, worry tainting his voice. "Are any of ye hurt?"

They all reassured him they were unhurt. Lachlan pulled Joan into his embrace, proving the bonnie serving gel had won the heart of Lochaber's darling Lachlan Cameron.

"Hilary," Constantine said, "bring Ismay back to the castle. I need to see to things."

"See to things, like MacRae's death?" Ismay asked him.

"Aye, things like that. And the imprisonment of his accomplice to kill ye. Lady Marjorie MacPherson. He admitted she paid him to kill ye and then me. But he went after ye first."

"Thankfully," Lachlan muttered with a smirk, "MacRae is a poor archer."

"I willna let him live again, wife. He has a price. Men like him are dangerous."

She nodded, believing he was right and let Hilary lead her back. "Fergive me fer making ye come outside, Hil."

Her friend slapped her arm. "He was coming no matter what, gel. Be thankful the fool attempted his nefarious deeds with the men around."

Ismay was grateful that none of them were hurt. She was grateful she would never have to run from Alistar MacRae again. She wouldn't apologize for it. She was glad he would be out of her life now. And if Marjorie wanted Ismay dead so badly, then the safest place for her was indeed prison.

Two hours later, she blew a deep breath out of her mouth and looked around the Great Hall. The emissaries had gone and Constantine was still interrogating MacRae. She should go to bed.

She left her chair and started for the door. He appeared there a moment later, tall, dark, and virile, scanning the faces until his gaze found her. Her heart thumped loudly enough for him to hear it. It seemed he may have indeed heard it for he smiled suddenly, as if he'd just seen home after a grueling battle.

Would it be too bold to jump into his arms? To kiss his face— och, every inch of it, as if she hadn't seen him for a time too long to bear. She took a tentative step and lifted her fingers to her lips. Remembering how he kissed her.

He reached her, filling her nostrils with a scent meant only for her. Sandalwood? Peat? Pine? Mayhap all three. It went straight to her head and made her feel drunk on wine.

He took her hand and brought it to his lips.

Every eye in the Great Hall was set on them. Constantine didn't seem to care.

"Were ye waitin' fer me, lass?"

His deep voice bathed her in warmth, comfort, and safety. It filled her veins with fire.

"Come, let's retire to bed," he suggested, sliding a sensual gaze to hers as he led her away.

"Aye." She didn't resist or refuse. She never would. She would always want him in her arms, her bed.

The instant they were out of the Great Hall, he tried to pull her in for a kiss, but she escaped his grasp and made him chase her up the stairs. If he wanted her, he'd have to work a wee bit. She was no pushover.

He caught her at the top of the stairs. He could have caught her sooner, but he let her have her fun. She wasn't the only one who laughed though. Constantine Cameron, Lochiel of Lochaber laughed too.

The sound filled the hall and reached the ears of the four men watching them from the Great Hall doorway.

"Where is my brother?" Fionn asked the man who had returned with the Lochiel a few moments earlier.

"He insisted on finding Lady Marjorie MacPherson of Raigmore," Hugh let him know.

"A woman?" Lewis asked curiously.

"An evil woman who wants Ismay…my lady, killed."

Lachlan and the others muttered about hoping Geoffry found her. Then they went back to drinking and singing ballads about their Lochiel and his courageous Lady Ismay Cameron.

The End

About the Author

Paula Quinn is a New York Times bestselling author and a sappy romantic moved by music, beautiful words, and the sight of a really nice pen. She lives in New York with her three beautiful children, six over-protective chihuahuas, and three adorable parrots. She loves to read romance and science fiction and has been writing since she was eleven. She's a faithful believer in God and thanks Him daily for all the blessings in her life. She loves all things medieval, but it is her love for Scotland that pulls at her heartstrings.

To date, four of her books have garnered Starred reviews from Publishers Weekly. She has been nominated as Historical Storyteller of the Year by RT Book Reviews, and all the books in her MacGregor and Children of the Mist series have received Top Picks from RT Book Reviews. Her work has also been honored as Amazons Best of the Year in Romance, and in 2008 she won the Gayle Wilson Award of Excellence for Historical Romance.

Website:
pa0854.wixsite.com/paulaquinn

www.ingramcontent.com/pod-product-compliance
Lightning Source LLC
Chambersburg PA
CBHW060340310726
48976CB00003B/661